BAD-ASS
Bitches

by

Nicole Michele

DORRANCE
PUBLISHING CO
EST. 1920
PITTSBURGH, PENNSYLVANIA 15238

Dorrance Publishing Co
585 Alpha Drive
Suite 103
Pittsburgh, PA 15238
Visit our website at *www.dorrancebookstore.com*

ISBN: 978-1-6386-7164-0
eISBN: 978-1-6386-7697-3

■ ACKNOWLEDGMENTS ■

First of all, I would like to thank the ten women in this book
who had the courage to tell their stories.
Hopefully, their journeys will inspire women
who have lost their way
to find their inner bad ass and
lead themselves to a better place.

Secondly, I'd like to thank my friend Taryn —
who over a glass of wine (or two) at the winery
during a PTA event, gave me the title to this book.

■ ■ ■

I wonder when the term *bitch* became so offensive towards women. If you look up the word *bitch* in the dictionary, the definition is: *the female of the dog or some other carnivorous mammals*. So somewhere along the lines of history, some man, who most likely had serious anger management issues and took out his frustrations on his poor dog, got really pissed off at a woman and called her a bitch. And I'm willing to bet that his woman, in all her loyal and dutiful ways, just shut her mouth and walked away, when she should have clocked him in the mouth with her frying pan. Thus came the birth of an offensive term used to describe a malicious, spiteful, or overbearing woman.

But since some men are not that smart, comparing us to dogs is really not the worst thing in the world. Let's face it—dogs are awesome! Kids adore them, we sleep with them, we cuddle up with them on the couch, and they are literally our best friends. They help us stay fit, they love us unconditionally, they listen to our problems, and they save us from danger. Haven't I just described the characteristics of most mothers? Loyalty, love, and devotion. Hell, I guess I'm a bitch!

So guess what, boys? I'm taking my word back and I'm going to redefine it! Malicious? When you mess with us, you're going to get the horns. You call it malicious, I call it reminding you that your tone of voice or your disrespectful ways need to be checked. A woman brought you into this world, and we have full authority to let you know if you've overstepped. Spiteful? Please! As if we have nothing better to do than to go out of our way to be mean to you just for fun. When the kids are taken care of, the dinners are made, the clothes are washed and put away, the bills are paid and organized, and the house tidied up, do you honestly think we have time to sit down and add being mean to our to-do lists? Overbearing? If we are tasked with the responsibility of taking care of our families, then you better believe that we fall under that umbrella! Can you organize a PTA meeting, complete with a fundraiser, a bake sale, and ladybug dance at the elementary school by yourself? Can you help your kids with their homework, attend their parent-teacher conferences via Zoom, and comfort your daughter during her first teenage breakup, all while cooking dinner for the in-laws, doing 5 loads of laundry, and soaking the dog in tomato juice after he just got sprayed by a skunk? Overbearing? Try saying thank you every now and then or even offering to help. Maybe then we wouldn't think of you as our fourth child.

So do you still think of us as bitches? Dogs would give their lives to their masters, just like mothers do to their families. Dogs never back down in the face of danger, even if the perpetrator is twice their size. Mothers get in Mama Bear mode when anyone messes with their babies. A dog's presence alone is a comforting factor, just like your mommy is when you've woken up from a bad dream. We are mistreated on so many levels, but we stay loyal to our families because it's in our blood. We are the gender that takes a back seat to men, we are the ones they call "crazy" when we show the slightest bit of emotion over the injustices. But when the black and blue marks start to fade and the broken bones mended, we come back stronger than before, undefeatable, unbreakable, and unstoppable. And that is the difference between a bitch —and a bad-ass bitch! ∎

▪ CHAPTER ONE ▪
Felicia

I don't think women usually consider themselves to be warriors. Most of the time, we are wives, housekeepers, mothers, psychologists, doctors, social workers, mechanics, cooks, therapists, friends, event planners, babysitters, and pet caretakers. We do these tasks because someone is depending on us, leaning on us, and in most cases, we're the only ones equipped to mentally handle these tasks without complaining. We need the world to be right and the universe to be balanced. Chaos does not suit us. We are the sun to many—when we shine down on the lives that depend on us, they are able to grow and be content. When others are content, we are content. That is the selfless gift that most women have been created with. It is innate, we were born with it, and we will die trying to protect it.

So when the clouds come in, and the downpours begin, and the category-5 hurricanes, and the 3-day blizzards, and the super tornados invade our lives—we rarely ever lay down and let nature pound us into the ground until we are lifeless and defeated. We are not feeble women or damsels in distress. Instead, we become warriors! We crush the chains that bind us and slay our opponents until we are standing on a mountain of their broken bones—their skulls beneath our feet. We rush to the nearby village and set free the innocent victims, vowing to protect them always, with every fiber of our beings. We go beyond the realm of warriors. We become badass- bitches!

Felicia found the man of her dreams while she was in college. He was tall, good-looking, had a great smile and a heart the size of Texas. He

1

hated school and was content being a farm hand. Felicia instantly fell in love with him, because he was kind to her and loved to go on adventures. On a whim, they would jump in the car and travel to Pennsylvania to pick up a part for a dump truck, and drive back the same day, exhausted and laughing about their conversations. They would talk about everything—work, money, family, and dreams. John came from a broken family. His mother was an alcoholic that moved from relationship to relationship. She ended up with 4 children—and 4 different baby daddies. John eventually was raised by his grandparents, an elderly couple who instilled hard lessons and tough love. Many nights, John slept in the barn, to enjoy the crickets chirping, the swish of tall grass, and the soft glow of the moon lighting up the darkness. This is how John escaped his unstable mother and all the things that made him different from the other kids. The bitterness of a life that was robbed from him—a father, a warm house, new school clothes, and family vacations that would never come.

Felicia opened up her heart to this lost puppy—took him in with her entire soul. She too could relate to his family issues. After all, her mother was neurotic about her health, and her father did the best he could to keep his wife from jumping off a cliff—literally. Finding John was like finding a golden ticket in a Wonka bar. She saw it as her chance to escape her chaotic home life, and possibly have a chance at something new and exciting.

They married quickly—both barely into their twenties. They settled down in a small apartment and made a home for themselves. She found a job in an engineering firm that created parts for aircraft, and he continued his job as a hand at a local farm. They put aside their money so that they could one day afford their own house—something they could put their names on to show the world that they too could contend in the world of real estate. After a few years, they were able to buy a small ranch on a suburban street in Montville. It definitely needed some work, but being low on funds, they did a lot of the home improvements by themselves. John learned a lot about plumbing, electrical, and carpentry with his new project. He quickly became a master at repairing just about anything. When their roof needed to be replaced, they enlisted the help of all their friends, and pretty much had a roofing party on the top of their house! The roof was completed in 3 days, at one quarter of the cost. For Felicia, it was another perfect memory to add to her fairytale life.

"Hey, honey?" Felicia called from the living room one day, when she heard John padding into the kitchen.

"Yah?" John answered.

"Can you come here for a sec?"

"Yah, hold on. Grand Theft Auto 4 just came out and I'm trying to download it."

Felicia sighed and flipped through her magazine nervously. After what seemed like an eternity, he finally came into the living room and sat next to her on the couch.

"Yah?"

"I have some news...." She picked at her fingernails and looked down. *Shit! My palms are starting to sweat. Why they hell is this so damn hard? What am I afraid of?*

"What?" John prodded.

Felicia looked up at him, tears in her eyes. "I'm going to have a baby."

"Oh... wow. That's great." He sat still and didn't move towards her.

"I'm scared, John. What if I don't know what to do?"

"Pfft. You'll know what to do... and I'll help you. It's not like you're alone." He put his arm around her and she immediately relaxed.

This won't be so bad. He's a good man. He'll help me. And we'll be such a cute little family. Oh, I could just picture it, she smiled.

≡ ≡ ≡

Their first daughter, Anna, was born in August of 2006. She was a cute little red-headed peanut. She was the spitting image of her father, and they both loved her to pieces. Felicia bought her all the latest toys and enrolled her in sports programs and camps. John bought her John Deere t-shirts and took her for rides on the tractor at work. For the first two years of Anna's life, the two young parents doted on their little princess and Felicia couldn't imagine how life could get any better.

≡ ≡ ≡

But life did get better.

"Babe?" John knocked on the bathroom door. "Are you all right?"

"One sec...." A toilet flushed and water in the sink splashed. After a few seconds, Felicia opened the door. She was pale and holding her stomach.

"You all right?" John asked.

"No. It must have been those leftovers I ate." Felicia looked up at him. "Do you feel sick too?"

"No. Why don't you sit down on the couch and relax. Do you want me to get you something?"

"No," she replied, and shuffled into the living room and sat on the couch.

Lines creased her forehead as she looked down at her belly. John followed her and sat down next to her.

"What is it?"

Felicia sat still for several seconds, all the while, rubbing her belly. Then she looked up at John.

"I think I'm pregnant."

"What?" John replied.

"I'm not sick from something I ate. This is different. It feels... different."

"How the fuck did this happen?"

Felicia recoiled from his words. *How did this happen? We've been doing it like rabbits lately! It's not like I could've done this by myself!*

"What do you mean?" she challenged.

"I thought you were on the pill?"

"I haven't been on the pill since we got married."

"What? Why didn't you tell me?"

"I thought you knew. I mean—we were trying. And then Anna came along. Why would I go back on the pill? Aren't we starting a family?"

"Yah, but...." John stood up. "Anna is only 2 years old. Taking care of her is tough. How are we going to manage two?"

Felicia stood up suddenly. "Are you telling me that you don't want this baby?"

John immediately softened. "No, no. Of course not. It will be fine. I just get worried about money sometimes, that's all. But it will all work out." He stood up and wrapped his arms around her and squeezed. Then his cell phone rang and he pulled away. "Oh, it's Steve.... Hey, man, what's up?"

Felicia watched as he walked away, chatting up a storm with his boss. Through fits of cackling and talking about the latest farm drama, she tamped down a small amount of rage that threatened to surface. *Weren't men supposed to be happy about having a baby? Is this just a girl thing? He acts like he doesn't even care!* At that moment, Anna began to whimper in the next room, waking up from her nap. John continued his meaningless blubbering on the phone, while Felicia dizzily went to get her daughter. She glanced at him before she entered Anna's room. John was different. He seemed... distant. But she shook her head and dismissed the thought. John had always been her rock. He would always be there for her, of this, she was sure.

■ ■ ■

Eight months later, they welcomed their second daughter into their lives. This one was the spitting image of Felicia. With dark hair and dark eyes, she was a chubby little angel—and they named her Halo. Soon, this small family became the apple of their community's eyes. Young, good-looking John and his girls visiting local fairs, spending a day petting calves, taking day trips at amusement parks, and living the dream as the model American family. Felicia basked in the sunlight of her blissful life.

Then one day… her utopia developed a crack.

Halo was two years old when she had her first seizure. At first, they were small and barely noticeable. But then they increased in the span of a few months. One day John was taking a lunch break in the green store and Felicia came to join him with the girls. They watched in horror as Halo collapsed to the ground, eyes rolled to the back of her head, and became unresponsive for forty minutes. They immediately brought her to the Children's Hospital in Hartford and waited anxiously for the team of doctors to diagnose their youngest daughter. The news that came back was a mother's worst nightmare. *Your daughter may have a brain disease, so we'll have to induce her in a coma and operate on her brain.* The category-5 hurricane came ripping into Felicia's heart and proceeded to dismantle every ounce of sense and stability from her young life. Rains poured into her tear ducts and threatened to flood the entire room. Winds pummeled her, lightning slashed her skin, and the incessant booming of the thunder deafened all the voices around her. This storm was enough to crush her.

But the warrior came out instead.

"Hello, Mom? Can you go to my house and pack me a week's worth of clothes? Yah, my good jeans, and my black yoga pants. Great. And I know it's a lot to ask, but can you take Anna for a while? I've got to be with my baby right now. She needs me. I'll send John to pick up my clothes. The ambulance leaves soon and I'll be on it. I love you too, Mom."

"Halo is leaving in 45 minutes. Will that be enough time for me to go home and get your things?" John asked.

"Probably not, but you can just meet me in Boston. That way you don't have to rush."

"Wait. You want me to drive all the way to Boston by myself?"

"Yup. Do you have a problem with that? Or would you like your daughter, her illness, and Boston Hospital to wait for you?" She had her hands on her hips, her shoulders squared and she was glaring at him. "And spend some time with Halo before you come. She's probably wondering what is going on." Felicia began to write out a list of items to pack, and a list of Anna's daily routine. "Here… give these to my mom." Then she turned to her youngest daughter, lying unresponsive in her hospital bed and walked over to her. She picked up the hair brush from the table and began to brush her hair with it. "Mommy's here, baby. Everything's going to be all right."

■ ■ ■

Over the next couple of weeks, Felicia remained in Boston at her daughter's side. When Halo had surgery, she waited anxiously in the waiting room, counting the seconds that went by. She never shed one tear, and instead, read the documents the doctor gave her on Halo's illness over and over again. When the surgery was completed, she breathed a sigh of relief when the doctors told her it went well. Felicia planted herself in her daughter's hospital room. Day and night, she watched over her angel, only leaving her side for the restroom. She refused help from her family members when they offered to stay with little Halo while she went out to stretch her legs. She held Halo's hand and spoke softly in her ear of all the fun things they would do when she woke up.

Halo did eventually wake up… but she was never again the same little girl that closed her eyes in Hartford. She was not able to talk, not able to walk, and she had to be fed with a feeding tube. The doctors told Felicia and John that it would take a lot of time, and a lot of special accommodations to make life comfortable for Halo. But the reality was, she would always be disabled. Disabled...disabled...disabled… disabled… disabled…. The words echoed repeatedly inside Felicia's head. *Will I be able to care for a disabled child? How will I pay for all this? Will other kids be mean to her? Will she ever marry? Will she live with me for the rest of her life?* These were the questions that took up residence inside Felicia's head. But the warrior inside her refused to allow these thoughts to invade her good judgment. Instead, she strapped on her sword, otherwise known as the internet, and began to research and Google and surf, until not one stone or piece of knowledge was left overturned. She spoke to doctors, read articles, applied for grants, changed the hours at her job to accommodate her daughter's schedule, met with teachers, and on top of all this—she was still the caretaker of her household and worked a fulltime job.

■ ■ ■

A year later, Halo had made some progress. She attended school that taught her how to every day communicate her needs. She continued to be fed with a feeding tube. But with physical therapy, she learned how to walk on her own. She wasn't ready to run marathons or take long strolls in the park, but she was able to move herself from one area to another without assistance. Felicia registered her for the Special Olympics, and taught her other daughter Anna how to help her sister and become an advocate for her. Life was tough, but she thanked God that her precious angelic daughter was still alive. Halo taught her the meaning of unconditional love, and she never asked for more than that. In Felicia's eyes, she was given a gift, and she would do everything in her power to keep her little gift happy and thriving.

But often times, when Utopia has a crack, the crack is rarely repaired. And when a crack develops from people that come from broken families, the issues that were never resolved act as crowbars to the fissure—stretching and tearing and widening until Utopia rips in half. Felicia didn't see this one coming. She didn't pay attention to the sadness in John's eyes. He was not the center of attention anymore—he now took a back seat to his daughter's needs. He wasn't able to go on vacations like they did in the past, because now they had a disabled child that had to have special accommodations. He couldn't go for long weekends with his wife, because being away from her daughter was something Felicia would not agree to. He didn't want to address his issues with a therapist or talk about his concerns with his wife. He kept everything inside and let it fester and increase in mass like a cancer. He spent more of his free time playing video games—well into the late hours of the night—often falling asleep on the couch. Video games became his outlet, his way to drown out all the ugliness that swirled around in his brain. People are told to close doors behind them for a reason—doors are meant to be shut. But John had had enough. In the winter of 2016, John opened a door when he met a new friend online. And this new friend was a female.

"Hey, do you know what time it is?" Felicia whispered, as she walked into the dark living room.

John gasped. "Geez, Felicia! You scared the hell out of me!" He rose from the couch, phone in hand, and walked into the kitchen.

"I'm sorry, but I think this is getting a little ridiculous. You do this every night, John."

"What?" he countered. "What are you talking about?"

"I never see you. You work all day, I work all day. I come home and I take care of Halo. You come home, and I put Halo to bed. When do we ever see each other or talk or do ANYTHING together?" She didn't realize her voice had risen or that her hands clenched into fists at her side. But John did.

"It's been tough, Felicia. I'm not going to deny that. Okay, I love that little girl too but you spend all your time with her. You never spend time with Anna, and all you do is take care of Halo and bitch and moan about shit. What would you like me to do?"

"How about be a husband! You spend all your fucking free time playing video games or on the fucking phone with God knows who! When's the last time you laid with me in bed and asked me how my day went? Huh? Shit, John! It's like you've bailed on us and I have no fucking clue where you went!"

John sighed. He put his head down and remained silent, staring at the floor. Felicia slowly walked over to him and put her hands on his face.

"Talk to me," she said softly.

"I can't. I don't know how."

Felicia put her hands in his and squeezed. He looked up at her, and she smiled.

"I know this has been tough on us both. It's been a really shitty couple of years. I miss you, John. I miss all the fun you and I used to have. I miss the talks we used to have. Sometimes I wish we could go back to that. But I wouldn't trade my girls for anything in the world."

"I know," he said.

"Hey. I've got an idea. Why don't we go away for the weekend— just the two of us? We could leave the girls with my parents. What do you think?"

"When?"

"This weekend! I'll make all the arrangements. Do you think Steve would give you some time off?"

"I guess I can ask him."

"Good. Ask him in the morning. This is going to be good for us, John. We need this! Just you and me."

"Yah."

"I'm going to bed. You coming?"

"Yah, I'll be there in a minute. I have to shut my computer down."

"Okay." Felicia smiled. She was so thrilled about her plans. She had always wanted to visit Niagara Falls, and now she would finally get to see it. *I hope the hotel isn't too expensive. Oh, who cares! We haven't been on a vacation together in a long time. If we spend a little bit more, it's totally worth it!* She glanced back at John, who was feverishly texting on his phone. *Strange—to be texting someone at 2:00 in the morning? It's probably his buddy Ben. I swear that guy never sleeps.* She threw herself on her bed and closed her eyes. She was so tired, she never noticed that John never came to bed that night.

■ ■ ■

Niagara Falls was amazing. The hotel was exquisite, the food was delicious, and the sights were heavenly. It was the perfect weekend. They took long walks by the falls and chatted about random things. They went shopping at the local shops. They even got their palms read by Madame Zelda for fun. Felicia felt like she had her old John back. She vowed that she would do this at least a couple times a year. Marriages always need work, and living with a disabled child makes it very easy to forget your partner. But John was the love of her life, and she would do anything to keep her family together. She would be a better wife, take better care of herself, and maybe tidy up the house a little more. Then John would see what a great woman she was. All she had to do was make a few adjustments and life would be grand once again.

■ ■ ■

Three weeks later, a multiple vortex F-5 super tornado ripped through Felicia's heart.

"Felicia?"

Felicia turned away from her pile of laundry and looked up at her husband.

"Yah?"

"Are the girls in bed?"

"Yah. Why?"

"I need to talk to you." His eyes searched hers for several seconds.

"Okay. What is it?"

"I...."

"John, you're scaring me. What's wrong?"

"I can't do this anymore, Felicia."

"You can't do what?"

"This house. This life. Us."

"What do you mean, John?" She stopped folding laundry and froze. A knot began to form in her stomach. Bile began to creep up into her esophagus. She felt lightheaded, and barely heard the words that came next.

"I found somebody else. I'm leaving you."

Wham! Watching your child transform from a disability that you cannot fix or prevent is a terrible thing. But watching your husband fall into the arms of another woman is enough to put even the toughest woman on her knees. Any normal person would have collapsed into a pool of her own tears, gone to bed for a month, and taken to the bottle for comfort. Other women would have gotten into the car and driven far, far away, most likely with a shiny, brand-new man that would make them forget about their troubles.

But Felicia was no ordinary woman.

"I'm sorry, I didn't hear you right. Did you just say you're leaving me for another woman?"

"Yes."

"Uh-huh. And you expect me to say what, John? Would you like me to congratulate you? Throw you a party? Tell you it's okay?"

"I'm so sorry, Felicia. I never meant to hurt you."

"GET OUT! You fucking bastard, GET OUT! I'm killing myself trying to keep this family together and you're out there fucking another woman? What about our children, huh? What are you going to tell them?"

"I'm not fucking her. She lives in Indiana. I've never met her in person. We just understand each other. She gets me."

Felicia stared at her husband, open mouthed. "I cannot believe what I'm hearing. Are you telling me that you are leaving me for a person you met online?"

"Yes."

"GET THE FUCK OUT OF HERE, YOU SICK BASTARD! AND DON'T YOU EVER COME BACK HERE AGAIN!!!"

The next day, Felicia contacted a lawyer. John spent the night at his friend Ben's house but he returned a couple of days later to get the rest of his things. The girls were confused. They couldn't understand why Daddy wasn't around anymore. The divorce process would only took 4 months to complete, and John promised not to fight her on anything. The separation agreement included the signing over of the marital house to Felicia, and that she be given full custody of the girls.

Felicia spent weeks and months learning how to operate and repair all the features in her house, and she made sure that the schools and daycare providers were aware of the situation, should her daughters begin slipping academically. She hired a therapist for Anna and communicated to Halo's behavioral clinician that any negative behaviors would have to be addressed. She enlisted the help of friends and family for support with the girls, or for a venting session. The night before John left for Indiana, he kissed his girls goodbye, and promised Felicia he would send her a payment for child support as soon as he could find a job. It was right before Christmas when he got in his truck and drove away.

Warrior Felicia was relieved when he left. Her biggest challenge was trying to explain to her daughters why Daddy left them. They directed their anger at their mother and often times she excused herself to her bedroom so she could have a 10-minute tear fest. But she always returned with a stoic face, ready to take on the next hurdle. She didn't have to see him anymore—didn't have to see the smile on his face when he gazed at his phone, when he thought no one was watching. She put on her big girl panties every morning as she got the girls ready for school and drove to work to put in a full day. At night, she crunched numbers and figured out what she could afford and what she could not. John had not found a job in the first 6 months living in Indiana, so the only source of income came from her job. There was still the mortgage to pay, utility bills, and daycare expenses.

When the first year was over, she began to smile again. She had healthy, happy girls who were involved in different programs and excelled at school, she was able to pay her bills, and she had one less man-child to take care of. She didn't hear from John often and that suited her just fine. He sent her a couple hundred dollars in the span of a year, but she didn't need his money. She was making ends meet on her own.

■ ■ ■

The following year, Felicia met a Navy Captain at a ball she was invited to through friends. She was taken by his smile and his kindness.

"Hi," he said, extending his hand. "My name is Dave."

"I'm Felicia."

"Felicia? What a great name. Is that Spanish?"

"Sort of. My dad is Puerto Rican. My mom is… a real mess."

Dave laughed out loud. "That's funny! Sounds like my mom!"

"I'm sure yours doesn't try to cut your steak for you when you're in a restaurant."

Dave howled with laughter, holding his stomach. "No, she does not!"

"I'm not even kidding."

"That's too funny." He stopped laughing and smiled at her. "So are you here with someone?"

"Yes. My friends Chris and Julie. They're right over there," she said pointing to a couple making out in the corner.

"Oh!" Dave said.

"Oh?"

"Yah!"

"How come you said it like that?"

"Like what?"

"Like you didn't expect me to be with them. I mean...," she said looking over at them, "I know they probably need to get a room but...."

"No, it's not that," Dave smiled. "I just thought you'd be here with your husband, or boyfriend or someone like that."

"No. No husband. No boyfriend either. I'm just here because I needed to get out of the house."

"Then I guess I'm the lucky one," he smiled.

Over the next few weeks, Dave asked Felicia on dates and she accepted, thinking that she couldn't be a hermit forever. She enjoyed her time with Dave, but was always skeptical at his sincerity. After all, she believed that most men were untrustworthy, and were only after a good time. After a couple of months of dating, Dave was promoted from Navy Captain to Rear Admiral. He was going to be honored at a special ceremony in Hawaii, of all places. And the only person he wanted to take with him was Felicia. She was reluctant, at first. She didn't want to leave her girls. But then, after much convincing from her parents, she decided to throw caution to the wind, and accepted Dave's invitation. The girls were staying with her parents, so she decided to indulge herself. She bought a new dress, got her hair done, and packed her bags. It was a trip that changed her life. They wined and dined, they took in some of the island sights, swam in the beautiful blue waters, and enjoyed the long quiet nights together. She watched him receive a high honor, and thought, *If nothing else, he could be a great companion.* They returned after 5 days, and continued to see each other often.

Dave became more involved with Felicia's girls, accompanying them to different school events and helping Halo participate in Special Olympics. He didn't push Felicia too hard, as he knew her wounds were still fresh. He was patient and understanding, and did his very best to listen and offer his support. Occasionally, Felicia pushed him away, or told him they were moving too fast. But Dave, being a calm and understanding man, waited until she took the time she needed to strip off her armor and put her weapons back inside their holsters. Felicia had been conditioned to fight and protect her girls at all costs, and trusting someone again would be almost impossible.

But love has a way of pervading even the hardest of hearts. Walls of steel with a thousand padlocks securing the gates are no match for the greatest gift of all. Love can raze impenetrable barriers, and allow even the toughest warrior to succumb to her warmth. To be truthful, Felicia liked when Dave was around. She liked spending time as a family, and she liked telling him all her fears and dreams. She liked to have someone there to depend on and lean on when times got tough. It took some time for Felicia to realize that she wasn't giving in when she let Dave share her world—but rather, she was letting love rule her life, rather than sadness and despair. It didn't matter that John had not sent a child support payment in two years, and it didn't matter that he only saw his girls once a year. She had won the battle. She had won complete control of her girls' wellbeing, she was self-supporting, and she had the love of a man that would offer her the moon.

"It's been a year, you know," Dave smiled.

"Yes, it has."

"I propose a toast," he stated as he raised his wine glass. "To us. May we find more happiness than this very moment."

"More happiness? I really can't imagine any more, Dave," she chuckled.

"Oh, I can," he said, reaching into his pocket and taking out a small, blue box. He slowly opened the lid and looked deeply into her eyes. "I know you had it rough. But I'm going to tell you for the hundredth time that I love you and I'm not going anywhere without you. You're my best friend, Felicia. There is nothing I won't do for you and the girls." He then got down on one knee. "Will you do me the honor of becoming my wife?"

Felicia stared at the man in front of her. A year ago, she swore she would never love again. She poured all of her energy into her girls and convinced herself that she would never need anyone else in her life. She vowed that she would never suffer the pain of being betrayed, or putting trust in a human being only to have it thrown back in her face. But a year later, a man came into her life and changed all of that. He taught her how to trust again, to have faith again, to depend on others again, and most of all he helped her tear down her wall, so that love could weave its way back into her injured heart.

"Yes, Dave," Felicia whispered, tears streaming down her face. She placed her hands on his cheeks and pulled him closer until their lips met. "I will be your wife."

■ ■ ■

Faced with the most debilitating life traumas, Felicia never faltered in her quest to make a good life for her and her girls. She looked defeat straight in the face and roared at it. She spat back at the demon that tried to ruin her. In the end, the demon shriveled down to the size of nothing and disappeared. She had all she needed—her girls, her future husband, supportive friends and family, a great career, financial security, and happiness. Felicia secured her place in history amongst all the warrior women who battled against their captors, and made it to the top. But to her friends, she was simply known as *one bad-ass bitch*—an indestructible woman who flipped off her cheating husband while screaming, "You want a piece of me? BRING IT!" ∎

■ CHAPTER TWO ■
Allura

W hen Allura's mother gave birth to her, the nurses in the ward couldn't take their eyes off of her sweet baby. She was the face of royal tranquility, and quiet beauty. They all fought over who would hold her so they could stare into her angelic face, as if God himself were speaking through her. Her mother settled on the name Allura, because she seemed to lure people in and mesmerize them.

As the years passed, Allura grew into her name. Her medium build, skinny frame, and long dark locks were appealing, but they took a backseat to her dark, obsidian eyes. They could entrance the devil himself. But Allura wasn't interested in being a temptress. She was determined to rise above her family's station. Her parents came from Italy. Her mother worked three jobs and had no time to counsel Allura. Her father worked as well, and was seldom home. The couple made enough money to pay the mortgage on their home and put food on the table. They had very little left over for pretty dresses and Barbie dolls. Allura set her eyes on living the American dream, for her parents' sake—a good career, respectful husband, a couple of kids, and a house with her name on the deed. She didn't want to struggle making ends meet. She intended to be financially secure and have plenty of time to spend with her family.

When she entered college, she poured herself into her studies, and excelled in school. Although she had plenty of friends that begged her to participate in the college party life, she always declined their invitations. On Friday nights, while her friends piled into someone's car to locate the nearest keg, Allura would spend long hours in the library reading her textbooks. On one occasion, a young man stopped at her table.

"Hi."

Allura looked up. "Hi."

"I see you here every Friday night."

"Uh-huh."

"I think you're in my philosophy class, but I sit in the back so you may not have noticed me. My name is Jasper. Jasper Metcalf."

"Oh, I'm Allura."

"Allura? That's an interesting name. Is that Greek?"

"No, it's Italian."

"Wow. It reminds me of that show I used to watch as a kid—*Voltron*."

"Yah?"

"Yah. I think the princess's name was Allura."

"Oh."

"So what do you think of Professor Camden? A bit of a nut job, eh?"

"I'm sorry … Jasper, is it? I'm in the middle of a project right now and I really need to get back to work."

"Oh, sure. I'm sorry. I just wanted to introduce myself."

"Well, it was nice to meet you."

"And if you ever want to get a cup of coffee, just let me know."

"Will do. Thanks."

Jasper left her table, but didn't go too far. He planted himself three tables down and made it look like he was studying. He watched Allura's every move. The way she put her extra pencils in her hair, the way she furrowed her brows when she was heavy in thought, or even the delicate way she flipped pages in her book. There was something about her. And then there were her eyes. They seemed to pierce him like an arrow. Her eyes burned into his mind and he longed to stare at them again. It was like staring into the sun—he wanted to keep looking at such a beautiful star, at the risk of destroying his self-control.

■ ■ ■

It took a year for Allura to finally accept Jasper's coffee invitation. They met at Sanchez's Espresso Bar on Main Street. At first, Allura found him dull and kind of nerdy. All he talked about was basketball and *The Lord of the Rings*. They were two subjects that Allura had no background knowledge on. But then he began to talk about his family and their traditions, and Allura found herself intrigued. Jasper too had hardworking parents, and they saved all their extra money to send him to college. They also made a big deal at Christmas. Their house was always bursting at the seams on Christmas Eve with relatives from all over New England. Granted, Jasper's family didn't put out the Italian spread that Allura feasted on each year. But an American buffet that consisted of ham, mashed potatoes, and deviled eggs was good enough for the Metcalf family.

Allura and Jasper began to see each other regularly. After a few months, the regular meetings included a kiss of some sort. Before the year was out, they were full blown into dating. Allura liked having Jasper around. He was like a comfortable old blanket. And Jasper loved to dote on her. He often bought her books or surprised her with a blizzard from Dairy Queen. One fall evening, when they were lounging around in his dorm room, she took her clothes off and rocked his world. He was on fire after that, craving more of her with each passing day. But Allura was only interested in one thing—independence. So when the roll in the hay was over, she simply put on her clothes, grabbed her keys, and headed on over to the library.

After they graduated in the summer of 1995, Jasper took Allura to their favorite restaurant, and got down on one knee.

"Allura, I love you with all my heart. Will you marry me?"

"Yes, I will," she replied. The words came out of her mouth, but they were chalky and forced. Truthfully, Allura was not in love with Jasper. He didn't set her soul on fire like some of the characters in the romance novels she occasionally read. That kind of passion wasn't real, she told herself. But Jasper adored her and he was educated and could provide for her. It was a smart match, as her mother would say. And Jasper was the key to living her American dream.

Or so she thought.

■ ■ ■

They married the following summer. Allura found a job teaching in a Catholic school, and Jasper became the manager of a grocery store. They bought a small home in East Hampton. It had a small yard and only two bedrooms but it was perfect for the newlyweds. In the first few years of their marriage, they traveled quite a bit. They took trips to the shore, or Upstate New York for hiking, or cozy cabins in New Hampshire. Allura was content with her life, but still, the picture of the American dream was not yet complete. Jasper would have been happy waiting a bit longer to start a family. But Allura wanted more. So in the winter of the year 2000, Allura finally got her wish.

"Jasper? Is that you?"

"Yah."

"How was work?"

"Same old, same old. How about you?"

"Great!"

"Great? Wow, that's a switch. Usually you're tired and annoyed when you come home."

"Well, today is different. I have news."

"Oh?"

"I'm pregnant."

Jasper stared at her speechless. Allura stared back. This wasn't exactly the reaction she pictured. Wasn't the father-to-be supposed to pick her up and spin her around the room, wearing a grin from ear to ear?

"Hon? Aren't you going to say anything?"

"Uh, wow. That's great, honey. Wow. A baby. That's ... uh ... great."

"You seem disappointed."

"No," he rushed over to her and took her hands in his. "I'm sorry, you just caught me by surprise, that's all. It'll take a few days for it to sink in. I'm happy, though."

"Okay, good, because I am so excited. Jasper, we're going to be parents!"

"Yah, amazing, isn't it?" He hugged her, then pulled away quickly. "So what's for dinner?"

■ ■ ■

During the next 8 months, Allura made sure she took extra good care of herself. She only gained about 25 pounds, and ate only organic foods. She was determined to do all she could to have a healthy baby. Jasper helped her decorate the nursery and often went shopping with her so she didn't have to lift anything heavy. Her pregnancy went fairly well, and in October of that year, she gave birth to a beautiful baby boy. They named him Jack.

For the first year of Jack's life, Allura couldn't get enough of her little angel. He was perfect. At first, his eyes were the standard blue that all babies were born with. But by the time he hit 6 months old, it was obvious that he inherited the same dark eyes as his mother. He was a good baby, and both parents loved bringing him to family functions to show him off. The small family was very happy. But the American dream never stops at just one child. Two years later, Allura gave birth to her second child. This time she was a girl, and they named her Ella.

Their family was expanding, and their little two-bedroom house was no longer adequate. Allura and Jeff decided to build a house on a parcel of land that they bought. Allura threw herself into the designs of the new house with a vengeance. She spoke to engineers and builders. She bought books on interior design and wrote down ideas in a notebook. She researched all the latest bathroom gear—from faucets to sinks. She imagined what family functions would look like and tailored the house to accommodate get togethers. In Allura's mind, the house had to be absolutely perfect.

"Do you think we should add another 5 feet to the kitchen?"

"Babe, it's late. Can we talk about this in the morning?"

"No, Jasper. This is important. Can you just hear me out?"

"Ugh. Do I have a choice?"

"No," she shifted in their bed so she was sitting up now and facing him. "So I was thinking that at Christmas time, when we have my family over, we have to accommodate Uncle Frank. So if we add 5 more feet, then he can move around with his wheelchair and not feel like he has to park somewhere and stay there all night."

"That's it? You want to add more square footage because you're worried about your uncle in a wheelchair?"

"Yah! I mean it's Uncle Frank. He's like a second father to me."

"I thought this was our house. Why are we building a house to suit your extended family? It doesn't make any sense."

"Well, it makes perfect sense to me! I like having my family over!"

"Fine. Okay. You win. I don't want to fight with you over this. We'll extend the kitchen 5 feet."

"Thanks. I knew you would understand."

The house was built in 10 months, and when Ella turned 2, she celebrated her birthday in her new house. Allura had finally achieved her dream. The career, the house with her name on the deed, the respectful husband, and two kids—a boy and a girl. Life couldn't get any better than this. She spent all her free time with her children. She enrolled them in play groups, signed them up for sports, and went on little adventures with them. Who would have thought an Italian girl with parents that barely spoke English could achieve all this? But she did. And she was pretty content with her amazing life.

Often times, where there is a strong woman commandeering a household, there is sometimes a weak man living in her shadows. Jasper was expected to go to work every day because his job was to support his family. If he had an idea of some sort, he had to run it by Allura first. Sometimes she agreed, and sometimes she did not. But ultimately, Jasper knew who was in charge of his life. It wasn't him, and he wasn't sure if he liked it.

"I was thinking that we could have your parents take the kids for the weekend and we could go up North to New Hampshire. Just the two of us, like we used to. We could rent one of those cottages," Jasper grinned.

"I don't wanna go."

"Why?"

"The kids are too young and my parents are not that healthy. My mom has a ton of issues with her thyroid and my dad takes care of her."

"Allura, we haven't gone away since before Jack was born."

"There will be plenty of time for that when the kids get older. They're only little for a short time."

"So what are you saying? That we can have a romantic weekend when Ella turns 18?"

"Not that old! Maybe in a few years, we can go. But not right now. I don't wanna go."

Jasper was shot down quite a bit. Allura usually had her way. At first, he took it pretty well. There was no way he could ever win against her. The only thing that he did command was his job. At least in that arena, Allura didn't have any say in what went on there. So he spent more time at work, acquiring extra hours here and there, and spending more time getting to know his coworkers. One day, he even brought one of them home to meet Allura.

"Babe, I'm home."

"I'm in here. I had a meeting at school, so dinner will just be a few minutes late," she called from the kitchen.

"Uh, Allura, this is Crystal. Crystal, this is my wife, Allura," Jasper announced as he entered the room.

Allura looked up from the lower cabinet, where she was trying to locate her favorite pan. "Oh…." She stood up. "Hi. I didn't know we were having company."

"Hi!" Crystal extended her hand for Allura to shake. "Your home is gorgeous!"

"Thanks. So you work with Jasper?"

"Yes. I just became the general store manager."

"Oh, congratulations."

"Thanks. Yah, Jasper is one of my best employees. He has a file I needed for my report so that's why I'm here."

"Oh, yes," Jasper cut in. "Let me run and get that for you." And with that, he left the two women alone in the kitchen.

"Are you married, Crystal?"

"No. I was engaged once but that fell through."

"No kids?"

"No. I would love to have some someday. God, I would kill to have something like this. Beautiful home, kids…. Jasper is a lucky guy."

"Well, it took a lot of hard work on both our parts. This didn't happen overnight."

"Oh, of course. Yes. I just hope I am as fortunate as you two one day."

"Here it is," Jasper said as he reentered the room. "All the projections are here too."

"Thanks. Well, I don't want to take up any more of your time. I know that you're getting ready to have dinner."

"Oh, why don't you stay?" Jasper replied. Allura shot him a look and he instantly retracted his offer. "I mean…."

"No, no, I don't want to impose. Besides, I still have a lot of numbers to crunch. I'll probably be up all night." Crystal looked at Jasper—playing the part of the damsel in distress. Surely, he would come to her rescue and invite her again for dinner. In which she would graciously accept.

"Well, it was nice to meet you, Crystal. We don't want to keep you from your work," Allura said.

Crystal glanced at Jasper, who was now looking at the ground.

"Likewise, Allura."

"I'll walk you out," Jasper replied.

Allura watched the strange woman walk away with her husband. There was something about her that she didn't quite like. But she shrugged it off and blamed it on her time of the month. *God, I hope I didn't come across as a bitch. Oh well, she was a little too nice for my taste. I hope I never see her again.*

≡ ≡ ≡

A month later, she noticed that Jasper was spending more time on his phone. When she asked him who he was talking to all the time, he answered, "My boss," and explained how their store was in the middle of a merger and he was helping Crystal make the transition smoother. It didn't sit well with her, but she figured it was the same with her workplace. Allura's boss was a man. If she had to spend time talking to him on the phone because of some important event, she would want Jasper to understand too. So she let it go.

Three months later, Allura was cleaning her bedroom and Jasper was in the shower. As she was gathering up some clothes he left on the floor, she noticed his phone had fallen out of one the pockets. At first, she just stared at it, trying to decide if it happened to land there for a reason. Then she glanced at the door and stooped to pick it up. She immediately punched in his password and went to the text messages. Crystal's name was at the very top, so she knew they had just spoken. She took a deep breath and opened the messages.

Why do you put up with her?

Idk. She's my wife?

She doesn't have any respect for you. You're a puppet. You deserve better.

Maybe.

Come over tonight.

What?

Come over.

Wham! The breath that should have flowed effortlessly in Allura's lungs had suddenly disappeared. Could this be happening? Was her husband having an affair with this tramp?? The same tramp that had entered her home and spoke to her? Her instincts had been right after all—she was no good. Her husband had not answered when she asked him to come over. Did that mean that he refused her? Or did that mean that he was thinking about it? Heat started rising in Allura's head. Anger replaced all common sense. This bitch was not about to take her family from her. This was HER family, and no one else's.

At that moment, Jasper opened the bathroom door with just a towel wrapped around him. Allura looked at him with her molten rock eyes, and they were on fire. It was a look he saw occasionally, and didn't care to tangle with.

"Why is Crystal asking you to go over her place?"

"What?"

"Text messages, Jasper. Now answer my question."

"Why are you looking at my text messages?"

"Because I'm your wife and what's yours is mine. Now answer the FUCKING question!"

"I don't know! She asked me to come over, that's all! It's not like I did it!"

"I don't want you to have anything else to do with this woman, do you hear me?"

"She's my boss, Allura. I have to talk to her."

"You will ask for a transfer or find a new job. Am I making myself clear?"

"I didn't do anything wrong, Allura!"

"You may not have done anything YET, but if you don't stop this now, she will continue. And then it will turn into something. Are you getting this?"

"Fine. Okay, I will tell her tomorrow."

Tomorrow came and went. The text messages between Jasper and Crystal stopped. He still spent long hours at work, but at least they were not communicating after work. A couple of months went by and all was quiet on the home front. A little too quiet. Then there was that little voice inside Allura's brain niggling her. She recalled Crystal's face, standing in her kitchen. She was devious, and calculating. Surely she wouldn't stop if Jasper asked her to. Jasper was a weakling. He couldn't command an army of ants! Somehow, she had to know the truth. Someone was lying, and she had to know who!

The next day, she took a half-day off of work and went to A&E Detective Agency. She sat down with a man named Allan and explained her story to him. She then paid him $500 in cash and asked him to get back to her within the week. The not knowing was eating her alive. And the fate of her American dream was at stake. The next seven days went by slow as molasses. Each day was more agonizing than the next. Finally, she got the call she was waiting for.

"Mrs. Metcalf?"

"Yes?"

"Detective Jones here."

"Yes, Detective. I was expecting your call."

"I spent the week trailing your husband. Mostly, he went to work and back home again."

Allura exhaled. So far, the news was hopeful. Maybe things would work out after all.

"But on Thursday, he took a different route."

The blood drained out of Allura's face.

"Go on."

"I followed him to an apartment building on the South Side. The woman you mentioned, Crystal, resides there."

"Please go on."

"When he got out of his car, another pulled up next to him. It was Crystal. They both entered the apartment building, hand in hand. He did not exit the building for approximately 2 hours."

Allura did not say a word. Her head was spinning into oblivion. *My husband betrayed me, my husband broke vows, my husband committed adultery, my husband let someone else touch him, my husband touched another woman, my husband wants to be with another woman, my husband cheated on me.*

"Mrs. Metcalf?"

"I'm here."

"I'm very sorry. Would you like me to continue following him?"

"No. Thank you very much for your service." She hung up the phone and went into her bedroom. The kids were out in the backyard so she had a moment to herself. She closed the door, leaned against the wall, and sunk down to the ground. A slow moan came out at first, then the tears fell, then the wails. Her world was crumbling beneath her. Her perfect American dream was nothing more than broken glass shattering beneath her feet.

She didn't know how long she sat there, but when she heard the commotion of kids entering the house and Jasper's voice, she knew she had to face the music. She heard him come up the steps and enter the bedroom.

"Allura?"

She simply looked at him. Her eyes were dark and foreboding. It sent a shiver down his spine.

"What's wrong?"

She stood up and faced him. "Is there something you want to tell me?"

"About what?"

"About your trip to Crystal's apartment."

He stared at her for a moment, considering his response.

"Seven years of marriage, two children, a beautiful house—all down the drain. That's what we mean to you? You can discard us like we're trash?"

"Allura, it's not what you think."

She took a step forward and slapped him across the face. The force of the blow sent him stumbling backwards.

"Don't you dare lie to me! I hired a private investigator to follow you this week! Don't you dare lie to me!"

"Yes, I went to her apartment! Yes, I slept with her. But Allura, I don't love her! I made a mistake and I'm really sorry. Please don't end this. I swear I will never see her again!"

Allura turned towards the bed and sat down. She was tired. Her heart hurt so badly. She didn't know how it would ever heal. This man who she shared a life with had broken his promises to her. How could she ever trust him again? What if he was the kind of guy who wanted the wife at home and the whore on the side?

"You betrayed me. You betrayed your children. What am I going to tell them?"

Jasper fell to his knees and wrapped his arms around Allura's legs. "I love you, Allura. I made a mistake!" he sobbed into her knees. "I swear to you, I will never look at another woman again! Please!"

"Tell me how this happened, Jasper. Is it because I wouldn't go away with you? Is it because I became boring? Was I too bitchy?"

"No!" he looked up at her. "No, it was me. I was weak. I didn't make my feelings clear to you. I let you lead, but instead of walking beside you, I fell behind you. Then when I wanted to catch up, you were already gone. Crystal distracted me—I couldn't catch up to you."

Allura stood up suddenly. "Don't ever mention that whore's name to me ever again, do you hear me?"

"Yes, I'm sorry. Please forgive me. I need you in my life. The kids need me too."

Allura did not know what to do. She needed time to think.

"I'll think about it."

The next day, Allura went to work. She had a hard time not thinking about things, but she welcomed the distraction of everyday life. She picked up the kids from school, asked them about their day, made dinner, and folded laundry. On the outside, she looked like she was in control. On the inside, she was screaming in pain, and trying desperately to find a way out of hell. Two weeks went by like this. Jasper came home earlier from work, and engaged with the kids more. At night, he tried to cuddle with Allura, but she continued to keep him at arm's length. One morning, she woke up and decided that enough was enough. For the sake of her family, she would give Jasper another chance. It's not that she loved him—she actually didn't. But she loved her kids more than life, and would do anything to make them happy. She waited until Jasper came home that evening to tell him.

"Hi. I have something to tell you," she said.

Jasper walked slowly into the kitchen. He didn't take his eyes off of her.

"I've decided that I can move past this. You're my husband and I'm your wife and there's no reason we can't work this out. For the sake of the kids, anyway."

Silence. Jasper's lips began to quiver. Tears pooled into his eyes. Something was wrong.

"Jasper? What's wrong?"

"I wish with all my heart that I could stay here with you," he whispered. "But I can't."

"What do you mean?"

"She's pregnant. She just told me today. The baby is mine."

And there it was. Sometimes, a sign from the heavens is all it takes for a person to take a deeper look inside of themselves. God is always in control, not the humans He created. And God wanted something better for his beautiful creation. Allura didn't speak to Jasper much after he broke the news to her. She kindly asked him to get his belongings and get out. Jasper was gone within the week. She allowed herself two days to lay in her pajamas and give in to her sadness. She felt as though the black hole of despair was getting ready to devour her, and she welcomed it. *What if I throw myself under a bus or take extra sleeping pills. Would that make the pain go away? What about my kids? Would they miss me? Or should I just let the darkness take me now?*

On the third day, she woke up early and lay staring at the ceiling. Thoughts swirled around her mind like bees. They were talking to her— trying to sway her so that she picked a side. One side coaxed her to fall into an abyss of depression, and accept that the American dream she wanted so badly was built on lies. This side also wanted to blame her for everything— she was too mean, she wasn't pretty enough, she was bad in bed. But the other side was an iron-clad giant of a woman—much like a soldier. She slapped her in the face with reason and stared into her lifeless eyes. *You aren't a quitter. You are a warrior. Get up! This loser doesn't deserve you. You are a descendent of the Italian culture—a culture that has seen wars and famine and poverty. Survival runs through your veins as it has in theirs. You have fire within you! Look within you and find your strength again, and you will rise!* With that, Allura rose, took a shower, got her kids off to school, and went to work.

■ ■ ■

Over the next month, Allura was all business. She discontinued Jasper's medical insurance, filed for divorce, hired an attorney, and met with a financial adviser. She spent more time with her kids to compensate for the time their father was not spending with them. She enlisted the help of her own father and mother to care for the kids when she had meetings at school or if she needed help shuttling them to sports. By the time she reached their final court date, Allura was broke, exhausted, and incredibly relieved.

Jasper married his lover and they had two children together. He lost his job for a period of time, so Allura had to pay for her children all by herself. Her children hated seeing their father on the weekends because he didn't seem to have time for them. But Allura always made time for Jack and Ella, and she raised them to be hard workers and above all—honest. Jasper tried to get Allura back several times while he was married to Crystal. But Allura felt nothing but pity for him. She had no interest in men with no balls. Overall, the biggest lesson she learned in this bittersweet experience was that the American dream she wanted so badly for her life had always been in her hands. She didn't need a man to make it complete. She needed to believe in herself, be a good mother, further her education, keep teaching, and enjoy life for everything it had to offer.

Ten years later, Allura walked into the old high school for her annual August Professional Development. She had on her tight jeans, favorite white tank top, and her cute Egyptian sandals on. She had straightened her hair, just because, and it fell in a thick, dark mass down her back. Her face was tan and her eyes were bright with the enthusiasm of seeing her old colleagues and starting a brand-new school year. She walked through the door of the computer lab and saw Mason—a fellow teacher who had piqued her interest for the last 8 years. Their eyes locked immediately. The smiles on both their faces lit up the entire room.

"Well, well—look who's here?" Mason grinned.

"Wow. This is a twist of fate."

"Are you actually going to sit next to me?"

"Bad idea?"

"Really bad. I'm not going to pay attention at all."

"Oh, c'mon. Stop teasing me!"

"Are you still dating that city dude?"

"No. We broke up last week."

"That's a tragedy."

"What about you? Aren't you supposed to be engaged?"

"Turns out, she wasn't the girl for me."

"Is that so?"

He smiled then and looked deeply in her obsidian eyes. "It's been eight years of one failed relationship after another. I feel like I've been all over the place with everything in my life."

"Tell me about it. Ever since my divorce, I feel like I've been searching for someone to make me happy. I forgot that being true to myself is the only thing that makes me happy. I've got to own my feelings, say them out loud, and accept the person that I am."

"And who are you?"

"I'm Allura. I work hard, I love my job, I hate drinking, I like to stay in my pjs, I like to sleep late on weekends, I'm a good mom, I love my Italian family, I drink tea, I hate liars, sometimes I'm bitchy, I'm good in bed, I love the beach, I dance to 80s music, and I always tell the truth."

Mason stared at her with his mouth open. He was stunned. He never heard a woman speak so truthfully about her character.

"Your turn," she said.

He took a deep breath. "My name is Mason. I met you eight years ago and I haven't stopped thinking about you ever since. Sometimes I would dream about you at night, but when I woke up and realized it wasn't real, I was sad. I think you are so beautiful. Your children are wonderful. I feel bad that you've felt lost for so many years. I admire your courage and your strength. I am drawn to your fire. Will you go on a date with me?"

Now it was Allura's turn to be stunned. She had developed a secret crush on Mason years ago, but she never thought the feelings were mutual.

"Well? Are you going to answer me?"

"I'll think about it," she smiled.

He smiled back and nodded his head. Allura looked over at her friend Noel sitting across from her. She had eavesdropped on the entire conversation, and sat giggling inside herself.

"Bad-ass bitch," Noel mouthed to her, and Allura sat back and laughed. ■

▪ CHAPTER THREE ▪

Tyra

Tyra was your typical bad-ass teenager. Her mother left her when she was only 12 years old, and her father did the best he could with her. But not even his unconditional love could quell the demons swirling inside of her. She rebelled against anything that was tranquil and organized, and preferred instead to live inside chaos and anger. Her temper grew stronger as the years went on, and by the time she hit high school, she was a force to be reckoned with. She put the mean girls to shame, caroused with the dangerous boys, and made her teachers wish for an early retirement.

One boy, however, Jordan, seemed to tickle her interest. He was a skinny, short, dorky kid that loved to ride snowmobiles, and loved Tyra even more. They shared a common interest in turning wrench on anything mechanical, and his part-time job at a local farm. Jordan was dirty and daring, but his heart was soft and quiet. She longed to taste even an ounce of the peace he had within him.

"So... you wanna go to the prom with me?" he asked her one day.

"Prom? Who the hell goes to the prom these days? Isn't that for losers?"

"C'mon, babe," he chuckled. "I ain't no loser, and I ain't gonna stop asking 'til you say yes."

"Jesus. I suppose you want me to wear a dress?"

"Naw, I prefer you to be naked, but I don't think Mr. Salisbury would let you in."

"Aw, you're funny."

"C'mon, T. Go to the prom with me."

"I'll think about it."

How Jordan possessed the patience to stay with her is one of the world's greatest mysteries. She drove him insane with her wild ideas and obstinance. It was like taking care of a child at times. But when the woman in her came out, it was enough to put Jordan on his knees, and he fell completely in love with her. So when she dropped out of high school and told him goodbye, Jordan's world came tumbling down.

"Why weren't you in school yesterday?" he asked.

"I'm done."

"What do you mean you're done? With what?"

"With everything."

"Well, what happened?"

"Nothing happened. I'm just done with this place. I hate it."

"So you're dropping out?"

"Yeah."

"And what are you going to do? Work?"

"Yah, I guess. Whatever. I'll figure it out."

"T, c'mon. Stay with me. It can't be that bad."

"You can't even imagine how bad it is. I'm done, we're done, I'm moving on."

"What do you mean *we're* done?"

"Jordan, don't make this hard for me, okay?"

"Are you breaking up with me?"

"You belong here with all the guys—Johnny, Roger, and Sled. You got your boys. I need something different. I gotta get out of here. And where I'm going, you can't come. You have to finish school."

"Please, T. Don't do this. I love you. I can't live without you."

"I'm sorry, Jordan. I have to go."

She left him there in the parking lot, sobbing uncontrollably on the hood of his car. Even though her heart bled for him, watching him crumble before her very eyes, her defiance dragged her away. She got into her car, and swiftly drove away. She never looked back, for fear that the small, angelic voice inside of her would convince her to stay. So she just continued down Route 207, turned up the volume on LL Cool J, and thought about the next chapter in her life.

■ ■ ■

Over the next few months, Tyra secured a job at a fast-food restaurant. She had moved in with a friend of hers, worked during the day, and partied all night. She drove to the city on weekends, caught up with some people that she had just met the night before, and tried really hard to avoid trouble at all costs. This is where she felt in control—in a world of impulsivity and risk. Spending time with people that were just as lost as she was. It was safer this way. Love only complicated things—made her think of her mother. One day she was there, and the next day... she was not.

Guillermo was a smooth-talking ladies' man. He was good looking, he drove a sleek black Honda Prelude, and he always kept a wad of twenties on a money clip with a Brazilian flag. He wasn't really from Brazil but he loved to tell people that to make him sound foreign and exotic. His mother was Puerto Rican and his father was Mexican. He worked as a cellphone salesman at Techno World. Tyra walked into his shop one day to inquire about a new cellphone. Her phone got smashed when she accidentally left it on her car and drove off. She found it the next day, cracked and missing some keys.

"Well, hello, young lady. What can I help you with?" Guillermo smiled as she walked in.

Tyra eyed him suspiciously and reached into her pocket. She took out her injured phone and slid it across the glass case.

"You think you can fix this?"

"Let's take a look." Guillermo proceeded to examine the phone, turning it over and over in his hands. "Hmmm. I'm afraid this can't be fixed. Even if I send it away to have the keyboard replaced, it would cost you more than a brand-new phone."

"Shit. I don't think I can afford a new phone."

"Our cheapest model is only $100."

"Yah, well, your cheapest model is half my rent. I'll have to figure something else out."

"How about a used phone?"

"You got one?"

"Yah, but not here. Let me take you out to dinner tonight and I'll bring it."

"Dinner? I ain't no fancy girl!"

"You're funny," he laughed. "Even tough girls like you need to be wined and dined sometimes."

"Not this tough girl. I don't do wine."

"We don't have to drink at all. I would just like the pleasure of a beautiful girl's company. C'mon. What other plans do you have tonight anyway?"

"I could sit in my apartment and watch *In Living Color* and eat a bag of chips."

He raised an eyebrow at her and smiled.

"What? *In Living Color* is hilarious."

"I know it is," he purred. "But you can always record it… and watch it later. Let me take you out. Please. Where else can you get a free meal and a phone to go with it?"

Something deep inside Tyra screamed for her not to accept his invitation. But it was so faint and muffled that she ignored its little bite. What could it hurt? And she really did need a phone.

"Fine. But we're staying local, got it?"

"As you wish. I'll meet you here in two hours."

■ ■ ■

He didn't take her to McDonald's or the Royal Buffet. Instead, he took her to a Chinese restaurant with dim lights and great service. After drinking a couple rounds of Saki, Tyra found herself laughing at his corny jokes and playing footsies under the table. Two hours later, he paid the bill, led her to his car, and they both landed at his apartment. They barely made it in the door before her shirt came off and they were both clawing at each other like a couple of grizzly bears. *What the hell? It's been a long time anyway. Besides, maybe I can get away with getting this used phone for free.* So she left caution to flutter into the wind, and allowed herself to get tangled up in Guillermo's world.

■ ■ ■

A couple of months later, she got up quickly and barely made it to the toilet before she started puking her brains out. She cleaned herself up, made her way into the kitchen and poured herself a glass of orange juice. She was practically living with Guillermo at this point, so she didn't want to wake him just yet. *What the fuck is wrong with me? It must have been the chicken I ate last night. Shit! I don't have time to be sick. Unless….* Worry began to creep up inside of her. There was a chance that this had nothing to do with the meal she had the night before. She paced in the living room and tried to count the days before her last period. Was it possible? *Dear God, please let it not be. I'm too young and immature for this. I can't even take care of myself, let alone a baby!* She made a conscious decision to stop at the pharmacy on her way home from work.

That evening, she sat motionless on the toilet, staring at the white stick before her. It was after 8 P.M. and she could hear the apartment door opening and Guillermo throwing his keys on the counter.

"Querida? Where are you?" he called.

"In the bathroom."

"Okay, well, I have to go so hurry up."

Tyra flushed the toilet and opened the door. "It's all yours."

"Thanks, babe. I gotta go," he rushed past her, closed the door and unzipped his pants to relieve himself. Then he turned his head to notice the white stick sitting on the edge of the sink.

"What the fuck is this?" his voice boomed through the closed door.

No answer.

Guillermo opened the door and rushed into the living room, where Tyra was sitting on the couch staring off into space.

"WHAT THE FUCK IS THIS, TYRA!"

"What the fuck does it look like, asshole? It's a fucking pregnancy test! I'm pregnant, mother fucker!"

"Christ Almighty. Is it mine?"

Tyra shot up off the couch. "YOU DUMB BASTARD! OF COURSE IT'S YOURS!"

"Holy shit, what the fuck am I gonna do?" he mumbled, rubbing his forehead. "I can't be a father. I don't even know what to do."

"Well, you better figure it out soon, Daddy-o. Cuz I ain't having this baby by myself!"

With that, she slipped on her red Timberlands, grabbed her jacket and walked out the door. She had to get some air and clear her head.

She walked across the street to the park. The moon was half full, and it had just enough light to lead her to the playground. She found the swing set, and sat down on one of the seats. She dangled her boots in the sand below and rested her forehead on the cold chain. She closed her eyes and inhaled. Snow. The metallic, damp smell of snow permeated the air. A lump began to form in her throat. Snow meant packed trails, and packed trails invited snowmobiles to dance on them. *Jordan!* She squeezed her eyes shut. *This is not how my life was supposed to go. It should have been Jordan's baby, not Guillermo's! Jordan would have taken care of me. Jordan would have taken care of this baby.* She let the tears roll down her face for several minutes. She allowed herself just 10 minutes at the pity party she created for herself. Then she wiped her face with her hands, stood up with her head held high, and walked back across the street to her apartment.

"I'll figure it out myself," she muttered, as a snowflake began to fall from the sky.

■ ■ ■

Nine months later, Tyra welcomed Aiden into her life. He was a good baby. He barely ever cried, and smiled all the time. He captured his mother's heart right away, and she vowed to always take care of him and never abandon him. Guillermo was a typical young father—went to work, paid the bills, and left all the cooing and kissing to his son's mother. Aiden grew fast with each passing month, and by the time he was one year old, his young father was having a hard time letting go of his playful world.

"You're late. Where have you been?" Tyra blasted as he came home from work one night. It was well after 10 P.M.

"Working. Where else would I be?"

"You tell me!"

"Hey, I don't need this, okay? I'm tired and I wanna go to bed."

"Yah? Well, I'd like to go out and make money too. But see, I can't do that because I have to take care of OUR child!"

"Get off my back, Tyra! It's because I work that you can sit on your ass all day long and watch your damn soap operas. It's not like you clean anything around here. This place is a shit hole!"

"Sit on my ass, mother fucker? Where are all your dirty clothes? Huh? Oh, that's right, they're washed, dried, folded, and neatly placed in your closet! You hungry? Your dinner is waiting for you in the oven, where I left it over 4 hours ago! This place is a shit hole because you're a cheap bastard who supposedly works so much but can't cough up any money to put a down payment on a house or a better apartment for his family!"

"SHUT UP, BITCH! SHUT YOUR FUCKING MOUTH OR I'LL SHUT IT FOR YOU!"

"BRING IT, ASSHOLE! I AIN'T AFRAID OF YOU!"

With that, Guillermo lunged at Tyra and had her by the throat. She proceeded to punch him in the head until he finally let go, and then he lunged at her again. This time, he took her down and rolled himself on top of her. He then slapped her repeatedly in the face. The pain that exploded on her cheeks was immense, but the anger that boiled within her superseded what little fear of him she had. With a swift jerk of her knee, she thrust into his family jewels and sent him doubling over, writhing in pain. Then she quickly got up and grabbed her cellphone.

"You touch me one more time, mother-fucker, and I'll send your ass to jail. You hear me?"

There was no answer from Guillermo, as he continued to clutch his privates and moan like a sick dog. Tyra made her way into the bathroom and flicked on the lights. She gasped at her reflection in the mirror. Her cheeks were bright red and bruised. She turned on the faucet and splashed cold water on her face. Then she turned off the water, sat on the toilet and began to shake uncontrollably as the adrenalin began to ebb away. She didn't know what to do. She had a baby, no job, and an abusive boyfriend that she didn't even love. Somehow she had to pull herself out of this mess. She could easily call her dad for help, but she was too proud for that. She wasn't the type to crawl back to Daddy with her tail between her legs. She thought about getting a job. With a baby, it would be tough, but it certainly would give her some cash, and not to mention space away from Guillermo. Guillermo! Was he outside the door waiting for her? There was only one way to find out. She took a deep breath, stood up, and opened the door.

The apartment was empty and he was gone.

Guillermo returned two days later. When Tyra asked him where he had been, he simply said *a friend's house*. In that short time of reprieve, Tyra had secured a job at the laundromat down the street. It was part-time work, but she could bring Aiden with her. If she stuck with it for a few months, maybe she could make enough money to pay someone to watch him.

■ ■ ■

Another year went by and things were no better between Guillermo and Tyra. He was more distant than ever, refusing to spend any time with Aiden or Tyra. He didn't come home until well after 10 P.M., and some days he didn't come home at all. She suspected that there was another woman, but confronting him could mean another boxing match between them, so she simply dismissed the thought. But one night, she couldn't ignore the warning signs anymore. Because one night, Guillermo decided to come home early, and he wasn't alone.

"Who is this?"

"Tyra, meet Patsy. Patsy, this is Tyra."

Tyra was in shock. A loosely clad, light-skinned woman entered the apartment, hanging on Guillermo's arm. Her large bosom hung haphazardly out of her too tight dress, and the smile she wore on her lips indicated that she was more than just friends with him.

"So this is your new fuck buddy?" Tyra shot out.

"Jealous?" he purred. "Or maybe you'd like to watch."

"I suggest you get your whore out of here before I rip every hair out of her head. And take your nasty self over to her place and stay there too. You'll find your clothes out on the street in the morning."

"No, querida. This is my apartment, and I'll stay if I want."

Something inside Tyra snapped, and she picked up a glass ashtray and wailed it at the couple. They both ducked as the ashtray shattered against the wall behind them.

"You still thinking of staying, babe?" she challenged.

At this moment, Aiden, who had woken up from the crash of glass, called for his mother from the other room.

"Wait, there's a kid in here?" Patsy asked.

"Yes, our son," Tyra replied. "Would you like to explain to him what you're doing here with his daddy?"

"Honey, I'm outta here," Patsy said, looking at Guillermo. "You coming?"

She opened the door and quickly stepped out. Guillermo shot Tyra a look.

"You may have won this round, querida. But I'll be back again." He turned to leave but then looked back at her. "Oh, and you may want to wash those sheets before you sleep in them." He chuckled as he left the apartment and closed the door behind him.

Tyra exhaled. She ran to her son's room and picked him up in her arms. Then she carried him to the couch and snuggled under some blankets with him.

"Don't worry, sweetie. Mommy's here."

"Where did Daddy go?"

"He had to go visit a friend."

"Is he coming back?"

"I don't know, baby. But what I do know is that Mommy is never going to leave you. It's just you and me. We're a team. Wherever Mommy goes, Aiden will go too. Okay?"

"Okay, Mommy."

She nestled underneath the covers with him and held him close. After several minutes, he fell asleep. But Tyra's mind was running a million miles an hour. There was only one option for her now—she had to leave. If not, she would never be able to look at herself in the mirror again. She would never be able to teach her son that bullies need to be stood up to. And she was no wimp! Her dad taught her better than that. At the thought of her father, her heart began to ache. How she missed him. When she was little, her father was her hero. There was no problem he couldn't fix. But she abandoned him—probably hurt him badly when she left. Would he even want to help her?

The next morning, Tyra woke up early and rose from the couch. Aiden was still asleep, so she went into her bedroom with her cellphone in hand. Even though it was early, she knew he'd be getting ready for work.

"Dad?"

"Tyra?"

"How have you been?"

"Fine. How about you?"

"Good."

"You're lying to me."

"Dad… I."

"Do I need to come get you?"

Hearing her father's soft words was too much for her. She had always wanted to prove to him that she was capable of making a life for herself and for her family. She wanted to show him how independent she could be. But the weight of it all—the lie that she was living—the pathetic human being she shared space with—it was too much for Tyra. She was never one to ask for help. But this time, she had someone other than herself to think about. Aiden. He deserved better. He deserved a family of people that loved him. He deserved a doting grandfather, cousins, and neighborhood friends. What kind of life would he have if she stayed? All day long in a laundromat and all night long in some dingy little apartment, with a volatile, cheating father?

"Dad, can I come stay with you for a little while?"

"Of course you can. Stay as long as you like. Do I need to come get you?"

"No. I can get a taxi."

"No, you won't. How much time do you need to get all your stuff together?"

"About an hour."

"I'm leaving in 10 minutes. What's the address?"

"What about work? Dad, I feel bad!"

"Do you know how much sick time I have? Don't ask me silly questions. Give me the address."

Later that day, Tyra was sitting on the couch in her dad's living room, sipping on a Coke. All of her belongings were in bags, scattered around the living and dining rooms. Her dad was outside mowing the grass with Aiden on his lap. She looked around the room. It looked exactly the same as when she left. There were school pictures of herself in frames on the table next to her. She picked one of them up. It was her fifth-grade picture. The girl smiling back at her had no worries at all. She played with her friends, rode horses across the street, went to church on Sundays, and annoyed her older sister. How peaceful things were back then. She wondered how she ever became …derailed.

Over the next few days, Tyra got settled in her dad's house. She couldn't afford daycare so she stayed with him during the day, and when her dad came home in the evening, she went to work as a bonds woman. It was perfect because she usually worked until about midnight every night and made good money. She knew her son was in good hands so she breathed a bit easier. Her plan was to save up some money so she could get a small apartment for herself and Aiden. She also filed papers at the local courthouse to get child support and full custody of her son, in case Guillermo ever came around looking for him.

One Sunday morning, she walked into her dad's kitchen and noticed that he was making his world-famous spaghetti sauce.

"Ooooo, Dad! Are you making Sunday dinner?"

"Yes, ma'am. I do Sunday dinner every Sunday."

"God, I missed that," she looked away. "I missed a lot of things."

"You took a walk."

"What?"

"You took a walk, and you went around the block," her father said. "You had to see what was around the corner. It's what you've always done—even as a kid. If you didn't go, you would have never seen what was there. And it was because of what you saw that led you back around the block, and back to me." She threw her arms around her father and hugged him tight. "I'm so sorry, Dad," she whispered. "I'm sorry I left you. I didn't mean to hurt you."

He held her tightly. "It's okay. You're here now, that's all that matters."

"No, Dad!" she pulled back. "I did what Mom did. She left you and broke your heart. Then I left you too. I tried so hard to not be her. But now I think I've become her carbon copy. I'm so sorry!"

"Stop it! You are not your mother, and I'll tell you why. Your mother left because she had a volcano erupting inside of her. She didn't let any of that steam out—ever! She never talked to me or anyone else about how lonely she felt. And then it was too late. Once she detonated, she was gone for good. But you—you knew you had dragons to slay, so you went on a journey. You've seen some hard times, but you came back. You have no regrets. You'll never leave that little boy. You've done your time."

"You really think so?"

"I know so! You're my daughter. Tough as nails. Stubborn too, but you are not your mother."

She hugged him again, and squeezed even tighter. She silently vowed to always take care of him and never leave him again. Her father was always her rock, and as long as she was near him, she would be all right.

They were interrupted by the ring of the doorbell. Tyra pulled away and looked at her father.

"Who's that?"

"Oh, I'm expecting my usual Sunday afternoon company." He smiled at her, then turned and walked to the door. He grabbed the doorknob, but before he opened the door, he looked back at her.

"And another thing. Sometimes second chances come around when you least expect them to. Keep your eyes open and watch for them."

He then opened the door and a young man walked in. Tyra gasped and stood motionless for a few seconds.

"Tyra?"

"Jordan?"

"I didn't know you were here."

"What are you doing here?"

"I have dinner with your father every Sunday."

Tyra looked at her father, standing on the sidelines with a giant grin on his face. "He's been coming ever since you left him."

"You've been having dinner with my father for three years?"

"Yes."

"Well, I have to go check on the sauce," her father said. "Tyra, take our guest to the living room. I'm sure you have some catching up to do." Then he disappeared into another room.

Tyra led him to the couch and they sat and talked. She filled him in on the difficult, disastrous parts of the past three years, as well as the one miracle that came out of it all. She introduced Aiden to Jordan, and Aiden immediately took to him. They spent hours talking, before dinner, after dinner, and into the wee hours of the night. When midnight rolled around, she walked him to his truck.

"It was good to see you, Jordan."

"Good to see you too, T." He stared at her for several seconds. "I missed you."

"I thought about you too." She smiled. "Especially when the snow fell."

"Well, maybe this year I'll take you for a ride on my new sled. It's really fast."

"I'm glad you never gave up that part of your life."

"I never gave up on a lot of things. Why do you think I came here every Sunday?"

She gasped.

"I knew you would come back someday," he whispered.

"How did you know?"

"As crazy as you were back then, you always had a soft spot for your old man."

"He wasn't the only one I had a soft spot for."

Jordan smiled then, and Tyra's heart melted. This is where she belonged. Never again would she long for the fast life, and unpredictable, immoral people. Never again would she settle for anything less than proper respect for women. She had wandered through fire and got burned many times. But she came out on the other side. She became a mother, found a job she enjoyed working at, and best of all, she reconnected with her beloved father. She had a court date scheduled with Guillermo, but she wasn't afraid of him anymore. He couldn't touch her. She was a warrior, and she would spend the next few years battling him over their son, and taking him down with every cheap shot he threw at her. On the day she went to the tattoo shop to celebrate yet another victory in court over her son, she was indecisive over what she wanted. She needed an emblem to symbolize a fighter. A powerful Chinese saying? A warrior queen? A mother holding her son? But the tattoo artist took one look at her, gave her a toothless smile, and solved her dilemma almost immediately.

"How about a bad-ass bitch?" he asked.

Tyra smiled. "Yah. That'll do." ∎

▪ CHAPTER FOUR ▪
Jillian

If ever there existed a woman who didn't have a mean bone in her body, that would be Jillian. She would listen to a friend tell a tale as if she were taking notes in a college class. And if the friend wanted to go on and on, Jillian would never complain or seem frustrated. She would simply listen until the story was over.

And then there was the way she moved—all graceful, like a gazelle. With her head held high, she would enter any arena with purpose and dignity. Her eyes were as blue as the ocean at sunset. They would captivate her audience and melt even the most frozen heart. Everyone wanted to be Jillian's friend—including Maurice.

They met in high school. She was a sophomore and he was a senior. He was tall and thin and an upperclassman. She was young and innocent and looked up to him. It was the perfect setup. He would mold her into what he wanted her to be, and she would never leave him.

"Why are you wearing that skirt today?"

"I don't know. I thought you might like it."

"I'm sure the other boys in this school like it too."

"Oh. I didn't think about that. Should I go and change into my gym clothes?"

"Do whatever you want. I just think it makes you look cheap."

And off she would go into the bathroom and put on her sweats. This went on for a year. So what if she had to watch her words when she spoke to him. She was dating a senior! That in itself was something to be proud of.

After Maurice graduated from high school, he attended UCONN for a year. The couple remained together because he commuted, so they still saw each other in their hometown. But when the year was over, he got kicked out for having bad grades. He had a terrible relationship with his parents, so he begged Jillian's father if he could live in their basement. Her father agreed because he knew it meant so much to his daughter. In retrospect, those giant red flags should have prompted Jillian to rethink her decision to stay on with him. But like so many other women, she simply ignored them and moved forward.

During Jillian's senior year of high school, Maurice attended another school, specifically for IT training. He graduated at the same time that Jillian graduated from high school. He immediately got an IT job in Stafford Springs and began to save up money for a home of his own. Jillian enrolled at UCONN in the nursing program, but commuted from home. Maurice continued to reside in her basement.

In the fall of her last year at college, Maurice surprised her one day at work. She was working as a park ranger at a community center, so he brought by a picnic lunch. He made her a grilled cheese sandwich on the grill. When she was ready for dessert, he reached into the picnic basket and pulled out a small box.

"Jillian, will you marry me?"

"Yes."

And that was where she went wrong.

■ ■ ■

Maurice had purchased a house shortly after they became engaged in North Windham. It was a great starter home—perfect for a couple starting out their lives together. Jillian finished her final year at UCONN and they were married that summer. She decided to take the rest of the summer off, and just enjoy being a newlywed in her own home.

"So, are you ever going to get a job?"

"I guess so. I was just going to take the rest of the summer off."

"Must be nice not to have any responsibilities in life."

"What do you mean? Don't I take care of things around here?"

"That's nothing compared to how hard I work all day."

"Do you want me to get a job?"

"Oh, I'm not telling you what to do. But if you want to contribute to this household, you should probably get a job. Of course, it will be hard for you because you have no experience, but you should start getting yourself out there."

"Oh, okay. I'll pick 5 places I'm interested in and apply in the morning."

"You'll probably have to up that to 50. A girl fresh out of college, with no experience? You'll be lucky if anyone even looks at you."

Ouch! That one stung. But again, Maurice was wiser in a way. He already had a job. Surely he was just giving her honest advice. She should appreciate the fact that he was preparing her for the worst. After all, that would just make her work harder in finding a job.

Jillian ending up sending only one resume, to Windham Hospital. She didn't need to apply elsewhere because she got a call that week and was hired on the spot. She began working on September 1. Life was good once again. Both of them had good jobs, they enjoyed free time on the weekends, and they were free to travel wherever they wanted. This carefree lifestyle went on for three magical years.

While they were within this three-year blissful era, Jillian's mind often drifted off to what she craved the most in life—having a family. The baby bug had left its mark on her and she convinced Maurice that they should try for one. At first, he hesitated—stating that it was too early in their marriage. Then he got into the spirit of things when he saw how much he could benefit from this, sexually. But after years of no luck, Jillian knew that something was wrong with one of them. They decided to go to a fertility doctor to get checked out.

"I'd like to go over the test results with you," Dr. Collins said. "Jillian, you are in great shape and your reproductive system is working just fine."

"Oh, that's a relief."

"The problem is not Jillian," Dr. Collins shot a serious look at Maurice. "Maurice, you're going to need a 'procedure' done."

"What kind of procedure?"

"Let's just say there are some lines that are not flowing freely. We just need to go in and unclog some of the masses that have formed."

"What if I don't have it done?"

"Well, then you and Jillian can never have children."

"Hmm. Well, thank you for your time, Doctor. Jillian and I will go home and discuss this."

Neither one of them spoke in the car. Jillian mulled over different scenarios in her head, but she decided it was best to keep quiet until he spoke first. After all, she wasn't the one getting operated on. Maurice seemed heavy in thought until he reached home.

"I've decided I don't want to do this," he finally said as he turned off the ignition.

"What?"

"You heard me," he looked at her squarely in the eyes. "There's a reason why I'm not able to have kids. I'm fine the way I am, Jillian. We can adopt a puppy or a little kitten. Kids are too much work anyway."

Jillian was stunned. "I don't know what to say."

"There's nothing to say. Besides, the final episode of *Friends* is on. We better get inside before we miss it." And with that, he got out of the car and went inside the house.

Jillian just sat in the car staring at the walls of her garage. *Is he kidding? Is this some stupid joke? What if he is serious? We're never going to have kids? I'll never be a mother? That just can't happen.*

Jillian made sure not to talk about it for a week. She wanted to give Maurice time to process things. Maybe he would have a change of heart. She waited until Sunday afternoon to bring up the subject one more time.

"I want you to have the surgery."

"What?"

"I want a family, Maurice. It's all I ever wanted. I want to be a mother, and I want you to be a father. Please consider my feelings in this."

"So I should just do this for you, even though I don't want to?"

"But why don't you want to?"

"I told you—I'm fine the way I am. I like having no kids. We're free to do whatever we want. Have you considered that?"

"No, I haven't. Because I'm not that selfish."

"Oh, so now I'm selfish?"

"Please, Maurice. I don't want to fight with you. I just want to have a baby. I swear I'll take care of him or her. You don't have to do a thing."

"Yeah, right. You say that now, but you'll make me get up in the middle of the night and feed the kid."

"No, I won't. I'll do that. Please just think about it. For me."

Maurice stormed out of the room, went into the bedroom, and slammed the door. Jillian knew that he needed time to process things so she began to make dinner. An hour went by and he still hadn't emerged from his room. She went over and knocked lightly on the door.

"Maurice? Are you okay?" she asked.

"Yah," his voice sounded through the door.

"Can I come in?"

"Yah."

Jillian entered the room. He was on the phone with someone.

"I'll call you later," he said and hung up.

"Who was that?"

"A friend."

"Which one?"

"Did you come here to talk or give me the third degree?"

"Listen. I know you're upset. I probably would be too if I had to have surgery. But this is our future family we're talking about. When I married you, I pictured you and me and our children—like the perfect little family. I mean… don't you want that too?"

"Nothing is ever perfect, Jillian. But I'll have the damn surgery if that's what you really want."

"But I want you to want it too."

"What's for dinner? I'm hungry." And with that, he rose from the bed and padded off into the kitchen.

How strange he seems. It's almost as if he's pissed off with the world. It's probably my fault. I'm putting too much pressure on him. I should remember to do nice things for him in the next few weeks, she thought.

■ ■ ■

Maurice had the surgery, and within a month, Jillian was pregnant. Their first son, Nathan, was born in 2008. He was a good baby—very quiet and agreeable. Jillian spent most of her time doting on him. As promised, she was the one that got up for night-time feedings, she was the one that changed his diapers, and she was the one that loved him up. Maurice basically went to work, and held him every once in a while when Jillian was busy with something. He was fine with one child, and he seriously believed this was it. But about 9 months later, Jillian was pregnant again. Nathan was almost 2 years old when Lionel was born. Maurice was okay with the fact that he now had two boys instead of one, but he put his foot down after Lionel was born.

"This is absolutely the last child we're having."

Looking back, Jillian often wondered what would have happened if they had stopped at 2 kids. Would their relationship have continued? Would they have been happy, and would the picture of the perfect family been realized? But perfect families and sociopath men never go hand in hand, and Jillian learned this lesson the hard way. It was during the pregnancy of their third child, Anya, that Jillian's somewhat happy life turned into the prison sentence she was about to be served.

"Are you fucking kidding me?" Maurice screamed. "What did I say, Jill? I'm pretty sure I said no more kids after Lionel!"

"I didn't do this by myself."

"You most certainly did! You're the only one that knows what time of the month it is! You did this on purpose! To piss me off! Congratulations! You got what you wanted!"

"I'm sorry, Maurice. I didn't do this on purpose. This is a surprise to me too. Maybe next time you shouldn't have sex with me."

"Well, I won't. I've been doing it with someone else anyway."

Silence. *Wait. What? Did he just say what I think he said? He's doing it with someone else? As in, cheating on me? As in, I'm pregnant with his child and he's moved on to another woman?*

"Don't look at me like that! You drove me to this! I never wanted kids in the first place, but you insisted! I never wanted to have that surgery, but you made me! You drove me into Alicia's bed! This is all your fault!"

"Alicia? You mean, your intern?"

"Yah."

"But she's a child!"

"She's twenty. She's a grown woman!"

"I don't know what to say. Are you in love with her? Are you leaving me?"

"I don't know yet. She certainly doesn't piss me off the way you do!"

Crash! There it was. The punch in the gut, the slap in the face, the knee to the groin, all rolled into one. The pain that exploded inside her veins felt like poison traveling in her blood. She was going to have three kids—alone. Her husband did not want to be with her—he did not want to be a part of this family. What on earth was she going to do?

"She gets me, okay? She knows what I'm thinking even before I say it out loud. I really believe she's my soulmate."

"But what about me?"

"It was fine in the beginning. But things change, Jillian. People change. You became different. You're not the one for me."

"But you knew I wanted children from the beginning. I haven't changed at all!"

"And I was willing to deal with one. Not this army that you created!"

"You make it sound like this is all my fault."

"Well, it is your fault. You wouldn't hear me! You just wanted what you wanted and you never took my feelings into consideration at all! Shanaya was right about you too."

"What do you mean? What does Shanaya have to do with this?"

"We spent some time talking about you. She told me you were going to go behind my back and get yourself pregnant—more than once. She said you seduced me when you knew you were fertile."

"What? My best friend said that about me? I never said any of that stuff!"

"Yes, you did. You were spending less and less time with her. You dropped her for the kids. What did you expect from her?"

"I expected my best friend to support our little family. Not to create lies and tell them to my husband!"

"Well, she had a different agenda."

"And what was on her agenda?"

"Forget it. You wouldn't understand."

"Please tell me."

"When Nathan was a baby, you went away. Remember? I was home by myself and I swear I almost packed my clothes and left. I was that miserable."

"I didn't know."

"Yah, well, Shanaya knew. And she came over with Rick that first night. And we talked about it, and she made me realize that I was missing out on a very active sex life. I mean, I'm gonna be honest, Jillian. You don't really turn me on anymore. You don't do *exciting* things."

Jillian's heart was pounding a million miles an hour. *What is he saying? He tells my best friend and her husband about our sex life? Why?*

"But Shanaya is into stuff like that. So we did it. And it blew my fucking mind!"

"You did what?" Jillian screamed.

"I fucked the shit out of her. We both did. It was fucking amazing. I've never felt so satisfied with a woman before in my life."

"You slept with my best friend in front of her husband?"

"No. He participated. I was in the front and he was in the back at first. It was glorious! We did it a few times, then we switched sides. Just watching the pleasure on her face made me hard."

"I think I'm going to be sick." And with that, Jillian ran to the bathroom and locked the door. She sat with her face staring at the toilet for a few minutes, trying to breathe in and breathe out. She kept her eyes squeezed shut, trying to focus on something good and pure, instead of the filth she just heard from her husband's lips. Who was this man? Surely he wasn't the same person that she married. What kind of a man becomes that evil over time? She didn't want to see him anymore. She wanted him out of her house!

After about an hour, Jillian emerged out of the bathroom. She was numb. She felt as if someone had tasered her. She had no idea what to do now. Maurice was on the phone in the living room.

"I'll call you back," he said when he saw her. "Look. I'm not trying to be the bad guy here. But I hate lying to you. I just wanted to come clean and tell you what's been going on with me. I don't want to have any secrets anymore."

Jillian sat on the couch and looked out the window. She felt deflated and had nothing to say.

"If you want me to leave, I can."

Jillian looked at him then. "You mean like a divorce?"

"Well, I guess we can think about that. It costs a lot to get a divorce so maybe we should take things slow. I was going to move out for a while—give you time to think about things. Then we can see what happens."

"Where will you go?"

"I'll go and live with Alicia. It's closer to work anyway."

"What about the kids? Am I supposed to raise them by myself?"

"I can come home on the weekends so you can go to work, and I can stay with them. If you want."

"What about the bills? I can't afford this house by myself."

"I'll pay the bills... for now."

"Sounds like you thought about everything. I guess there's nothing more to say."

"I'm sorry it came to this, Jillian."

She did not respond. She simply stared at him for several seconds, then watched him walk into their bedroom. She could hear him unzipping luggage and filling it up with his belongings. Jillian just sat and stared out the window.

Ten minutes after Maurice got into his car and drove away, her two boys came home. They were with their grandparents for the day. They came bounding into the house, giggling, and holding lollipops in their hands.

"Look, Mommy! Look what Grandpa got us!" Nathan beamed.

"Oh, that's yummy. Grandpa is so good to you," she looked at her father. She must have given him a look because in the next moment, he stopped smiling and steered the boys into the kitchen with their grandma. He then came and sat down beside her on the couch.

"Pumpkin, what is it?"

She didn't even have a chance to say a word. Seeing her dad standing there like a great big rock, the lump in her throat grew bigger. Then the tears came gushing out, as she flung herself into his arms. He held her for several seconds, just stroking her hair. Finally, when she had no more tears to cry, she looked up at him. He sat her down on the couch.

"Tell me everything."

And she did.

■ ■ ■

Seven months later, Jillian sat in her favorite arm chair in the living room, holding her baby girl. She had been thinking about her dad's words of advice for weeks now. He had told her that she was strong and that she would survive this. He told her that human lives belong to us and God and no one else, and that only we can dictate how things should go in our lives. God just puts it in writing. But in the end, we decide which path to go on, we decide what to do about our problems. And no one should solve our problems except us. She looked down on the angelic face before her. She smiled, and she instantly knew that no one was more important than her three precious children, and they deserved the best life possible. This, she would promise them.

A car door slammed outside. Maurice was home for the weekend. He entered the house, and shuffled into the living room where she sat.

"How's it going?"

"Fine. I was hoping to talk to you before I head out to work."

"What about?" he said hesitantly, as he sat on the arm of the couch.

"I've been thinking a lot about our situation. We have three beautiful children, and they deserve a good home with parents that love them and want to be a part of their lives. I am willing to work things out with you, if you would like. We can go to counseling and learn how to communicate. I can also try to *learn* things that would excite you. I am willing to do anything for the sake of this family."

She waited for him to process her words. He looked down at his feet, and then back up at her.

"I'm sorry, Jillian. I just can't do that. I like being with Alicia." He stood up and began to walk into the kitchen. He took a few steps, then turned to her. "But I will still pay the bills and take care of the kids on the weekends. I know you just had a baby, so I know it's hard." Then he walked away.

"Our baby," she whispered.

■ ■ ■

Three years. Three years she lived like this. Two strangers passing on the weekends. The good news was that she didn't have to share a bed with him, and she didn't have to share a living space with him on the weekdays. They barely spoke to each other. Jillian knew the kids could feel the tension but she just figured that they would be all right. After all, divorce was horrible on children. It was probably better to stay in the same house together than force them to live in two separate houses.

In the fall of the third year, Jillian enrolled Anya in preschool. She knew that Anya was shy, but she figured she would open up with the other children. In October, Jillian attended Anya's parent-teacher conference.

"Thanks for coming, Mrs. DeLeone. Anya is adjusting very well to preschool. She has made some friends and plays with them in the classroom and out at recess. She enjoys listening to stories, and she seems to understand math concepts."

"That's great."

"There is one thing that concerns me about your daughter, Mrs. DeLeone."

"What is it?"

"She doesn't talk."

"Well, she's very shy. It will take her a while to open up."

"She will not even take the oral reading assessments so it's hard to pinpoint her reading level."

"She just needs more time."

"Mrs. DeLeone, Anya does not present herself as a shy girl. I've been doing this for a long time, and I know the difference. Anya acts as if…"

"As if what?"

"As if she has been through trauma. Kids with severe trauma will shut down and refuse to speak. They do this because it is the only thing in their lives that they can control. I don't mean to overstep or to upset you in any way. I just wanted to make you aware, so that you can find someone to help her. Maybe an outside counselor."

Trauma. Refuse to speak. Outside counselor. The words reverberated in Jillian's head. *Somebody hurt her baby, and now she was broken. Was she to blame? Did she accidentally do this to her? Did Maurice do this to her? Her poor baby was in pain.*

"Shall I get some information from the school psychologist for you?"

"I… I would appreciate that. Thank you."

"I'm sorry, Mrs. DeLeone," the teacher reached over and touched her arm. "I know this is a lot to take in. But she's only three. She's still young enough to change her behavior with the right intervention."

"Yes, of course. Thank you for your time."

On the ride home, Jillian's mind was spinning a million miles an hour. She could remember that horrible day, about two and a half years ago, when Maurice came home one weekend and didn't want to deal with Anya because she was sick. Jillian was holding her in her arms while Maurice was screaming at her. *She's the reason why we're in this mess! I never wanted her in my life! I never wanted a daughter!* She was just a baby then. Did she somehow understand what her father was saying? Did she know he was talking about her? Is that why she wouldn't speak in public? Because she knew she was an unwanted child? The tears came cascading out of her eyes then. She pulled over to the side of the road and sobbed violently. She rocked herself gently and allowed the anguish to wash over her. How did she get to this point? How could she allow her children to be hurt by their own father. How could she allow this lifestyle to continue? It would have to end—for the sake of her wonderful children. It had to end.

She pulled a tissue out of her purse and blew her nose. She wiped her eyes and took a deep breath. She was about to steer the car onto the road when her cell phone rang.

"Hello?"

"Jillian, it's Mom. It's your dad. He's in the hospital."

Jillian raced to the emergency room of the hospital and barely parked the car. She ran inside and sprinted up the stairwell to the fourth floor. She found her mother crying silently in the lobby.

"Mom?"

"He's gone, Jillian. It was a heart attack. He just couldn't hang on any longer."

"No!" Jillian sank to her knees and buried her face in her hands. Her rock—her big bear of a father was gone. The only loving man her children had known was gone. Her father was her angel—he was always there for her. And she could tell him anything. His wisdom was amazing. He always had the best advice. Now who would she turn to? The emotional stress of the day was just too much for Jillian to bear. She allowed the darkness to penetrate her, welcomed the gray fog into her soul until she was numb. The light exited her vibrant, blue eyes, as did any shred of happiness that remained in her tattered heart. She accepted the nothingness that enveloped her and watched her spirit die.

After the funeral, Jillian said her final goodbyes to the remaining family members, and went home with her three children. It was a comfort to have them around. They were quiet and somber, but they stayed close to Jillian by either holding her hand or resting their heads on her arm. Somehow they knew that their heartbroken mother needed some extra comfort. They ate a simple dinner that night and then she tucked them all into bed. She read them stories and then watched them fall asleep.

She went into her bedroom and sat on the bed. A picture of her dad rested on her bureau. He was holding a bass with one hand and a beer in the other. The smile on his face lit up the entire picture. That was her dad—always took life by the horns and mixed in a little laughter. She spent an hour staring at him. *Hi, Dad. It's me, Jillian. I know you're in such a better place right now. I bet you and Jesus are getting ready for an arm wrestling contest. That's how I always want to remember you, Dad—strong, like a warrior. Nothing ever scared you. I wish you were here to tell me what to do. I'm lost without you. I wish I could go to where you are. I don't think I'm meant for this life. It's too hard.*

She hesitated a moment and thought. *But then there are my little angels—and I just can't leave them.* At that moment, a tree branch scraped against her window. She turned suddenly, startled by the noise, then relaxed. She glanced back at the picture of her father, then back at the tree branch scraping the window. It was a sign! It felt as if a dose of clarity was immediately injected into her brain, and she smiled. *Thanks, Dad. I know what I have to do now. I won't let you down.*

The next day, she made a trip down to the courthouse and filed for divorce. She didn't even bother to give Maurice a heads-up. He'd find out soon enough. Then she made a trip to the hospital. She still had time off for bereavement, but she wanted to talk to her boss. She found her in her office.

"Hey, Pam. Do you have a minute?"

"Yes, of course, Jillian. Please come in."

"I was wondering if there are any positions available that I can work from home. I really love this job, but I have three kids to raise, and I'd like to do it without being dependent on their father."

"As a matter of fact, the board and I were just talking about a position that is opening up. It involves inputting information in medical records. You would make up your own hours, but you can do all your work from home. You would only have to come in to the office once a week to drop off and pick up files. How does that sound?"

"Perfect! When can I start?"

"If all goes well, we should have you starting your new position in two weeks."

"I'll take it! Thank you so much!"

That weekend, Maurice came over as he always did. Jillian was getting ready for work. He knocked on her bedroom door.

"Hey, Jill? Can we talk for a minute?"

"Yah, what's up?"

"I don't think I had a chance to tell you how sorry I was about your dad. It must have been really hard to lose him. How are you doing?"

"I'm fine, Maurice. Is there anything else?"

"Yah. Uh… I know this may come as a shock to you but Alicia and I broke up. She was way too young for me, and I am so much more mature than her. I realized she's not the one for me after all."

"Oh. I'm sorry to hear that."

"So I've been doing some thinking and…." He smiled at her. "Maybe you and I should get back together. The kids would probably love it! We should really think about their needs first. I realize I haven't been that great to you in the past but I guess I could try and be a better husband. I mean, a family is what you've always wanted. We could probably have that now. So what do you think?"

Jillian took a long hard look at the father of her children. He was right—she had always wanted to have a family, and her children did come first. But then her mind flashed to the picture of her father, holding the bass and beer, and she thought about the kind of man that he was. He was a star—the kind of father she wanted for her own children. Maurice did not possess a fraction of the qualities her father had. And his wandering eye would surely wander again someday. Her children deserved better, she deserved better, and she was not going to be his victim anymore.

"Thank you for your offer, Maurice, but my answer is no."

"What do you mean? I know you're still in love with me! We have history!"

Jillian turned and grabbed her coat and purse. Then she looked at him one more time. "See you in court, Maurice," then she walked out.

≡ ≡ ≡

A year later, Jillian sat in a folding chair at her friend Noel's summer barbeque. She had an iced tea in her hand and she was watching her children splashing playfully in the pool. She noticed the branches rustling in the summer breeze, and couldn't help but think about her father. She smiled. How far she had come. Maurice was on his third or fourth relationship. The poor guy couldn't get it together. She sold the family house and bought another one—with just her name on it. Her children were involved in sports, they had many friends, and they laughed a lot more. Her mother helped her take care of the children more, now that she was alone. It was a beautiful summer day, and the gray fog that trapped her soul was now lifted.

"Hey, Jillian!" Noel beamed.

"Hey, Noel!"

"I'd like to introduce you to a friend of mine. Jillian, this is Blake. Blake, this is Jillian."

"It's nice to meet you, Jillian," the dark, handsome man said.

"Likewise."

"So which of these rugrats are yours?"

"The three in the pool," she pointed.

"Oh, Lionel is yours?"

"Yes."

"My son Cole and Lionel have been buds for years. They've been in each other's classes, I think."

"Yes, they have."

"Forgive me for saying this, but you have the most amazing eyes."

"Oh, thank you." Jillian blushed.

"Can you two excuse me?" Noel smiled. "One of my guests is leaving." And she left the couple alone. She walked over to her other friend, Lara, grinning from ear to ear.

"What did you do?" Lara asked.

"Oh, nothing," Noel said. "Just sometimes, fate needs a little shove, that's all."

They watched Jillian and Blake laugh over something silly.

"You are one bad-ass bitch, you know that?" Lara smiled.

"No. Not me," Noel answered. "That girl over there," and she pointed to Jillian. "Went through hell and came out like a tiger," she shot out. "That girl over there—that's your bad-ass bitch." ■

▪ CHAPTER FIVE ▪
Thalia

*O*h *say does that star-spangled banner yet wave … O'er the land of the free and the home of the brave?* The famous words of Mr. Francis Scott Key, adopted as the American fight song. Where is the home of the brave? Is it the vast sands of the desert, stretching for miles and miles, where lonely soldiers trek? Is it a place where men wear tattered fatigues and carry dusty rifles on their backs? Or are they the women, who defend their honor against those who would try to take it from them? Or the single mothers, who hold their babies close to them while they face the darkness of the oncoming battle? The real home of the brave are the warrior women who *unsheathe* their swords, and refuse to let a man strip them of their armor.

Thalia enlisted in the Air Force in 1997. She was a young, spitfire girl, with Native American bloodlines. Her dark hair and dark eyes were a deep contrast to the cheerful smile she wore. She was joy and spirit and strength, all rolled into one, like a Christmas ornament made out of polished steel. Ten years, she served her country well. She worked hard, wasn't afraid of combat, and she loved to travel abroad. They sent her to foreign places like Belgium, France, and Italy. An American Air Force base in Italy claimed her in May 2007—special duty assignment to Korea. She made special trips to Korea for various missions, and on a hot July night, her captivating smile caught the eye of a Lieutenant named Justin.

"You know how to shoot that thing?" he smiled.

"No. I'm just a porn star that knows how to jump out of cakes. This is just my costume," she shot back.

Justin laughed heartily. He instantly liked her. The girl had spunk, and a sense of humor. Most female soldiers lacked that. They perfected the art of seriousness in order to prove their worth to the male population.

"Where are you stationed?"

"Italy. But I'm here on special assignment."

"Staying in the lower barracks?"

"Yup."

"Football fan?"

"Yup?"

"Do you drink whiskey or beer?"

"Am I a contestant on *The Dating Game* or something?"

"No," Justin laughed again. "I'm just trying to get to know you."

"Well, get to know me when my shift is over. I have to report to my captain now." And with that, Thalia left him standing there.

Over the next six months, Thalia and Justin saw quite a bit of each other. She liked his companionship, as well as his entertaining side. They would watch football together on her couch. Sometimes they would even recreate the WWF and attack each other on the living room floor. They would go to bars together and have a few drinks, then they'd go back to one of their apartments and see how close they could get to breaking the bed.

In January, Justin got orders to ship out of Korea. He promised to keep in touch with Thalia either by calling or writing letters. On the night before he left, he took her to a quiet Korean restaurant on the south side. Then they finished the evening by having sex in as many different positions as they could think of. When they ran out of condoms in the middle of their sexual marathon, they simply threw caution to the wind and did it some more.

■ ■ ■

A month later, Thalia sat in the bathroom with her brows furrowed. Something was wrong. She wasn't feeling right, and she wasn't as energetic as she usually was. She began to count the days from her last period and froze.

"Oh, shit."

She got up from the toilet, pulled her pants up, and walked out of the apartment. She walked quickly to the pharmacy on base and picked up a pregnancy kit. She looked around to see if she recognized anyone but no one seemed familiar. She paid for it, hid it inside her jacket, and walked back to her apartment. She peed on the stick and waited five excruciatingly long minutes. One line meant you're not, two lines meant you are. She watched in horror as the white area materialized into two clear blue lines.

"Mother fucker," she whispered. "What the hell am I going to do now?" She sat on the floor in the bathroom for several minutes, with her hands on her head. All kinds of scenarios whipped through her mind. What will her captain say? She's in a combat zone—surely he wouldn't allow her to stay. And could she have this baby on base? Who would help her take care of it? Should she call her parents? Should she leave the Air Force? The questions came at her in a barrage. Finally she couldn't take it anymore, so she stood up and went out of the apartment. She walked over to her captain's quarters and knocked on the door. He answered the door quickly.

"Lieutenant Whales."

"Captain Stiles. I have an issue I need to discuss with you. Is now a good time?"

"Please come in."

She entered his simple, little apartment and located the nearest chair and sat. She rubbed her knees, not really sure how to approach this.

"Uh. I have a medical condition and I'm not sure what to do about it. I need your advice."

"I'm listening."

"Well, you see, sir … I'm pregnant."

Silence. The Captain stared at her for several seconds before he responded.

"I see," he said. "Are you planning on keeping it?"

"Yes, sir."

"Are you absolutely sure? Lieutenant, you are one of the best soldiers in my unit. I would hate to lose you. If you decide to keep the baby, you will get stationed elsewhere."

"I understand that, sir. And thank you for the compliment. But I do not believe in abortion and I would like to keep my child."

"Very well. I'll contact the officials and you should be reassigned before the week is out."

"Thank you, sir," she said, standing up. She saluted him and turned towards the door.

"Lieutenant?"

"Yes, sir?"

"Best of luck. I hope everything works out for you."

"Me too, sir," she smiled. She had the overpowering urge to hug the man and beg him to take her in so she didn't have to go through this alone. But she shook it off and walked out the door.

■ ■ ■

Six months later, Thalia sat at her desk and stared at her phone. She had been sent back to the United States and now worked in the office, as an Administrative Specialist. She was seven months pregnant. A pang began to form in her gut weeks ago—the urge to tell Justin about her situation. She chalked it up to the nesting syndrome—what expectant mothers do to get ready for their baby. In this case, Thalia was feeling as though she should at least inform Justin.

She waited until she went home that evening. Then she sat on the couch, grabbed her phone, and dialed his number. He answered on the second ring.

"Hey, stranger," he said.

"Hey, you."

"How have you been?"

"Oh, you know. Never a dull moment."

"I can imagine. I was in Korea a few months ago but they told me that you were reassigned."

"Yah. I left six months ago."

"Another combat mission?"

"No. I'm back in the States."

"Why?"

"Justin, I have to tell you something. And I would appreciate it if you just let me get this out before you say anything. Can you do that?"

"Yah, sure."

"Okay." She took a deep breath. *Here goes nothing.* "So, the last night that you and I were together, something awesome happened. We were so caught up in the moment … we didn't realize … anyway, I'm seven months pregnant. Yes, you are the father and yes, I am keeping him. You can be involved in this baby's life or not. Nobody gets to dictate whether you have rights to this child or not, because I'm telling you that you will always be allowed to see your son … if you choose to." She let out a sigh of relief. "There, I'm done."

Silence on the other end. No doubt, she had shocked the man so she waited a few minutes.

"Justin?"

"Yah, I'm here."

"Well? Do you have anything to say?"

"Yes. Will you marry me?"

Woah! I wasn't expecting that one! He must be in terrible shock right now!

"Uh, Justin? That is the last thing on earth we should be thinking about. People get married because they love each other and they want to spend the rest of their lives with each other. Not because they are getting pigeonholed into fatherhood."

"But it's the right thing to do."

"No, it's not. In fact, it's the worst thing we could do. Why don't we just see how this goes. Take some time to think things over and then maybe you can call me in a few days and tell me what you come up with. I'll still be here, okay?"

"Okay."

She hung up the phone feeling pretty satisfied. Her conscience was clear—the father was informed. Now she just had to give him some time to think things over. *Justin's a good man. He'll want to be in our lives, I'm almost certain of that. Then maybe he'll get a special pass to see the birth of our son and we can spend some time catching up. Everything will turn out fine!*

A few days later, Justin didn't call. Thalia didn't really think much of it. After all, the news she delivered to him was huge. He probably needed more time to think things over.

A week later, he still didn't call. Now she was getting nervous. *Did he regret his actions? Does he not want anything more to do with us?*

A week and a half went by with no call. *Well, maybe he's on a dangerous mission. Yah, that's it. That's the only reason he's not calling. I just have to be more patient.*

Two weeks later, he called.

"Hey."

"Hey! Is everything okay?"

"Depends on what you're talking about."

"Were you in a combat zone?"

"No."

"Oh. Were you on a mission of some sort?"

"No."

"Okay. Why haven't you called??"

"I've been kinda busy with something else."

"I see. Well, did you think about what I said?"

"Yah."

"And?"

"Thalia … I gotta tell you something."

"I'm listening."

"Shit! I can't believe this is happening."

"Can you just spit it out already?"

"A few months ago, I met this girl. She's pretty cool. I want to stay with her."

"Wait … what?" Thalia said. "Hold on a second. Two weeks ago, you asked me to marry you, and now you're telling me there's been another girl for a few months?"

"She's pregnant, Thalia. The baby is mine."

Whack! A boot to the gut would have been less painful. Thalia was speechless. She definitely had misjudged him. She had thought all along that there was a connection between the two of them, that they would somehow be together someday. But to hear that he had gotten another girl pregnant, and had no problems ditching the former girlfriend carrying his child as well? Well, that just made him out to be a first-class scum bag!

"Thalia, I'm so sorry. I never meant to hurt you."

"Sure you did. You're just too stupid to realize it."

"I know you're mad…."

"I'm not mad, Justin. I kinda feel sorry for you. Two times in the same period of time? Who does that?"

"You're just mad that I didn't pick you."

That was a low blow. Now Thalia was feeling rage!

"Listen to me, asshole! I don't need you or anyone else to help me raise this baby! I've been doing just fine all along and I'll continue this way! A real man would take care of ALL his kids, not just one! But if you wanna go ahead and live your life pretending your kid doesn't exist, that's on you!"

"Don't be mad, okay? This is hard for me too! I'm trying not to fuck this up. She doesn't know about you, and she's not as strong as you. I don't want her to leave me."

Thalia thought about his words. He was right—she was strong. And it dawned on her in that moment that he was weak. She didn't want a weak man in her life. That's a whole lot of unnecessary hurt that she didn't want to deal with.

"Don't worry about it. I won't tell her. I'll talk to you another time," and she hung up the phone.

≡ ≡ ≡

Over the next couple of months, Justin called Thalia to check in with her. The conversations were brief—a lot of awkward chitchat like, "How's the weather where you are?" and "What are you going to do today?" Thalia had pretty much grown numb to him. She entertained his calls for the sake of keeping her son's father in the loop, but she had no desire to beg for him to come back to her or to take responsibility for their child. In fact, Thalia began to look forward to having her baby all to herself. She would raise him with her traditions and her beliefs, and no one would be able to argue with her.

A month after Tyler's birth, Thalia received another call from Justin. This time, there was no awkward chitchat.

"I need you to do me a favor," he said.

"What?"

"This is going to sound strange but, I never told my family about you."

"What's so strange about that?"

"They don't know about you and the baby."

"His name is Tyler."

"Well, I was arguing with my mom the other day and it just kinda slipped out. I told her that I just found out myself—like recently."

"Why did you lie to her?"

"I don't know. I just blurted it out ...."

"Or maybe it was easier to pass the blame off to someone else."

"Please, Thalia. My mom wants to talk to you on the phone. Will you please talk to her? She's the ba—I mean, Tyler's grandmother. Can you please go along with this for the sake of my family?"

Thalia thought about it. To go along with this may award Tyler with the missing side of his family. So what if Justin was a coward? It's not like she had to attach herself to him. It was just a phone call.

"Fine. Give me her number."

A few minutes later, Thalia dialed the number.

"Hello?"

"Mrs. Stevens?"

"Yes?"

"My name is Thalia Wales. Your son told me you were expecting my call."

"Yes. Thank you for calling. Are you expecting? Or have you had the baby already?"

"I gave birth a month ago. His name is Tyler."

"My son knew all along, didn't he?"

Wow! She didn't beat around the bush at all! "No, not really. I didn't tell him right away."

"But he didn't just find out the other day, did he?"

"I really think you should ask him."

"I know my son. He's an idiot! He runs away from all his problems. He always has! And now he has two babies!"

"My child is not his problem, Mrs. Stevens. I made that very clear to him. If he wants to be in Tyler's life, that's great. But if he does not, I am perfectly capable of raising him without any help."

"That's very noble of you, Thalia. But my son needs to take responsibility for his actions!"

"Listen, Mrs. Stevens, I'm going to be very blunt. I'm not sure what family issues you and your son have, but I would appreciate leaving my baby out of them. I'll give you the same statement I gave your son. If you would like to be a part of your grandson's life, then I welcome you. But if you do not, please leave us alone. We are doing just fine and we don't need family drama to complicate our lives. Am I making myself clear?"

There was silence on the other line. Then Mrs. Stevens said, "Thank you for your time," and hung up the phone.

■ ■ ■

Eight months went by before Thalia heard from Justin again. In this time, she began dating Sam, a fellow Air Force recruit. He was very good to her son Tyler, and she was very content. One night, while they were staying in a hotel room, Justin called Thalia. He was drunk and he began spewing out crazy statements like "I should have picked you." and "Who are you there with?" and "You're nothing but a slut." Thalia told him to never call her again and that he needed some psychological help.

When Tyler turned one, Thalia got another phone call from Justin. This time he wasn't drunk.

"I have another issue and I need your help."

"Good Lord, man! When are you going to get yourself together?"

"It's my wife, Janey. I just told her about you and Tyler. She's freaking out! She wants to talk to you."

"Are you kidding me? I'm not a fucking therapist, Justin!"

"Please, Thalia! Just talk to her. It could save my marriage!"

"Jesus Christ! You're such a fucking idiot!"

"Please, Thalia."

"Ugh! Give her my number!"

He hung up the phone and she waited. Tyler was taking a nap and was due to wake up soon. Hopefully this wouldn't take long. Her phone rang a few minutes later.

"Hello?"

"Thalia?"

"Janey?"

"Yes. Justin just told me about your son. I just wanted to hear your side of the story."

"There's really nothing to tell. I was with Justin way before he met you."

"When was your son born?"

"May 12, 2008."

"My son Joey was born on May 20, 2008."

Son of a bitch! My bed wasn't even cold yet before he jumped into hers! What a dick!

"I see," she answered calmly.

"Do you want him back? Because frankly, you can have him!"

"I assure you. I do not want your husband."

"I seriously don't know what to do. My marriage sucks! He won't give me any money, he yells at me a lot, I stay home and take care of our son with no help from him—I'm all alone!" she sobbed.

"Okay, just calm down. Listen, there are resources on base that you can tap into. Soldiers are not allowed to mistreat their wives on base. It's like a code of honor with the military."

"So what do I do?"

"Well, first you should sit him down and figure out what's really bothering him. If that doesn't work, you can always go to his captain and file a grievance."

"I know what's bothering him, his conscience is eating him alive! He has a family here, but yet he can't stop thinking about his bastard baby!"

That's when Thalia saw red. Overall, she was a pretty chill person. But anyone who dared attack her child was met with a raging mama bear!

"DON'T YOU EVER ADDRESS MY CHILD THAT WAY AGAIN, YOU FUCKING WHORE! IF YOU EVER CALL MY CHILD BY ANY TERM OTHER THAN HIS BIRTH NAME, I WILL HUNT YOU DOWN AND MAKE YOU WISH YOU WERE NEVER BORN! AM I MAKING MYSELF CLEAR?"

"I … I didn't mean …."

"This call is over. Goodbye."

Janey called Tahlia one more time a few months later to complain about Justin, but Thalia told her she was complaining to the wrong person. She never heard from Janey again after that. When Tyler turned two, Justin and his family moved to Japan. Thalia was somewhat relieved. He chose to support his wife and son, and Thalia never had to have another conversation with that hateful woman again. She also hoped that Justin would find some peace in his life. Maybe a fresh start in a new country would allow him to start over and become a good husband and father. Thalia was not tormented by her past actions, so she couldn't imagine what demons were eating away at Justin's mind. She felt sorry for him once again.

When Tyler was 2 and a half, Thalia's duty in the Air Force came to an end. She moved back to Lebanon, CT, where her parents lived. She moved in with them until she could get her feet underneath her. She got a job because she wanted to be able to pay for a home for herself and Tyler. Sam had moved back to Lebanon with her and he stayed with her in her parents' home. But they had begun to have problems in their relationship, so he spent the majority of their time together living with his own parents. Tyler adored Sam, which was why it was so hard to end their relationship. And Sam was always looking out for his little man.

"Hey, I gotta talk to you," Sam said one night.

"What about?"

"Tyler. He said something tonight that kinda caught me off guard."

"What?"

"He said that he didn't deserve a daddy."

"What did you say to that?"

"I didn't know what to say so I told him that everyone deserves a daddy. I also told him that he was like a son to me and I may not be his real daddy but I loved him like a real daddy should."

It were statements like that that really moved Thalia. She wanted so badly for Tyler to have a good male role model in his life. Sam was great with him. But he wasn't great with Thalia, and she had promised herself that she would never settle for a man that didn't appreciate her. She gave him another year, then she told him they were better off being friends than boyfriend/girlfriend. He agreed, and they parted ways. But he continued to keep in touch with Sam.

Shortly after the breakup, Thalia's parents sat her down one evening. They wanted Thalia to be settled in her own home but they didn't want her to move far away. So they proposed to build an addition to their home, that way, she and Tyler could live next door, but have their own space as well. Thalia was excited about the idea, and it took the construction company six months to build the addition.

When Tyler was in first grade, Thalia got a strange call from her father.

"Justin called me today … at work."

"What? Why?"

"He's looking for you. He wants to talk to you."

"Doesn't he have my number?"

"His wife made him erase it when they moved to Japan."

"What a loser. Give me the number."

A few minutes later, Thalia pressed his digits.

"Hello?"

"Justin, it's Thalia."

"Thalia! It's so good to hear from you."

"Please don't tell me you have another family member that wants to talk to me because the answer is no."

"No. No family members. Just me this time."

"What is it?"

"Thalia, I fucked up."

"What did you do now?"

"I fucked up with us, I mean. Sometimes I sit alone outside and wonder why I ever let you go. You're so patient and wise. I feel like I can tell you anything. You know I'm fucked up but yet you still take my calls, and take my shit too."

"Well, you're the father of my son. If I were to get rid of you completely, my son would have a piece of him missing forever. And I don't want him ever to feel pain like that. Not when I can take it away from him."

"I wanna talk to him. Is he around?"

"Yah. He's right here. You sure you want to do this?"

"My marriage is already half destroyed. Janey hates my guts. I guess there's a part of me that hates her too. She made me choose between my son Joey and Tyler. She made me choose Joey."

"No, Justin. She didn't make you choose Joey. YOU chose Joey. Don't put the blame on your wife. You're a coward if you do. You had the choice to be a part of both of their lives. But because you weren't honest in the beginning, you dug yourself a nice little hole. Now you're trying to get out of it but your ladder has been burned."

"Well, I'm going to try and do the right thing now. I want to be a part of Tyler's life too. Please let me talk to him."

A lump began to form in Thalia's throat. She ached for this moment—to be able to give her son the one person that was missing from his little life. But she was skeptical too. What if Justin ended up hurting him? What if he made him promises that he couldn't keep?

"If I do this, you better not hurt him. So help me God, I will kill you."

"I won't hurt him, Thalia. Please."

She looked at Tyler playing Legos in the other room. She called to him.

"Your daddy wants to talk to you, sweetie," she said as she handed him the phone.

"You mean Sam?"

"No, honey. Your real daddy."

Tyler looked at her confused. Then he grabbed the phone. "Hello?"

"Tyler. It's your dad. How are you?"

"Good. Where are you?"

"I'm in Japan."

"Where's that?"

"It's far away from you."

"Oh. Are you going to come and visit us?"

"Would you like me to?"

"Yah."

"I'll see what I can do. Work is pretty busy right now. Would it be okay if I called you every now and then?"

"Sure."

"Great. I'll talk to you soon, Tyler." And he hung up the phone.

Over the next few months, Justin was true to his word. He called Tyler once a month. They spent time talking about school, sports, and traveling. At first, Thalia was okay with the arrangement. She saw a change in Tyler. He was thrilled to have his father in his life, and he looked forward to his phone calls. But after a while, she began to worry about the influence of Justin's wife over Tyler's innocent little mind. Justin wasn't strong enough to put his foot down whenever his wife made smart remarks, but Thalia had no problem voicing her concerns.

"Hey, we gotta talk," she said one day.

"What's up?" Justin asked.

"I overheard what Janey said in the background yesterday when you called Tyler."

"What did she say?"

"She told her daughters that they had to leave the room because their daddy had to talk to his girlfriend."

"She was just being an asshole."

"And I don't need my son to hear shit like that!"

"Why are you getting so upset?"

"Because I'm not your girlfriend! I don't need anyone putting thoughts in my son's head about their mother. I am not anyone's girlfriend, and I don't have affairs with married men! If you can't put a leash on that bitch, I will!"

"Calm down, Thalia. I'm sure Tyler doesn't think like that."

"Calling my son three times does not make you an expert on his thoughts. He's a little boy, and he's just getting to know you. He doesn't need her filling his head with ideas that might confuse him. I have a good reputation here. I have a job, I have nice friends, and I am home every night for my child. From now on, you can call Tyler when your asshole wife is not around."

"Understood."

"Good."

Justin continued calling Tyler to check in every once in a while. He complied with Thalia's wishes and only called when he was at work. That way, neither Janey nor Thalia would have any problems. Three years later, Justin called Thalia out of the blue and informed her that he was moving back to the United States. He had gotten a divorce and would be living by himself on base. His sister was graduating from high school and he wanted both Tyler and Thalia to fly down to Louisiana to attend the celebration. Thalia was a bit nervous about meeting his entire family, but she decided that now was as good a time as any to meet Tyler's grandparents and aunts and uncles.

Thalia bought her plane tickets in June and flew down for a week. Justin's parents had arranged for a hotel room for both Tyler and Thalia to stay in. They even picked her up at the airport. The moment Thalia met them, she instantly fell in love with them. They were so amazingly kind and generous. They asked so many questions and wanted to know everything about both of them. Finally they pulled up to a small, white cape in a suburban neighborhood and turned off the car. They got out of the car and led Thalia and her son to the front door. The door immediately opened and a young girl stood there.

"Tyler? Thalia?"

"Yes," Thalia answered.

"Oh my God, I'm so glad you could come to my graduation!" She hugged them both. "My name is Jean. I'm Justin's sister."

"It's so nice to meet you, Jean," Thalia responded.

"And this is Justin's brother, Nick," she said as a young man that looked similar to Justin came walking into the entrance.

"Hi, Thalia. I heard a lot about you," he smiled.

"I bet you have," Thalia laughed.

Just as he was about to respond, a back door opened and Justin appeared. Tyler took one look at him and instantly knew he was looking at his father. He ran towards him and dove into his arms.

"Daddy!" Tyler yelled.

"Oh, son. It's so great to finally meet you," Justin whispered and held him tight for several seconds. Then he set him down and let go.

"God, look at you. You're so big!"

"I'm seven."

"I know," he studied him. "You look like your mom." He then looked up and saw Thalia standing next to Nick.

"What took you so long?" he smiled.

"I had to wait until you got over all your girl drama," she shot back.

He laughed. "True." Then he looked down at Tyler. "I'm thinking I'm gonna take a break from the girl drama so I can focus on other people for a while."

Thalia and Tyler spent a wonderful week with the Stevens family. They attended Jean's graduation, they went out to dinner, and they laughed over silly stories. It was perfect. Thalia actually felt like she was part of the family. Tyler adored his aunt and uncle and his grandparents, but he gravitated towards his father all the time. His smile was immense, and anyone could see the happiness dancing around in his eyes. The night before they left, Thalia had a chance to sit down with Justin alone. They went down to a local bar and ordered a beer.

"So. Is this crazy or what?" he asked.

"What do you mean?"

"Who would have thought that you and I would be sitting here having a beer together, after the shit we've been through?"

"Oh, I don't know. I'm pretty chill about things."

"Yah, but I left you alone to take care of my child. I never offered to pay for anything. I chose another family over you and Tyler."

"Well, I never said you weren't a dick."

He chuckled. "Agreed." Then his face turned serious and he looked at her long and hard. "I'm sorry, Thalia. I never meant to hurt you. You of all people. You always made me laugh, you always had my back. Hell, I told you things that I never told anyone—not even my wife. You were my best friend."

"Don't beat yourself up too much."

"I do! You didn't deserve any of this!"

"Listen. My mother's people believe that we are put on this earth for a reason. And sometimes the reason is not very clear at first. Sometimes, we have to make great sacrifices or go on long journeys to find out what that reason is. You and I have come full circle. I learned so much about myself in that circle, and hopefully, you learned something about yourself too. I learned that there is nothing I can't do in this life. I may be a small woman but I am strong too. You have probably begun to see that you have to be honest with yourself and speak your truth. Only you can look inside yourself and see your good spirit. The bad one lives there too. But if you choose to follow your good spirit, your life will be filled with true happiness—and love. That little boy loves you. What you choose to do with that love is entirely up to you."

"You're so wise, and so incredibly brave. I wish I wasn't such an asshole back then. I would have stayed with you."

"Well, who's to say we would have made it? Maybe back then was not our time. And maybe this moment here is what we were meant to be. You will always have my friendship. And we have a son together. What more could we ask from each other?"

"True. I guess a friendship with you is the best I could ask for."

"And you will always have it."

"You know what, Thalia? You are one bad-ass bitch," he smiled.

"You bet your sweet ass I am," she smiled back.

"You wanna see more of my sweet ass?" he purred.

"No, but you can buy me another beer," she replied. "And don't try anything stupid. I'm not cleaning up any more of your messes."

"Affirmative, Lieutenant."

■ ■ ■

Thalia returned every year with Tyler to where Justin was stationed. She believed that Tyler needed to spend time with his father to have a good, positive role model in his life. She also believed that Justin needed Tyler to feel like he was a worthy father. Eventually, Tyler met his half-brother, Joey, and they got along well. Justin continued to care for all of his children, and keep in close contact with them.

As for Thalia, she continued to fight many battles as the years went on. They were not battles in faraway countries, or for the United States government, but rather, battles to defend the freedom she held so dearly within herself. She held tight to her family and close friends, and stood her ground against those that tried to bully her. She was a good mother, a faithful friend, a dutiful citizen, and she never let anyone or anything stand in her way. She was a soldier, a warrior, a survivor—and one bad-ass bitch! ■

■ CHAPTER SIX ■
Ireland

The secrets of the past trickle into our lives, like a leaky faucet that cannot be fixed. They drip, drip, drip until the surface becomes drenched. And then the mold sets in like a cancer, and spreads. It spreads into all the avenues of our lives. Black spots that taint us, mark us, brand us with their infections. Until one day, we rip the pipe right out of the house, reroute the water line and wait for the mold to dry up and flake away in the wind. Then the secret is nothing more than a whispered memory in the darkness of the night.

Ireland was cursed at birth. Her father knew it the day he laid eyes on her for the first time. Something wasn't right. She was too thin, too tall, too pale, and too blonde. Genetics are funny sometimes. You can have a set of kids that look nothing like each other. Chalk it up to some ancestry that came from another part of the world. But this was different—and he knew it. He knew it from the start, although his wife would deny it all. Ireland, named after the country of her ancestry, wasn't really his.

"I'm out of here!" she cried.

"Please, honey. Don't do this. You're my flesh and blood," her mama replied.

"I've had enough of that asshole!"

"Don't swear. It's not ladylike."

"I don't give a fuck what's ladylike and what's not! I don't know what crawled up his ass in the last 15 years, but I'm not gonna take it no more!"

"He's just having a bad day, that's all."

"He treats me different, Ma! Wake up! It's like I'm not even his daughter!" Ireland spat out.

Her mother gasped and rammed a fist into her mouth. Ireland waited for her mother's comeback, but received none. She almost wanted to ask her what she meant by it, but instead, she chose to ignore her eerie silence.

"Where will you stay? You have no money."

"I'll figure it out. That's what's good about tough love, dear mother— it teaches you how to survive on your own."

"Take this," she said as she stuffed a hundred-dollar bill in her daughter's jean pocket. "Don't spend it on that funny stuff, though!"

"Ma, c'mon. You can't afford this."

"Take it. You can pay me back when your life gets settled."

Ten minutes later, Ireland left home. She was 15 years old and scared to death. For a few days, she crashed on a friend's couch. But then she was told about a cheap apartment on the east side of town. It wasn't very clean, but she could fix that easily. It would be her own place. A place where no one could tell her that she didn't belong, and a place where she could discover what she was really made of.

It was 1973, and the smell of freedom permeated the air. She found a job at a local grocery store that she could walk to. She went to high school during the day, and worked at night after school and on weekends. She hung out with friends when she had some free time, and called her mother every Sunday. She was street smart, knew how to have fun, and worked hard.

■ ■ ■

Three years later, Ireland graduated from high school. Money was getting a bit tight, the rent had gone up, and her mother begged her to come home. Against her better judgment, she packed up her belongings and moved back home. She promised herself that this was only temporary, and made sure she found activities to occupy her time so that she didn't have any more run-ins with her father. She found a job as a nurse's aide at a convalescent home and began dating a biker named Manny. They dated for only a few short months before he asked her to marry him. Ireland saw it as her "get out of jail free" card, more than lovers destined to be together. So she said yes. Why not? So what if Manny was a bit possessive of her, and tried to stifle her free spirit? At least he didn't ignore her.

One night, Ireland was at a party with some friends. Her drink was empty, so she decided to go into the kitchen for a refill. While she was pouring herself some whiskey and Coke, a voice spoke to her from behind.

"I couldn't help but notice that you're not here with anybody."

Ireland turned around and saw a young man standing in front of her. He was tall and skinny like her, light-colored hair, but too clean cut for her standards. He looked like someone that belonged in a library or on a chess team. But he had a wide smile and looked like a kid at Christmas.

"Yah. So?"

"Well, I was wondering if I could talk to you for a bit."

She took a long drink from her cup, never taking her eyes from his face while she did. "I'm listening."

"My name is Gus. Gus Spencer."

"Ireland."

"What about it?"

"That's my name."

"Oh, really? That's a beautiful name. Your parents must have loved that country."

"They've never been there."

"Really? Then why did they name you that?"

"I don't know. I guess my mom really liked that name."

"Are you Irish?"

"No. I'm a hundred-percent Italian."

"Like hell you are!"

"Excuse me?"

"Say what you want but that light hair and fair skin? You've got Irish in ya, lassie!" he chuckled.

Ireland stared at him, speechless. Either this guy was crazy or he had the social skills of a gnat. How dare he question her heritage! Who did he think he was?

"So do you have a boyfriend? A gorgeous girl like yourself must be taken."

"Yah, I got one."

"Is he here?"

"No. He's at the bar with his friends."

"Why isn't he here with you? I wouldn't let you out of my sight if you were mine."

"Well, he thinks his biker friends are more interesting. Frankly, I don't even give a shit."

"Oh, so it's not that serious?"

"Do you call engaged serious?"

"Yes!"

"Well, we are."

"Are you in love with him?"

"Hell no! I'm just getting married so I can get the fuck out of my parents' house!"

"That's stupid! You should marry for love."

"I said yes, so I guess I'm stuck with him."

"Not necessarily! Just tell him you've had a change of heart."

"Ha!" Ireland laughed. "He's a big guy. I'm sure that wouldn't go smooth with him."

"Then I'll do it for you!"

"What?" she laughed again. "He'd kill you. And I wouldn't want to be responsible for a man's death."

"If I have to prove my love for you, I'll do what I have to do. Now, which bar is he at?"

Prove his love? I just met the guy! Now I'm really thinking he's crazy. But maybe he's a step up from Manny. Intellectual people go pretty far in life, don't they? Good job, good money. I'd never have to move home again! What if he's "the one?" Hmmm. Maybe I should see where this goes.

"Okay, let's go. You driving?" she said.

"Yah!"

Thirty minutes later, they pulled up to Road Kill, a biker bar just outside of Chaplin. Ireland insisted on staying in the car, just in case her fiancé was pissed off enough to come after her next. But after watching Gus walk slowly into the bar alone, she shot out of the car and walked in after him. It was certainly a sight to see. Gus, a skeleton of a man standing up to Manny (aka Hercules), surrounded by all his biker friends. Gus told Manny that he didn't want any trouble, but that he would use violence if necessary. His terms were to let Ireland out of her engagement, or suffer the consequences. Manny took one look at Gus and laughed. But Gus was insidious. He declared that Ireland was single once again, and turned and walked her right out of the bar. It was like a scene from *The Twilight Zone!* But Manny was too drunk to argue, and Gus and Ireland drove away, unscathed.

Days later, when Manny finally sobered up, he tried to patch up his relationship with Ireland, but she didn't receive any of his calls. Having a nerd as a bodyguard gave her a renewed sense of self-worth. Manny eventually got tired of Ireland's lack of interest, and moved on to a voluptuous tramp that shot pool and drank whiskey from the bottle.

Ireland was not exactly attracted to Gus, but she was definitely impressed by his bravery. So when he asked her to move in with him a couple weeks later, she accepted. Living with a knight in shining armor and freedom from her parents? Not a bad gig. They found a small apartment on School Street in Manchester. He worked for a construction company, and she worked at a retirement facility. Life was blissful for a year.

About 11 months later, Ireland announced that she was pregnant. Gus received the news with joy. He loved Ireland and couldn't get enough of her. Having a baby with her would fuse him to her for life! They married a few months later. It was a small wedding, with only family members present. At twenty-one years old, Ireland gave birth to a baby boy. They named him Hogan. They quickly took to parenthood. Ireland quit her job and cared for her little baby son all day long. At night, when Gus came home, he would join in the baby fun as well, helping her as much as he knew how. The young family was so happy that they didn't notice that Ireland was pregnant once again. This time, she gave birth to a little girl, and they named her Eleanor.

At this point, the little apartment on School Street could no longer hold a family of 4. So they found another apartment on Cooper Street that was much bigger and had 3 bedrooms. Here, Ireland began to expand her knowledge of herbs. She took a class that taught her the origins of different plant life and the different uses for each. In addition to being a full-time mother, she created a garden outdoors as well as indoors. She began to make remedies for common ailments. Gus thought she was absolutely adorable.

"Do you think things can ever get any better?" he asked her one night.

"We could hit it big with the lottery," she joked.

"Nah. I wouldn't want a lot of money. I like things just the way they are."

"Really? You wouldn't want to escape the city and live in a house in the country?"

"Oh, but we will. I started looking already."

"You have?" she sat up in bed. "Where? And why didn't you tell me?"

"I wanted to surprise you."

"Well, shouldn't we look together?"

"I suppose we have to, now that the cat is out of the bag," he sighed.

"Speaking of letting the cat out of the bag…."

"Uh-oh. What did you do?"

"No, dear. What did we do," she smiled.

He looked at her, puzzled. He searched her eyes and saw the brightness of her smile, and he knew.

"Only one thing can make you that happy," he grinned as he reached for her.

"Besides the two we already have?"

He enveloped her in his arms. "Guess we'll be needing that house pretty quick, then." Then he kissed her and snuggled deeper under the covers with her.

The lake was as enchanting as Ireland's disposition, so Gus bought a house on it. She loved it. By the time she was ready to deliver their third child, she had planted a variety of herbs in her garden outdoors, and the inside of her house was sprinkled with various antiques. Ireland had become a modern-day Caroline Ingalls from *Little House on the Prairie.* Even the birth of little Ives was almost archaic. He was born inside their home from a midwife. To Ireland, simplicity was at the core of her being. She loved home cooked meals, sitting in a chair outdoors watching the sunset, observing a butterfly collecting nectar, and feeling her baby draw nourishment from her breast. Life was quiet, and peaceful.

At least it was until that fateful day in the fall.

Marty was the neighbor's kid. He was in his early twenties, very respectful, and happy to help others. Gus instantly took a liking to him, and he often invited him over to ask for assistance on various projects. On a rainy fall afternoon in mid-October, Gus decided to raise his foundation. It wasn't the best weather conditions for the job, but Gus was a "get it done" type of guy. Marty's father had a cement mixer, so Gus borrowed it for the afternoon.

"Well, here she is, Gus. A real beauty, eh?" Marty laughed.

"Oh, yah. She'll do the job, all right."

"My dad says she sparks a bit, but it's no big deal."

"Oh, really? Let's have a look." Gus flipped on the switch of the mixer and watched as sparks occasionally sizzled out of the motor. He scratched his head. "Well, that don't look good."

"Ah, it's nothing. Dad's been using this thing for years like this."

"All right then. But let me do the scooping, just in case. I've got longer arms than you."

"Gotcha!"

They worked for a few hours, pouring concrete into the forms. The rain began to come down harder, and the two men were soaked. Both were looking forward to ending the task soon, so they worker faster.

"I think a couple more batches ought to do it," Gus said while scooping up the cement into the bucket.

"Hey, why don't you let me get the last load. We can be done in 10 minutes."

"Yah, all right. Just stay away from the motor. She's pretty hot now. I wouldn't want you to get any burns."

"Oh, I'll be careful. I watched my dad do this a million times," Marty chuckled.

Gus walked away slowly, balancing the heavy bucket with his right arm. He couldn't wait to be done so he could crack open a beer and admire the finished product. He wondered what Ireland was making for supper. Suddenly, he heard an awful scream, and turned around, dropping the bucket on the ground. Marty's body was convulsing into electric shocks against the metal rim of the cement mixer. Gus ran towards him and grabbed the plug and yanked it free from the extension cord. But he was too late, Marty's body slid off of the mixer and crumpled to the ground.

"IRELAND! CALL 911!"

Gus grabbed Marty's face and began to slap it, screaming for him to come to. He even tried to administer CPR. Over and over, pumping his chest, and breathing into his mouth, but Marty didn't even flinch. The paramedics came and tried to revive him, but it was too late. Marty was gone.

Hours later, after the ambulance took Marty's lifeless body away, and Marty's parents were given the bad news, Gus dragged his broken heart over to the refrigerator and opened it. He took out a six-pack of Budweiser and went and sat on the couch. He cracked open one and guzzled it down in one gulp. He then cracked open a second one and did the same. Ireland entered the room. She sat next to him and gently took his hand. He didn't look at her, just continued to drink the contents of the metal can in his hand.

"Honey, it wasn't your fault," she whispered.

"Like hell it wasn't," he replied, as he reached for a third beer.

"He just wanted to help, baby, that's all."

"Help?" he spat, as he rose up from his seat. "Help? That boy will never help anybody ever again. He will never see another birthday, he will never get married, never have kids, and never help his neighbor with an outdoor project!"

"It was an accident, Gus. Please! Can't you see that?" Ireland placed a hand on his arm, but he yanked it away quickly.

"This was all my fault. The mixer was sparking. I knew that was bad. I'm a construction worker, for God's sake! It was raining outside! Water and sparks just don't go together! And when he asked if he could do the last load, I should have said NO! He's shorter than me! I knew there were risks involved!"

"But he wanted to, baby!" Ireland pleaded. "He's like that—always wanting to learn new skills or prove himself. You can't blame yourself for that!"

He looked at her, and took a giant swig from his beer. "But I bet his father can," and he walked away.

In the weeks that followed, Gus and Ireland did their best to move on from the tragedy of losing Marty. Ireland continued to care for her family. She cooked and cleaned after 3 small children and a husband who refused to forgive himself. Gus got up every morning, and went to work building houses. He brought home enough money for the family to survive on, so Ireland never could complain that he was slacking in his duties. But she noticed how different he had become—the light was gone from his eyes. He began spending more time at Rusty's—the bar in their old neighborhood in Manchester. By 2:00, he was reeking of alcohol, but he never came home angry. He was never an abusive man. Ireland knew that time was the only thing that could heal his broken spirit, so she let him do what he had to do.

■ ■ ■

A few years later, Gus was still drinking on a daily basis. Ireland tried to divert his attention from the bottle by encouraging him to expand his business. At first, the new idea seemed to be working. Gus bought a three family investment house in Windham, and fixed it up. Ireland thought they made a good team—he fixed up the houses and she managed the business part of it. Gus wasn't back to his old self, but at least this was a start.

Ireland joined the PTA so she could be involved with her children's education. She began to hang out with the PTA moms and even invited them over for play dates, barbeques, and summertime lounging by the lake. One hot day, Ireland invited her friend Nelly over for some swimming. They sat by the edge and watched the kids jumping off the dock.

"You're kinda quiet today," Ireland said.

"Yah," Nelly replied.

"Something on your mind?"

"Uh, no. Just hot, I guess."

"Ain't that the truth. Hell, if it gets any hotter, we could probably grill the burgers on the pavement!"

Nelly stared into Ireland's eyes.

"What is it?" she asked. She noticed that Nelly looked away quickly and her hands began to tremble. "Nelly, for God's sake! Tell me what's wrong!"

"Sweet Jesus, I can't do this anymore," she sobbed. "I can't carry this around anymore!"

She stood up quickly and walked further down the edge, away from the kids. Ireland followed.

"Nelly, what's going on? Please tell me."

Nelly faced her friend, tears in her eyes. "I'm so sorry, Ireland," she whispered.

"About what?"

"Dave was with Gus two weeks ago. They were having a couple beers at Rusty's. He had him laughing too—you know—Gus has been so down lately. After a few, Dave had to go to the bathroom. When he came out...." she stopped and looked at Ireland, tears brimming in her eyes, her lower lip quivering.

"What happened?"

"Dave said there was this nasty-looking woman in a short skirt, too much makeup, and fried blond hair," Nelly sniffled.

Ireland swallowed.

"Gus was making out with her."

Wham! There it was—the wrecking ball right in the gut. Ireland gripped her heart.

"She left before Dave could walk up to them, but he couldn't believe his eyes. He finished his beer, paid the tab, and walked out. Gus asked why he was leaving so soon, and he couldn't even face him! Ireland, I'm so sorry!"

Ireland walked over to the lake, dumbfounded. *That bastard! Cheating on me while I'm at home trying to maintain a family and a future? You fucking dick! Wait until you get home!*

She was parched but her mouth couldn't produce any spit. She bent down low and scooped up the brownish water in her palm and put it to her lips. She slurped it down. It was most likely filled with urine and dirt but she didn't taste it nor did she care. Nelly sat crying softly next to her, apologizing profusely. Was the world spinning? Why did she feel so dizzy? Was she tired? Should she take a nap?

"I don't feel well," Ireland whispered. "I think I'd like to be alone for a while."

"Of course," Nelly sniffled. "Do you want me to take the kids?"

"No. I can manage."

"Oh. Okay. I'm so sorry, Ireland. If there's anything I can do to help, please let me. I feel terrible! I didn't know if I should have told you ... but if it were me, I'd want to know."

Ireland looked at her friend, anger bubbling up inside of her. She quickly tamped it down. This wasn't Nelly's fault. She was doing what any good friend would do. Only one person was to blame, or was it two? Could this have been her fault as well? Maybe if she was a little more caring, or maybe she should have insisted that he get help for his drinking. It couldn't have been all of his fault, right?

"Please, Nelly. Just give me some time to digest all of this, okay?"

"Yes, of course," Nelly said. Then she slowly walked up the bank, and disappeared around the house.

Later that evening, when the kids were in bed, the dishes were washed and the house was quiet, Ireland walked into her bedroom. Gus was supposedly at the bar doing what he did best. She flipped on the light in her closet and stared at the boxes on the top shelf. She reached up for the baby blue shoe box and pulled it down. She sat cross legged on her bedroom floor and ran her palm over the lid, sweeping away the light film of dust. Then she opened the box and smiled at its contents. She pulled out a picture of her and her sister Jen, smiling in the sun after a day of running through the sprinkler in her parents' backyard. Another was of her and her old dog, Buddy. Another was of her mom at Christmas. God, how she missed them all! She had gotten so wrapped up in her life with Gus and the kids that she only saw them at Christmas. She pulled out picture after picture of her life as a kid and laughed at each memory they produced.

At the bottom of the stack, was a picture of her father. He was dressed in a brown suit, looking as if he just came out of church. She stared at the picture. This was her father, and yet, searching deep inside her heart, she was amazed that she didn't hold one ounce of love for this man. *Why? Why did you hate me so much? Am I so unlovable? Is it the same reason why my husband doesn't love me anymore and found someone else?* The tears came pouring out and she wailed like a mother losing a child. It went on for a long time as she expelled all the hurt she had felt over the years. A parent that didn't love her, leaving home at such a young age, the death of the neighbor's son, and finally—her husband's infidelity. She sobbed until her eyes were raw and red, and there were no more tears to shed. Then she lay on the floor and closed her eyes.

She awoke to the sound of her front door opening and shutting, and boots being removed. She heard the truck keys being placed on the counter and the refrigerator door opening. Ireland staggered up, replaced the blue box and its contents back on the shelf and shuffled into the kitchen.

"Woah, hey...." Gus shook. "You scared the shit out of me."

"What are you doing up so late?" he asked, closing the refrigerator door.

"Waiting for you."

"Why? You never have in the past?"

"Where were you?"

"What?"

"You heard me."

"I was where I always am on a Saturday night."

Ireland walked towards him. She got close to his neck and inhaled. Although very faint, mixed in with the smell of whiskey was the distinct smell of a woman's cheap perfume. She recoiled quickly and stared at him.

"What? What is your problem?" Gus stepped back.

"Does she have a name or do you just call her Baby?"

"What are you talking about?"

"Why? That's all I need to know. Why? Why would you do this to me? Was I so terrible of a wife? Was I not good in bed? What was it, Gus?"

"I have no idea what you're saying right now!"

"SAY IT! Don't you dare lie to me. I know all about the whore you've been making out with at the bar. Next time, make sure you don't mix your friends with your sluts when you want to hide the truth!"

"Dave?"

"That's right! You want to tell me he's lying?" Ireland raged.

Gus snorted and looked away. Then he faced her once again.

"She was drunk and she grabbed me. What could I do?"

Ireland stared at him with her mouth open. Then she slowly walked over the kitchen table and sat down. She looked down at her hands and spoke.

"I'm going to ask you one time, Gus. If you lie to me, I will file for divorce in the morning." She looked up at him. "Is there another woman?"

Gus stared at her. After several seconds, he sighed.

"Yes."

Even though she already knew the answer, the words stabbed into her heart. Three children, a house by the lake, a business partnership, and happiness all seemed to swirl around into a giant typhoon of deceitfulness and dishonesty. The sacred bonds of marriage that she upheld for years disappeared into nothing. All of it—gone, with his one act of selfishness.

"Why?"

"Well, you did it first. I don't even know why you're so upset."

Ireland stood abruptly. "Excuse me?"

"Yah. You didn't think you could hide Ben from me, did you?"

"Ben? The lifeguard?"

"Yah! That day at the lake. I saw him give you his phone number!"

"For my sister Jen! He had to get rid of his guinea pig because he was going off to college and Jen was looking to buy one for her kid!"

"Well, it didn't look that innocent to me."

"Did I make out with him at the lake? Did I ever come home drunk, smelling like sex?" Ireland shouted. "What other proof do ya got?"

"Well, you didn't seem that interested in me so I thought you found someone else."

"And that's how you think a marriage works? I cheat on you so you cheat on me? What about communicating and working out our problems? After everything you and I have been through, don't you think I deserve at least that?"

Gus walked over to the kitchen table and sat down. He put his head between his hands and sighed. Then he looked up at Ireland.

"I'm sorry," he whispered. "I couldn't deal with Marty's death. It was all my fault. Drinking was the only way I could make it all go away."

Ireland sat down.

"I spent so much time at Rusty's that most of the time I didn't even know my own name. Then Jean and I started talking. She made me forget everything."

"I'll bet she did," Ireland muttered.

"You remind me of him!" Gus spat out. "You were there! Every time I'm around you I remember what I did to him!"

"Bullshit!" Ireland stood up. "That's the coward's way of trying to get out of something. You put blame on someone else!"

"No, I didn't mean to blame you," Gus stood up. "I just didn't know what to do anymore."

"Here's what's gonna happen. You're going to stop drinking, and you're not going to Rusty's anymore. You're going to never see that woman again, and you're going to get tested. I'll call the doctor in the morning and set up an appointment to go and talk to a therapist. I should have done that years ago but I never thought it would get to this point."

"No. Not a therapist," Gus stated. "I'll do everything else but that. I can quit on my own, I swear."

Ireland looked hard into his eyes. "If you don't, you and I are done. Am I making myself clear?"

"Yes. I know. I swear I'll change," he said.

She turned and walked towards the bedroom. "I'm going to bed. You can sleep on the couch tonight."

■ ■ ■

In the months that followed, Gus was on his best behavior. He got tested—all negative—and he quit drinking. He seemed to be working harder at his construction job and that made Ireland breathe a bit easier. She still had a hard time warming up to him, but she figured that would go away with time. After all, weren't lots of couples able to work these things out? A little positive thinking would fix everything! Ireland continued to focus on raising the kids and dabbling with her gardens.

One day, on her way to drop off some paperwork at the doctor's office, Ireland decided to take a detour and drive through her old neighborhood. She smiled as she drove down Cooper Street and saw how well the new tenants were treating her old apartment. She came to the stop sign and froze. Up ahead, on the right was Rusty's, and there in the front, Gus's truck was parked. It was one o'clock in the afternoon. Her heart began to beat a million miles an hour. She slowly drove past the bar and parked on a side street in direct view of his truck. She shut off the engine and sat, contemplating her next move. Should she go in, or wait for him to come out?

She made up her mind to go in and confront him, but as soon as her hand gripped the door handle, Gus came sailing out… and he wasn't alone. The woman looked to be 10 years older than him. She had red hair which looked like it got burnt by one too many perms. She had on a short denim skirt and a pink tank top which barely contained her ample breasts. She had on a pair of silver heels. Gus walked her over to the passenger side of the truck, but before opening the door, he placed his hands on her ass and moved in for a kiss. The woman wound her arms around his neck and shoved her tongue down his mouth.

Hell hath no fury as a woman scorned.

Ireland saw red.

She got out of the car and walked over to them. When she got within three feet of her husband and his tramp, Gus looked up and noticed her, then quickly moved away from the woman.

"Are you Jean?" she asked the woman.

"No. I'm Candace," she replied. "Who are you?"

Without responding to her, Ireland looked at Gus and shook her head, smirking.

"How many more are there, Gus?"

"Ireland, I—"

"Who is this, Gus?" Candace blurted.

"I'm his wife," Ireland answered. "And you can leave now."

The woman looked at Gus, who couldn't even look at her. Then she quickly clattered back into the bar on her shiny heels.

"So you managed to quit drinking but you didn't quit the women, did you?"

"This is all your fault, you know. A man can't live without sex!"

"We're done now," she stated, then turned and walked to her car.

Gus followed and grabbed her by the arm.

"Wait! I can change. I swear!"

"We're way past that."

"Okay, okay—how about you cheat on me now? Any guy you want! We can even the score. Then we can start all over again."

Horrified, Ireland stared at her husband. She searched his eyes for some glimpse of the man that she married—the one that adored her and loved being around her. But there was nothing left of that man. He was replaced with an irresponsible addict, haunted by demons. His lies defined his life now. She shook free of his hold and walked over to the driver's side.

"Ask Candace if you can stay with her for a while. I don't want the children to see this." Then she got in the car and drove off leaving him there.

■ ■ ■

In the months that followed, Ireland put on her strongest face and moved forward. She filed for divorce and did her best to distract the kids away from the fact that Daddy was now living in the basement. There was no arguing between them. In fact, they hardly ever spoke to each other. Ireland got a job as a bartender at night so she could make some extra money. She knew she had to find a way to live without his income. During the day, she found a job cleaning houses. She was not afraid of hard work, so she survived on very little sleep.

Six months later, Gus and Ireland found themselves in court. She got custody of the children and the home on the lake, and Gus got the house in Windham. He waived his rights over the children in exchange for not paying child support. Ireland scoffed at this idea, but in the end, no one was more important than her children, so she gladly agreed. Without his financial support, she was unable to keep the house, so she sold it and got an apartment in Hebron. The kids saw their father every once in a while, and Ireland accepted the fact that this was the way things were going to be. She never badmouthed Gus to the children. After all, he was their father.

She quit her bartending job as soon as she and Gus parted ways, but kept her house cleaning job during the day so she could pay the bills. Life returned to a somewhat form of stability once again. But late at night, when the kids were asleep and she lay staring at the ceiling all alone in her room, she had quiet conversations with God. *So this is it, eh? This is how my life is supposed to go? Why? What did I ever do to make you so mad at me? Did I not go to church as much? Did I forget to say a few prayers? I hurt so badly! Is there any male in this world that is honest and good? Why are they all so… so… horrible?*

One Sunday, while the kids were visiting their father, Ireland decided to pay her mother a visit. She drove to her childhood home, and found her mother watering some flowers in her backyard.

"Hey, Mom."

"Ireland!" her mother smiled at her. "What a wonderful surprise! Where are the kids?"

"They're visiting Gus. I have to go pick them up around 6."

"Oh. Would you like to stay for lunch? I'm making your favorite— tuna on rye!"

"Mom, I hate tuna."

"Since when? You always ate it as a kid!"

"That was Jen, not me."

"Oh, yes. You're right. Well, I also have turkey?"

"Mom, I need to ask you a question. Can we sit for a minute?"

"Yes, of course. Is something wrong?"

Ireland turned and walked over to the patio. She chose a chair in the direct sun and sat down. Her mother followed her and sat in a chair under the umbrella.

"Is Dad home?"

"No. He went to True Value. Why do you ask?"

Ireland sighed and leaned back in her chair. She tried to figure out where to begin.

"Mom, are you proud of me?"

"What? Why are you asking me that?" her mother chuckled.

"Because my life is not like Jen's. She had the perfect childhood and the perfect marriage and the perfect kids. I am so far from all of that."

"But I don't want you to be Jen. I want you to be Ireland."

"I guess that's why I'm here. Who is Ireland?"

"What do you mean?"

"Mom, my entire life has been filled with turbulence. I grew up with a father that never loved me and a mother who tried her best to cover it up. I went on to marry a man who didn't love me enough to keep his dick in his pants!"

A small gasp escaped her mother's lips but she didn't say a word. She turned her face and closed her eyes.

"Mom, please tell me. What terrible thing did I do to make Dad hate me so much?"

Tears began to stream down her mother's face. Now Ireland knew that something was wrong. A knot began to form inside her belly.

"I'm sorry," her mother whispered.

Ireland leaned forward and grabbed her mother's hand.

"What are you sorry about?"

"I'm sorry for not telling you sooner."

"Telling me what?"

"I was engaged to your father when I was 20 years old. I was young and I was scared. I didn't want to break away from my parents just yet, but I didn't think I would ever have the chance again, so I said yes. I loved him, but I just felt like we should have dated longer." Her mother turned to look at Ireland. Then she reached out to her daughter and smoothed back her hair and smiled. Her eyes seemed to be a million miles away.

"I met your father when I was working at the department store. He was a mechanic for the elevators and they seemed to be broken all the time." She laughed. "I began to tease him about it. One day it was raining really hard when I got off my shift. I couldn't start my car. He came around with his truck and asked if he could give me a ride home. I accepted and we talked about everything. I never wanted the ride to end," she said with a faraway look in her eyes.

"We would continue to see each other at work. He made me laugh. Sometimes I would find a daisy at the counter. He knew they were my favorite. Then came the day I will never forget."

"What day, Mom?"

"He asked me to marry him and I became engaged."

Ireland leaned back and stared at her mother.

"I don't understand. Weren't you happy? It seems like you guys had a real connection."

"We did." Tears began to form in her mother's eyes again. She looked squarely at her daughter. "He cried when I told him I was engaged to another man."

Wumpf. The air got sucked out of Ireland's lungs once again. She held her breath and stared at her mother, trying to comprehend the full meaning of her words. Then she looked up at the sky and closed her eyes for several seconds. She opened them and looked at her mother once more.

"Dad is not my father, is he?"

"No," her mother sobbed. "I couldn't let him go, Ireland, not just yet. He tried to convince me to break the engagement and run away with him but I couldn't. I couldn't bring that shame upon my parents. Then one day he came by my house late at night and I snuck out. He had his truck packed for California. He said his cousin landed him a good job fixing cars and that he was leaving for good. He asked me one last time if I would go with him. God, I wanted to so badly! He held me so tight. Then he kissed me. One thing led to another... and then he was gone. I never saw him again."

Ireland sat dumbfounded. Hearing about her perfect parent doing not-so-perfect things was a tough pill to swallow. She didn't know if she should be angry at her mother or just feel incredibly sorry for her.

"Dad found out?"

"No! We were married a month later. When you were born, it just seemed like I had given birth a month early, so he didn't really think anything of it. But as you turned from a baby to a little girl, he could clearly see how you didn't resemble either of us in any way. We had a terrible fight one night, in which he accused me of cheating on him. But I assured him that I would never do that and he let it go. But things were different after that night. He began to ignore you and didn't want much to do with you. I did my best to shield you from him. I distracted you and spent a lot of time with you and Jen. But now I see that I made things worse for you. I'm so sorry, Ireland. Can you ever forgive me?"

Ireland folded her mother into her arms.

"Of course, I can forgive you, Mom. You fell in love. How can anyone fault you on that?"

Her mother pulled away from her and looked into her eyes.

"There were so many times I wanted to find him. Track him down and tell him all about his baby girl. But in the end, I belonged to my husband and my family. So I did nothing," she said. Sadness filled her eyes.

"But every time I look at you, I see him," she smiled. "Blonde hair, dark eyes and tall—you look just like him. He was a good man, Ireland. Once he set his mind on something, he made it happen. He started with nothing, but he survived. He never allowed anyone to break his spirit. He had honor and kindness. So if you want to know who you are, my dear, you are your father's daughter."

The tight strings that held Ireland together finally snapped and she broke down sobbing. Her mother held onto her. Ireland cried for her father—an angry, self righteous man who couldn't accept the love of an innocent child. She also cried for her dad—a man that probably could have changed her life, if she ever could have met him. She pictured him as a smiling man, with a gentle heart, who never backed down in the face of danger. And she also cried for her mother. She couldn't imagine being in love with another man for all those years, and never allowing herself to experience that love. Although it was her choice, she was forced to live out her life with another man—a man that showed her very little tenderness and compassion. They both cried for what seemed like hours, extinguishing all the anguish they had endured over the years.

"Well, that's that," Ireland said, slowly pulling away.

"Honey, I'm sorry," her mother said, wiping her nose on her handkerchief.

"You know what, Mom?" she smiled. "I'm not."

Her mother looked at her, perplexed.

"All this time, I've been feeling sorry for myself—trying to figure out where I went wrong—to be so unlucky in life. But I've been looking at it all wrong! I survived, Mom. I left home at age 15 and made it by myself for years! Find me a kid that could do that today. I married a man who turned into an alcoholic and a cheater, and yet here I am with a job and a home and three kids who I adore! I'm not on welfare, I'm not on drugs, and I'm not wasting away on a couch with a bottle in my hand! I'm taking care of my kids and paying all my bills—BY MYSELF! And I don't care anymore. I'm not looking at the past anymore. It stays where it is. I'm moving forward and I'm going to overcome anything that gets thrown at me—because that's WHO I AM!"

"Yes, baby," her mother smiled, cupping her face. "That's exactly what your father would have said."

A week later, Ireland was cleaning an office in a new development that was being built. She had met the builder one day in the grocery store and he offered her the job on the spot. The money was good, the work was steady, and she could tailor her hours around her kids' schedules. She couldn't believe her luck! She decided to take a quick break outside so she sat on the curb and closed her eyes as the sunshine washed over her face.

"You waiting for the bus?" said a deep voice.

Ireland opened her eyes and saw a giant man standing over her. His t-shirt and jeans were covered with dirt, he had a short beard, and the most incredible blue eyes she had ever seen.

"No. I'm just taking a break," she smiled.

"Same here. Do you work for Reggie?" he asked.

"Well, sort of. I clean all the offices he's building."

"Oh, I see. We finished this one last year," he said pointing to the building in back of them.

"Yah, he told me. So what do you do?"

"I run the equipment—excavators, bulldozers, skid steers."

"Ah. Play in the dirt all day, right?" she smirked.

"Yup. I'm not the type to be in there crunching numbers!" he pointed to the building again.

"We all have our thing."

"I'm Sam, by the way," he said, extending his hand to her.

"Oh, I'm Ireland," she answered, shaking his hand. "But you can call me bitch."

Sam looked at her puzzled.

"No, I'm just kidding. If you call me that, you'll never see me again," she laughed.

"Oh, I wouldn't want that," he smiled. "But you aren't … mean, are you?"

"I'm really not. I've had a tough life, Sam. I've been through a lot of shit. But I ain't taking anymore of it because I have three kids and a good life now. Anyone messes with that, the bitch will certainly come out for sure."

"Woah, that's hot."

"What?"

"A bad-ass chick. I like that."

"You better believe it, stud," she laughed.

"Can I date you?"

Ireland got up from the curb, and smirked at him.

"Maybe someday. I gotta get back to work now," she said. She could feel his stare as she turned around and walked toward the office building.

Yep. I still got it. She smiled. *C'mon, take me down, I dare you.* ▪

■ CHAPTER SEVEN ■
$\mathcal{K}atrina$

Sometimes the unbelievable happens. Like when you're watching your sick calf's health deteriorate by the hour. Weak body, labored breathing, protruding bones, not having any desire to eat or drink anymore. You try everything—you even lay in the pen with her and sing lullabies. You trudge your weary self back into the house at two in the morning and fall asleep on the couch with your boots still on. And then it happens. You wake up at 6 A.M., drag yourself outside for the morning chores, fully expecting to find one less calf to take care of and wham! The calf is up, eating, drinking, looking more alive than ever—her ailment completely gone. Explanation? There is none. It just happens. Call it one of those gifts from God. We don't question it, we just rejoice in it. Because more often than not, we're burying those calves along with a little sliver of our hearts.

But every so often, the unbelievable surfaces.

Katrina was a cowgirl. She could stack 200 bales of hay in a wagon by herself in the middle of July. She could clean a barn, feed her animals, and rewire a fence that needed mending before the sun set for the day. She could drive any tractor, dump truck, skid steer or pretty much anything that required a grease gun and diesel. She wasn't the kind of girl that went to the mall—if she needed a bra, she bought it through Amazon. Daylight was precious—especially when there was farming to do.

She met Randy at the Washington County Fair in the summer of 2000. She was showing her prize short horn and he was pulling his chiannias. He was a good-looking man—fearless with the big boys, sporting a million-dollar smile. She noticed him right away, but was too shy to make a move. So she decided to win her competition to get his attention. It was no contest—with the amount of time she spent taking care of her animals, no one came close to her skill. She also won the Powder Puff competition, which was strictly for females and their animals. All the boys usually crowded around the fences for that one. Something about a girl in tight jeans, wielding a stick on an animal twice her size. It gets all the boys hot.

"Do they always behave like that?" Randy came up to her, as she was tying up her pair to the side of the trailer.

"Mostly. I guess today they were in a good mood," she responded.

"Looking good," he smiled.

"Yah, they should. I must have hosed them down about three times in the past 12 hours," she shouted as she moved the grain pails underneath their noses.

"I wasn't talking about your pair," he smiled.

"Oh," she looked up and blushed.

"I haven't seen you here before. Is this your first year?"

"No. I was here last year too."

"I didn't notice you."

"Well, how could you? With the redhead hanging on your arm," Kat smiled.

"Oh, Ashley? Well, she ain't hanging on my arm no more," he laughed.

"Clearly."

"I was gonna go up to the Lion's booth and get a cheeseburger. You wanna go?"

"Yah, why not?" she said. "I have to give them some water first. Do you mind giving me a hand?"

"Not at all."

"By the way, I'm Katrina. You can call me Kat."

"I'm Randy, but you can call me Master," he smiled.

"You're funny," she said and made her way towards the spigot.

He was nothing but a gentleman the entire day. He helped her with her animals, bought her lunch and dinner, and watched a couple of truck pull shows with her. Around midnight, she dragged herself into her camper with a smile on her face.

For the rest of the weekend, they watched each other's shows, helped each other take care of their animals, and laughed hysterically. They exchanged phone numbers and addresses and discovered that they lived within 20 minutes of one another in upstate Rhode Island. By Sunday, Katrina had fallen in love with him. She vowed to never let him go.

It was late August when Katrina began vomiting in the morning. At first, she thought it was a summer grippe or something that she caught from too many people at too many fairs. When it didn't go away after a week, she decided to buy a pregnancy test. It was positive and she was terrified. She texted Randy and told him to call her when he had a minute.

"Hey, girl! What's shaking?" he greeted her from a truck stop.

"We gotta talk."

"What's wrong?"

"I'm not a sugarcoat kinda girl so I'm gonna come right out and say this…. I'm pregnant."

….

"Randy? Are you there?"

"Yah. So it's mine, right?"

"You're a dick."

"Well, obviously mine is doing the job," he laughed.

"Can you stop with the jokes? This is serious."

"Okay. So, what are you thinking?"

"I'm not getting rid of it, if that's what you're asking," she said.

"I wasn't suggesting that."

"Good, cuz here's the deal. I'm keeping this baby and I'll raise it myself if I have to. You can see it once in a while or not at all, totally up to you." She held her breath. She was perfectly ready to have this baby alone, but she really wished he would swoop down and take care of her like all knights on shiny horses do.

"What if I want to be involved?"

"That would be cool," she breathed. "Do you?"

"Of course! I'm not one of those losers, you know," he said. "I take care of my kids."

Randy already had a daughter with his first wife. She was 10 years old and he saw her every other weekend. Katrina hadn't met her yet but she was convinced that he was the perfect dad. She was sure that the divorce was completely his ex-wife's fault, since he painted her out to be a crazy woman. Katrina was pleased that she was the one who had saved him from such a demon, since he was no doubt, the perfect man.

They entered the fall, business as usual. Katrina lived with her parents on the farm, and Randy lived at his house, on his own small farm. She practically lived with him on the weekends. During her third month, she noticed that he wasn't around on weekends anymore. He claimed that he was working long hours to get extra money for the baby. He drove eighteen-wheelers for a living, so it wasn't hard to believe. But she missed him nonetheless, and tried very hard to distract herself from the loneliness she felt.

One Saturday, she decided to pop over his house and surprise him. She made him dinner and was going to leave it in his fridge so he had something to eat when he came home. She pulled into his driveway and noticed that his truck was parked there, along with a blue sedan. She slowly got out of her truck, and walked up to the front door. She wondered if she should knock first, but then decided against it. After all, she was his girlfriend.

The door was unlocked so she entered the house.

"Hello?" she called.

A woman appeared from the back room of the house. She had on a lot of makeup, tight jeans, a glittery shirt, and her hair looked like she had just come from the salon.

"Hello?" she asked.

"Who are you?" Katrina questioned.

"Linda. Who are you?"

"Katrina. Are you a friend of Randy's?"

"I'm his fiancé."

An anvil slammed into her chest—just like in those Bugs Bunny movies. Fiancé. When the hell did he get a fiancé? Why didn't he tell her? All this time, she had been carrying his child, talking with him about how they would raise this baby. For what? Was it all a joke to him?

"I'm sorry, what did you say?" she asked.

"I'm his fiancé. Who are you?"

"I'm... I'm... I seriously can't do this," Katrina stammered. "I have to go," and she turned to leave. She walked out of the front door and made a beeline for her truck. The tears sprang up immediately and it felt like her heart was breaking in two. She got in and turned on the ignition, and almost peeled out of the driveway. Within 30 seconds her phone rang. It was Randy.

"What?" she cried.

"Were you just at my house?" he asked.

"Yup. And I had the pleasure of meeting your lovely fiancé!"

"Okay, I can explain."

"How could you do this to me?" she sobbed. "I thought you loved me? You told me you were going to take care of our baby?"

"I am! I will! It's just... well .... So here's what happened. I met Linda at the doctor's about two months back. Remember when I hurt my back? Well, she's the one that helped me get better."

"And?"

"And it just happened really fast. I wasn't looking for it, I swear! I can still take care of you and the baby, though."

"So you're marrying someone that you met two months ago?"

"She's my soulmate, Kat. I can't explain it."

"Goodbye, Randy. I'll call you when the baby is born," and with that, she hung up the phone.

She bawled the entire way back to her parents' house, while he continued to blow up her phone. She eventually turned it off. She parked her truck in the driveway, walked into her house and flung herself into her dad's arms. She poured the whole story onto him and cried some more. She was devastated and shocked, but more than anything, she was mad at herself for falling in love with such a con artist.

■ ■ ■

Five months later, Katrina gave birth to a beautiful baby boy, whom she named Jaden. Her parents and her sister were present at his birth. She texted Randy the next day to let him know, but that was it. He tried to call her a few times, but she never called him back. There was little to no communication between them, and she preferred it to stay that way.

Jaden grew up quickly. Katrina thanked God that she had the assistance of her family. Randy had come by one time to meet his son and another time to visit him. He also offered to send money if Katrina needed it. But she was proud and didn't need anyone's help to raise her son. So Randy continued to send presents for his birthday and Christmas.

Jaden was a handful! She loved to bring him down to the barn and show him her steer. He got so excited every time she did. For the first 4 years, she continued to raise her boy, work full time, and maintain her farm. But as soon as Jaden turned five, the fairs began to call her in her dreams. She missed hauling trailers, grooming her animals for the show, and hanging out with the people she considered her second family. She also wanted to introduce Jaden to steer showing, in hopes that maybe someday he'd like to give it a try himself!

That summer, she unloaded her animals at the Brooklyn Ag Days Fair. It was a low-key fair in Connecticut, and Katrina thought it was the perfect setting to introduce fair life to Jaden. He helped her tie up her short horns to the side of the trailer, and then she showed him how to fill up the water buckets from the spigot. On the way back to the trailer, she saw Randy's pickup truck pulling up to her trailer. She sighed and got ready to put on her best "I don't give a shit" face. As they neared the trailer, Randy got out of his truck.

"Hey there, little guy!" he shouted.

"Hi, Dad," Jaden squealed. "Look at me! I'm watering the boys!"

"Oh, good! Then you can come and water my boys too!"

Katrina ignored their entire conversation and tended to her animals. She figured it was good for her son to get reacquainted with his father. While Jaden ran off to get his favorite toy to show his father, Randy approached her.

"How's it going, Kat?"

"Very good. How's married life?" she said without even looking at him. She was cleaning up manure from under her animals.

"Yah, about that...," he said.

Katrina looked up.

"It didn't work out. She's moving to Florida," he said.

Katrina just shook her head, and continued cleaning her animals.

"I'm sure this is the part where you get to tell me what a fool I was, right?"

"Not at all. I'm sure your problems were mostly your fault."

"Not arguing that one."

"What did you do?"

"Oh, it's a long story. But let's talk about you. Jaden looks great. You're back in the action again. All good?"

"So far. We'll see how the boys perform. Up for debate."

"Need a hand?"

"I got it all under control," she replied. "Where are your animals?"

"With Tony. I was going to check on them. Do you mind if I bring Jaden with me?"

"If he wants to, go ahead," she responded.

Within five minutes, Randy and Jaden were skipping off to another trailer to inspect even more animals. Randy made sure to take his time showing off his kid to all his buddies. It was the perfect way to redeem the sins of his failed marriage.

Looking back, it was that moment that set the stage for Jaden's future. He took one look at the oversized white bulls and decided that this was the place for him. They spent all summer at various fairs that year. Jaden and Randy bonded over pulls and pulled pork sandwiches. Katrina was pleased. She wanted Jaden to know his father. It was better that way. She gave them their time together and focused on the fairs. She showed her steer and entered Powder Puff competitions. She won a few and came in second at a few more. Overall, it was a summer well spent and she was thrilled to be back in the ring.

After the season ended, Randy continued to see Jaden quite a bit. He even took him to the hockey rink where Randy played with a men's league. Jaden's eyes lit up when Randy appeared one day with a pair of hockey skates his size. He taught Jaden how to skate that winter, like a real father should. Katrina's feelings of indifference began to subside as the bond between father and son grew. She found herself laughing with Randy over cute stories about Jaden, just like they did when they first met. She actually found herself looking forward to seeing him again.

At the start of the following summer, Randy invited Katrina and Jaden over for some burgers. Jaden loved seeing the bulls, so the three of them spent the evening working them in preparation for the first fair of the season. Jaden went around the fields on a sled pulled by the bulls. On the last round, he fell asleep and Randy saw this as an opportunity to talk to Katrina.

"Remember that time you and I took a ride on the sled?" he laughed.

"That was crazy. Those bulls wanted to bolt into the next state! I can't believe they didn't."

"Then they stopped and refused to move another step!"

"We laughed so hard we almost peed our pants!" she chuckled.

"I remember we did other things on that sled," Randy smirked wickedly.

She looked at him and smiled.

"I haven't forgotten."

"Wanna stay over? We can put Jaden in the guestroom."

She turned to look at him.

"For a fling, Randy? I'm too old for that."

"No, not a fling. More like a … regular occurrence."

"What are you saying? I'm not filling the void until your next wife comes along. No thank you."

"Okay, I admit that was shitty—what I did. But you've got one over on everyone. You're the mother of my son. I love that kid, and I want to spend more time with him."

That was a low blow. Anyone knows that if you wanna earn points with the mother, you always go through the kids. Jaden needed a father, no doubt about that. But did she need him? Or was she better off going her own way? She still thought he was sexy as hell. Maybe being married to the crazy lady made him appreciate what he left behind.

"Where do you see this going?" she asked.

"I see it going where it should have gone to begin with. You. Me. And Jaden."

"I can't handle another heartbreak, Randy."

"I get it. I wouldn't do that to you again. Why don't we take it slow," he was awfully close to her. "And see where this goes?"

She stopped walking and he stopped the bulls. He then leaned in for a soft kiss. God, how she missed him! Maybe it wouldn't be so bad to spend one night with him. Besides, she hadn't been with a man in years! And he was the father of her son. It's not like she just pulled this man off the street.

"All right. You put the bulls away and I'll carry Jaden to the spare room."

"Deal! I'll see you in 30 minutes."

The next morning, she left Jaden with Randy and drove home to feed her animals. During the car ride, she questioned herself over and over in her head. Was she desperate for love or was she just plain stupid? All the girls Randy came in contact left him for one reason or another. What made her believe that she would be any different? Was he right? Was she special because she gave him a son? The son he always wanted? Or was she just so crazy in love with him that she couldn't listen to reason? She honestly didn't know if this was the right decision. And now there was another little person involved, not just her.

As soon as she got home, she decided to have a chat with her parents to get their take on things. When she announced that she was seeing Randy again, they exchanged worried glances at each other and cautioned her on her decision. But they weren't the judgy type, so they said their peace and left her alone to live her life as she wanted to. In the end, she drove back to Randy's house feeling confident that this was going to work this time. After all, Jaden loved the idea of "Mommy" and "Daddy" being in love again. How bad could this be?

■ ■ ■

For the next 8 years, Katrina and Randy became the oxen -pulling power family. They enrolled Jaden in the local 4H Teamster Club and he began to show and pull oxen. He also joined the school hockey team and practiced over the winter. Katrina continued to live at her parents' house, mostly because she didn't want Jaden to change schools, and also because she liked keeping an eye on her aging parents. But on Friday nights, she packed Jaden up and they both spent the weekend at Dad's house. Life was good. Sometimes Kat would bring up the idea of marriage. But after two failed marriages, Randy was in no hurry to put on a ring again. And Katrina, having the patience of a saint, understood and never pressured him.

Then things turned strange.

One afternoon, Katrina called her friend Lyle, the plumber. Randy had asked her to call him so he could make a house call. The toilet was leaking and Randy had no time to fix it.

"Hey, bud," she greeted him. "How's it going?"

"Oh, it's going, Kat," he said. "How are you?"

"I'm hanging in there. Hey, listen—Randy wanted to know if you have some time to come over. It seems like we have an unhappy toilet."

"Your house or Randy's?" Lyle asked.

"Randy's."

"I don't have time," he responded.

No time? Since when? "Uh.... okay, when do you have time?"

....

"Lyle?"

"Listen, sweetheart, I think you better find someone else to do the job. I'm just too swamped."

"Lyle, what's going on? This is me you're talking to. You've been Randy's friend for over 10 years."

"Not anymore," he muttered.

"Why? Did you guys have a fight?"

"I can't talk about it. I don't hate him—I just don't want to hang out with him anymore, okay?"

"Lyle, please!"

"Kat, you're a good woman. Probably one of the best I've ever met. He don't deserve you. I gotta go. I'll talk to you soon," and then Lyle hung up the phone.

Kat looked at the phone in confusion. What just happened? And what did he mean by saying Randy didn't deserve her?

Later than evening, she told Randy about the strange conversation. He didn't recall any fight between them and assured her that it was probably a misunderstanding. He promised her he'd talk to him in the morning.

The following day, Jaden broke his arm during hockey practice, and Katrina forgot all about the eerie phone call with Lyle.

Six months later, Katrina was having lunch with an old friend at the Main Street Pub. She noticed an old friend, Will, sitting at the bar, having a drink. Once she was done eating lunch, she said goodbye to her friend and made her way to the bar.

"Hey, stranger," she said, smiling at Will.

"Well, look who we have here!" he said, hugging her. "It's good to see you, Kat!"

"Mind if I join you for a minute?" she asked.

"Not at all! Please sit," he said. "Want a beer?"

"No. I have to get back to work soon."

"How's Jaden?"

"Growing like a weed. I wish I could eat a package of party-size Oreos and not gain a pound!" she said.

Will chuckled.

"Those days are long gone. I was telling Lyle the other day that I'd be lucky if I could get through a cheeseburger without taking antacid pills!"

Katrina laughed, then looked hard into Will's eyes.

"Yah, I talked to Lyle a few months ago. He acted really strange," she said.

"Oh?"

"Yah, it was weird, Will. He refused to come over and fix a toilet. And then he said something to me that bothered me."

"Well, that's not like him."

"I know!"

"What did he say?"

"He told me that Randy didn't deserve me."

Will looked away from her and took a sip of his beer. He didn't meet her eyes again, he simply looked down at his fingers.

"Now I know there's something going on," she said. "Will, please talk to me!"

"Listen, Kat, we love you," he said, finally turning to her. "You're like the daughter we never had. So we get overprotective of you sometimes."

"But what do I need to be protected from?"

Will eyed her and didn't say a word.

"Is it Randy?"

"Just keep your eyes open, that's all I'm saying. Ain't my business to begin with."

"But you're his friend!"

"Not anymore, darlin'."

She let the words sink in. This was now the second man that dropped Randy's friendship. And he was a good man too!

"Please tell me what he did," she whispered.

"He's no good for you, Kat. Let him go."

Then he threw a twenty on the counter, got up, and kissed her softly on the forehead. He headed out the door, leaving Kat trying desperately to swallow the bile that had suddenly started to creep up into her throat. She knew Randy wasn't perfect. Hell, he had two failed marriages! But lately, she had been having a hunch that things were not right. She knew it was silly, and quickly tamped down those thoughts when they surfaced.

But after her conversation with two of the most respected men she'd ever had the pleasure of being friends with, the red flags were now raised.

There was another woman.

Katrina didn't question Randy that evening. She simply observed him. But nothing seemed out of the ordinary. He still spent time with Jaden, he still went to work every day, and he still played hockey on Monday nights. He didn't spend hours on the phone and he wasn't acting shady. Was it possible that maybe she was wrong?

Then one day, on Christmas Eve, she was cleaning Randy's house in preparation for the Christmas Party they were about to have. Randy and Jaden were out picking up last-minute gifts so she had the house to herself. She was a thorough cleaner, so naturally, she made sure she cleaned all the cobwebs and took care of all the dust bunnies under the furniture. While she was vacuuming underneath the cushions of the sofa, she noticed an article of clothing all bunched up. She shook it loose and noticed that it was a gray, woman's t-shirt. And it wasn't hers.

She turned off the vacuum and sat down. The room began to spin. *Whose fucking shirt is this?* Anger welled up inside of her. She began to picture some leggy blonde bimbo, pulling off her shirt while making out with Randy. *Dammit! I'm such an idiot!* She ran out of the house and sat in her truck, and focused on just breathing for a few minutes. After thirty minutes, her parents pulled into the driveway. She didn't have the heart to cancel Christmas, even though she felt like she was going to be swallowed up by her grief. So she put on her big, fake smile and got out of the truck.

For the rest of the evening, she had an out-of-body experience. She watched herself taking out trays of food and offering them to her guests. She watched herself drinking the spiked Christmas punch—heavily. She watched herself ignoring Randy. And then she watched herself leaving the entire mess right where it was and passing out on the couch. All the while, her real self was perched into a corner of the room, sobbing hysterically over her poor, dead, broken heart.

That week, she had planned to use some vacation days to get some projects around the house done. But instead, she decided to use the time to do some investigating. She began with social media. Luckily, she had the password to all of his accounts, so she began to rifle through them all. She knew he wouldn't be smart enough to cover all of his tracks. After a few hours, she decided to tap into his Craigslist account. She had heard that sometimes truckers solicit call girls with it. What she discovered went beyond all realms of understanding.

Trucker looking for a buff, young-looking man to satisfy curiosity. New at this, taking it slow, but ready to play poker! Call 555-1317.

What...The...Fuck!!!!!!!!!!!

That's his number! Is this a joke? Is this the new thing that guys do for a good laugh? Or is he really...gay? But the shirt stuck under the couch was a woman's shirt—or was it? The need to take a shower overwhelmed Katrina. She quickly peeled off her clothes and got in, not even waiting for the water to turn warm. Her skin ached and her head began to pound. She vomited twice. She stood there feeling the water shooting into her scalp. About 20 minutes went by before she was settled enough to get out. She toweled dry and put on some clean jeans and her "farm girl" t-shirt. This asshole wasn't going to get the best of her. The fucker was going down!

Avoid, avoid, avoid. That was the theme that week. Her investigation was not done yet, and questioning would occur when she had all the facts before her. Luckily, Jaden spent a lot of time with friends so she was free to make calls and tap into his personal files. One night, she offered him a couple more beers at dinner time—explained it as a "New Year's good riddance to 2015" motion, so he wouldn't get suspicious. As predicted he passed out when he got into bed that night, and Katrina had the entire night to step into the mother ship of his secret world. She quietly stuck her hand into the front pocket of his jeans and whipped out his cell phone. Then she tiptoed downstairs, put on her boots, and slipped outside into the darkness.

She walked over to the old elm tree and leaned on it. She took a deep breath, for she knew that cellphones were the key to the underworld for any good cheater. She punched in his pass code and began with the text messages. She scrolled down the first few—clearly work related or farm related. But then there was one from Arabella—a girl they had known from the fairs. Why would she be texting him in late December?

Hey. You up for another round?

Yah. What time?

Around 5:30. Told Jim I'm working late.

I'll be waiting—naked.

And there was the proof. Although she fully expected to uncover an affair with a male, she was appalled at the conversation before her. She began to feel nauseous again. Arabella and Randy? What a slut! She was known at all the fairs as the *Wanker Wench*. She used to give blow jobs to all the boys before the pulls began—sort of a good-luck ritual. She was always wearing dirty clothes—probably from rolling around on the ground all the time. And Jim had been her boyfriend for over a year.

When did these two start hooking up? When did Randy's standards become so low?

She needed more. She scrolled down the list again. Jenny? Again, why is she texting him in December? These were people they only spoke to in the summer. Reluctantly, she opened up the messages.

I've been naughty again.

Oh, really?

This time I'm going to need a hard spanking.

It's gonna hurt.

I'm sorry, master. Bruise me if you need to, I deserve it.

I want you on your knees.

I will videotape it so you can hear my screams.

Oh, God! Jenny too? She's married! Have I been living in a cult all this time? These women are cheaters too! And they were our friends! They ate with us, watched shows with us, slept in the trailers with us, even took care of Jaden! What kind of a sick world am I living in?

Katrina's head began to spin. Tears began to well up in her eyes. She didn't know this man anymore. Not only did he deceive her, he performed vile acts on these women. This was the father of her child! She looked down at the phone. Video? She closed the text messages and opened up his photos. She gasped and held her hand over her mouth. She saw picture after picture of Randy in various nude poses, with his dick in his hand. These must be the pictures he used to solicit female (or male) companions. Scrolling down further, she found pictures of Jenny, dressed up as a dominatrix, or a leather-clad biker chick—with all her private areas fully exposed. Scrolling even further, she saw pictures of Arabella, fulfilling her fair given name of *Wanker Wench.*

Katrina looked away, tears cascading freely down her cheeks. These people were dirty, and shameful, and they had no regard for human beings. They were selfish, lustful whores that only wanted to satisfy their bodies, without any regard for commitment to other people. They tainted the innocence and old fashioned fun that the fairs were founded upon.

She looked back at the phone. What more was there to see? And then she remembered Lyle and Will, and their cautionary message to her. Did they somehow know? Is that why they unfriended Randy? She opened up his text messages once more and began to scroll past Arabella and Jenny. She was looking for Lyle or Wayne's names. Then she stopped cold, when a certain message caught her eye. It was from Beverly, Tony's wife, and it said *Don't let Tony find out.*

With heart in her mouth, Katrina drew in a ragged breath. Please, God, not her too? Tony was Randy's best friend. He and Bev had two beautiful girls. She hesitated while she stared at Beverly's name, then she clicked on the message.

Hey
Hey
You got company?
No. I'm alone
I wanna see you again.
I can't. I have the girls
Bring them to your moms at 2. Just for an hour
I don't know
I can't stop thinking about you. I need you
It's not right
I know but I can't help it. Please! I'll go crazy!
Okay. Just for an hour.
Ok!
Don't let Tony find out

Katrina's mind shattered. She threw down the phone and covered her face. This woman was the kindest and sweetest person on the planet. She had known her for 15 years! She attended her wedding to Tony, she visited her when she gave birth to her girls. If you looked up the word *"good"* in the dictionary, you would most likely see Beverly's picture. How could she have turned so easily? Anger began to bubble up inside of her. Randy! It all made sense now! Two failed marriages—not because his ex-wives were crazy, but because he couldn't keep his dick in his pants! Randy was a sex addict. He had no soul, no good conscience—only the need to fulfill his craving. This was a sickness. Was it hereditary or was it learned behavior? Jaden! Her thoughts quickly went to him. She would do whatever it took to protect her son from all of this!

Katrina wiped her wet cheeks and took a deep breath. She had to compose herself. One thing was certain—her relationship with Randy was over for good. There would never be a question of going back. The man lied to her over and over again. But Jaden was a different story. Did she sever their relationship too? Or should she pretend everything is fine and wait until he graduated from high school? She could probably suck it up for three more years, right? The man is grotesque, though. Three more years with him? But there is nothing a mother wouldn't do for the wellbeing of her child. Nothing.

Katrina went back in the house and never said a word about what she discovered that night. She slid his phone back in his jean pocket and went to bed. In the morning, she placed her heart in an ironclad box, chained it shut, and went about her day. Randy tried to touch her a few times, but she always claimed that she was tired. She also came up with excuses not to go over his house for the weekend, claiming that her parents needed her. But she always made sure to deliver Jaden to his father, so no one would suspect she was unhappy. Business as usual.

That summer, they attended the fair as a family. She retched when she caught a glimpse of Arabella or Jenny, but she busied herself with her animals or Jaden's pair so she barely had time to interact with them. She couldn't believe she made it through the fair season without any drama. Her saving grace was Daniel. He owned a farm in Connecticut and his sons pulled oxen. They had known each other for years but never had the time to talk. That summer, she spent a lot of time chatting with him and his wife, and if she had to be honest with herself, it was refreshing to talk to them. They seemed down to earth and not interested in making friends with Randy's shady crowd.

Another Christmas came and went and Katrina vowed to make it through 2017 in much the same way. Randy only called her when he needed something so it was pretty easy to avoid him. One day in late summer, he called her up.

"Hey, where is the registration for the trailers?" he asked.

"In the file cabinet. Why?" she replied.

"I just got a letter from DMV saying that they need to be registered."

"Okay."

"Can you take care of that?"

"I'll see what I can do. I'll have to sign your name. You okay with that?"

"Why wouldn't I be? Just get it done. I don't wanna get pulled over."

"Fine." Then she hung up and made herself a note to take care of the registration. Suddenly, a thought struck her. What were her ties to Randy? The trailers. One trailer was hers but they were both in his name because at the time, it was easier to put them both in his name. She needed her trailer to haul her animals to the fair. So why couldn't she fix that? He already gave her permission to use his signature. She quickly gathered up her documents and headed down to DMV. She produced a bill of sale with his signature on it and had the clerk process all the paperwork. In a matter of hours, the trailer was in her name and registered. She smiled as she left the office. Another string cut! Other than Jaden, she had no ties to him anymore.

A month later, Katrina was at Randy's house cleaning and gathering up the last of her belongings. There was no need to keep anything of hers there. She wouldn't be staying there anymore. She was so lost in her work that she didn't hear him coming inside.

"Kat!"

"What!" she said looking up.

"I thought you were taking care of the registration of the trailers!"

"I did," she replied coolly.

"No, you didn't! This one is expired!" he shouted, waving the document in front of her.

"I registered one of them—mine."

"That one is in my name too!" he yelled.

"Not anymore," she smiled. "That trailer is mine. I changed the title over into my name and registered it in MY name."

"What the hell has gotten into you?"

She looked at him deeply for a moment. "I think I'm done," she said. Then she got really close to him and said, "Why don't you get Arabella or Jenny to do that for you. Or even Beverly. I'm sure you've got a lot to hang over her head. You can blackmail her if she refuses."

"What?"

"Oh, by the way," she smiled. "Your dick pix are hot!"

She turned and made her way to Jaden's room to put away his laundry. Randy followed her.

"You went through my phone?"

"A long time ago. I have no desire to see what you've put on there lately. But I think this is my last trip here. Jaden has no idea so we'll just tell him we broke up," she said over her shoulder. "Cool with you?"

"Good riddance. You didn't do much for me anyway," he smirked.

"Well, that's probably because I'm a girl," she smiled.

"What do you mean by that?"

"It's been a while since I've seen a good poker game," she laughed. "What do you think all your fair friends would think if they knew?"

"They'd never believe you!"

"Well, computers are amazing things. They save things like Craigslist ads and pictures of your friends' wives dressed up in leather."

"You bitch!" Randy screamed.

"You better believe it, son. You're a lying, cheating bastard and you're a disgrace to your gender. No one with any dignity or pride wants to be associated with you. You're pathetic and you've fucked with me one too many times! Only now we have a kid mixed up in all this. So here's how this is gonna go—you're gonna do your part as a father and we're going to be nothing but cordial to each other. You're gonna attend all his games, graduation, conferences, whatever. When he needs you to be his father, you're gonna be there. And you're never gonna say one bad word against me. Because if you ever step out of line," she said, holding up her phone, "this little girl is gonna show all your friends who the real Randy is. You got me?"

He just stood there and stared at her. She could tell he was angry because his nostrils were flaring. But he had no comeback. She had pinned him to the wall with her cunning ways. She turned and headed towards the door.

"See you around," she turned to look at him one more time. "Oh, and by the way… if you wanna call me *master*… I'm totally okay with that," she smiled once more.

"How about bitch? That's more fitting, don't you think?"

She grinned.

"Only if you put 'bad-ass' in front of it." She sailed out the door with her head held high.

In that moment, Katrina felt absolutely liberated from such a fake and overinflated player. In the weeks that followed she thought of him less and less, until he was nothing more than the size of a pea (which equaled the size of his brain as well). Katrina vowed that she would never again fall into the trap of a smooth talker—someone who appears to be something that he is truly not. A gift was given to Katrina—although painful at first, she was convinced that she would perish like the little sick calf. However, the pain quickly turned into salvation, and it took hold of her lifeless soul, until she began to live a new life once again. ▪

▪ CHAPTER EIGHT ▪
Ariel

Speed. Defined as rapidity in motion, going, or traveling. As in, the need to grow up quickly so you can get to the cooler parts of your life. As in, the need to get in your car and drive very fast and far away so that you can leave the old life behind and get to the new one fast! As in, making decisions that alter the course of your life because you didn't slow down enough to think about your actions. And if you don't control your speed...

You crash.

Ariel was a bad-ass bitch when she came out of her mother's womb. She demanded attention, she beat up the boys in her neighborhood, and no bully would ever think about messing with her. As she grew up and went through high school, she did all the things that normal teenagers did to push the boundaries. She skipped school, she drank beer, she played pool at the pool hall, she pulled down her pants on a dare, and she dreamed of the day that she could leave her hometown of Colchester and spread her wings. The day she graduated from high school, her mother took her aside and looked at her hard.

"You got fire in your eyes, Ariel," she said.

"Yah, and speed in my blood," Ariel smiled. "You told me that a million times, Mama."

"You're too big for the playground and there's no more room in the playpen. Nothing is holding you back anymore."

"Mama, you're talking crazy! I ain't no baby!"

"Listen to me!" her mother grabbed her by the shoulders and gave her a little shake. "There's a big ugly world out there, and if you're not careful it'll chew you up and spit you out. I can't tell you what to do anymore because you're an adult. But before you decide to go running off to Timbuktu, you better see the road ahead of you—clearly! And if it ain't where you wanna be, don't get on it."

"I'll be alright, Mama," Ariel smiled softly. "Don't worry about me. I ain't gonna do nothing stupid, I promise."

Her mother stared into her eyes for a long time. Then she let her go and smiled weakly.

"Make sure you always know which road leads to home," she said.

■ ■ ■

Six months later, Ariel threw in the last suitcase in the trunk of her Honda Accord and shut the door. She took one good look at her mother's house and sighed. She didn't want to say goodbye to her so she waited until her mother left for work that morning before she packed up her things.

"You gonna miss this place?" her best friend Carly asked.

"Not the cold, that's for sure!" Ariel replied.

"You better call me when you get there," Carly scolded.

"Why don't you come with me?" Ariel smiled.

"Because Jerry would die without me and I don't feel like having a man's death on my hands."

"Girl, that boyfriend of yours is too much!" Ariel laughed.

"Yah, but he buys me anything I want and never gives me a hard time about nothing," Carly chuckled.

"Well, if you change your mind," Ariel said, getting into the driver's side of her car, "you know where to find me."

"Drive slowly! I know how you are!" Carly scolded again.

"Florida, here I come!" Ariel shouted and blew a kiss to her best friend. She turned on her car and put it in drive. She watched her friend waving to her from her rearview mirror, until she turned the corner and was out of sight.

A couple days later, Ariel pulled into her cousin's driveway in Portsmouth, Florida. She offered to help watch her kids when Jamie decided to return back to work. It seemed like a good deal—room and board in exchange for watching her kids 5 days a week. She would have her weekends free, so she could lay on the beach and work on her tan. The nearby beach even had a tiki bar, so she could use her fake ID to sit down and sip on some fruity drinks every once in a while. Ariel couldn't wait to live this carefree lifestyle.

Then she met Derek, and everything went to hell.

≡ ≡ ≡

Jamie was running late for work one morning. She had her heels in her hands and she was running down the stairs.

"Shit! If I don't get fired today, it'll be a miracle!" she blurted out of breath.

"Then go already," Ariel chuckled. "I've got things under control here."

Jamie was halfway out the front door when she skidded to halt.

"Oh, and make sure you're here around 9. The plumber is coming over to take care of that toilet."

"It's about time," Ariel said. "Now get out of here!" She finished feeding the baby as she heard Jamie's car peeling out of the driveway. Then she started to clean up the kitchen.

Around nine o'clock, Ariel was coloring in a Paw Patrol coloring book when the doorbell rang. She got up from the living room floor and padded over to the front door and opened it. A beefy-looking man stood there, holding a five-gallon bucket filled with tools. He had short brown hair and blue eyes, and a smile that could melt the sun.

"Morning. I'm here to fix a toilet," he said.

"Yah. Come on in," Ariel smiled back. She led him upstairs to the bathroom and pointed to the toilet. "Well, this is your patient. The darn thing won't work."

"How long has it been out of order?" he said, kneeling to the floor and looking around.

"As long as I've been here, I guess."

The plumber stopped what he was doing and looked up at her.

"You're not from around here?"

"No," Ariel replied. "I'm just helping my cousin out. I'm actually from Connecticut."

"No kidding," he said. "That's gotta be a climate shock."

"It's kinda nice. Back home it's 30 degrees and snowing. I'm not a cold-type girl."

"Huh. So you're not going back anytime soon?"

"Nope."

They locked eyes for a moment and a slow smile began to form on his lips. Then he got up and extended his hand.

"I'm Derek, by the way."

"I'm Ariel," she said, taking his hand.

"Great to meet you," he said.

"Yah, you too," she said. "Well, I have to go check on the kids and you have to get to work." She turned to leave and then stopped at the door. "If you need anything, let me know." Ariel turned and smiled at him, and then she descended the stairs.

Derek worked on the toilet all morning. It seemed like he made twenty trips to his truck in the driveway, just so he could walk past Ariel and smile. When lunchtime came around, he was finished. He grabbed his five-gallon bucket of tools and descended the stairs.

"Well, she's running," he called.

Ariel came out of the kitchen and met him at the front door, wiping her hands on a dish towel.

"That's great! Jamie will be thrilled."

Derek put his bucket of tools down and fished out a small piece of paper out of his front pocket.

"Oh, is this the bill?" Ariel asked, extending her hand towards the paper.

"No," he smiled. "It's my number."

Ariel stared at him and blushed.

"Tell your cousin I'll mail her the bill," he said, picking up his bucket once again. "But I sure hope to hear from you soon."

He grinned at her, then turned and went out the front door, whistling all the way to his truck. Ariel watched him walk away.

That evening, she was lying on her bed, watching the latest episode of *Counting Cars* on television. A piece of paper on her night table caught her eye and she rolled towards it to grab it. It was Derek's number. She stared at it as the gears in her head kept turning. *Should I call him? What if he turns out to be a serial killer? Well, he didn't look like one. And he has a full-time job.* She contemplated Googling how many plumbers turn out to be serial killers, but then opted against it.

"Oh, what the hell," she said. "You only live once, right?" She grabbed her phone and dialed the number. It rang once. *Shit! What the hell am I going to say to him?* She panicked and hung up the phone, feeling really stupid. Ten seconds later, her phone chimed. She looked at her phone and didn't recognize the number. But it had a Florida area code. Her mouth went dry. Slowly, she hit the green answer button.

"Hello?"

"Ariel?"

"Yes?"

"It's Derek."

Wham! It was like a fireball of bullets went ripping into her chest. He had such a deep, silky voice on the phone. She smiled and rolled onto her back.

"Hi," was all she could think of to say.

"Let me guess… you dialed my number and then couldn't think of what to say to me so you hung up and felt really stupid."

Ariel laughed. "Something like that."

"Well, I'm glad you called."

"Really?"

"Yah. I got home from work around five and I've been waiting by the phone ever since."

"You're lying!" Ariel laughed again.

"No, I'm not! Okay, I got something to eat and then I waited by the phone."

Ariel laughed again. "What did you eat?"

"Leftover pizza."

"Sounds like a bachelor's usual," she said, and then decided to get clarification. "You live alone, right?"

"Yup."

"Apartment or house?"

"Apartment. I'm saving up for a house, but around here, you need some serious cash."

"No kidding," she said. Visions of Derek and houses with white picket fences and dogs and kids all went swirling around in her head with giant hearts attached. She felt ridiculous, but she smiled anyway.

"Hey, what are you doing tomorrow night?" he asked.

"Not much." Her heart began to pound. *Oh my God, he's going to ask me out. He's going to ask me out!*

"Wanna go play some pool?"

"Yah, sure."

"Have you ever played before?"

"I've got some skill," she smiled.

"Awesome. I'll pick you up at seven."

"Okay."

"See you tomorrow, Ariel," he said, and then he hung up the phone.

Ariel rolled back onto her stomach. She couldn't stop smiling. Her first date in Florida! And with a hot guy! She wondered how many tattoos he had, and where. *Okay, stop! You're not gonna sleep with him on the first date.* She got up and went over to her dresser and started rummaging through the drawers. What does one wear to a pool hall? She finally decided on her gas monkey t-shirt and a pair of ripped jeans.

"Perfect," she smiled, and then got ready to go to bed.

The next night, Derek came to pick her up in his work truck. She hopped into the front seat and made herself comfortable. They chatted casually about their day and laughed about random things. Twenty minutes later, they pulled into the parking lot of Renny's Pool Hall.

"Okay, so I'll go easy on you the first time," he chuckled, as he racked up the balls in the triangle.

"Oh, really? Okay," she smiled. "You go ahead and do that." She had been to plenty of pool halls in her high school days to know a thing or two about the art of the game. But she wasn't about to tell him that.

"Can I get you a drink?"

"Sure. I'll take a Coke."

"Okay, I'll be right back," he said walking away. "Why don't you pick out a stick and try shooting the white ball with it?"

Ariel stared after him. The poor thing was in for a big surprise! She was no damsel in distress, that's for damn sure. She picked out a good stick and chalked up the tip. Derek returned a few minutes later with a couple of drinks and some shots. Ariel watched him set them down on the table.

"What are those for?" she asked.

"To ease the pain."

"What pain?"

"Loser has to take a shot," he grinned.

"Better give me the keys to your truck then."

"Why?"

"You're not driving me home drunk!" she shot at him, putting her hands on her hips.

His eyes widened and he laughed out loud. "Really? Well, I think I'll hold onto these keys. Because I'll be carrying *your ass* in the house."

"Game on!"

Ariel easily won the first three games. Derek quickly realized that she was very skilled with a pool stick and he tried to up his game. But years of unsupervised visits to the pool halls paid off for Ariel as she happily watched Derek drink down a third shot.

"You wanna hand over your keys now?" she grinned, extending her palm.

"Nope," he said firmly. "It's time for you to pay the piper."

"Rack 'em up then, bro."

Six games later, Ariel only had to drink two shots. Derek wearily had to drink four of them, but amazingly, he was not drunk. Ariel still worried about his driving abilities, so she asked for his keys. Without question, he handed them over to her.

"Where to?" she asked as he got into the passenger side of his truck.

"55 Verde Hills," he replied, reclining in the seat.

She punched it into her GPS and turned on the ignition. The truck roared to life, and she loved the sound of the power stroke engine rumbling as she stepped on the gas.

"So, I got my ass beat by an underage girl from the North," he laughed.

"Well, you shouldn't have assumed," she said. "And I'm 19. It's not like I'm a child."

"No, you certainly are not a child," he glanced at her with a sly smile.

"How old are you? I guess I never asked you."

"How old do you want me to be?" he continued smiling at her.

She glanced at him.

"Cute."

"I'm 27," he chuckled.

"No wonder I kicked your ass," she smirked. "You're practically over the hill."

"Dude, ouch!" he laughed. "You may have beat me in pool, little girl, but there are things that I can do that you can't even touch."

"Such as?"

"I didn't see you fixing that toilet."

"You got me there."

"And I could devour a large pepperoni pizza in under 6 minutes."

"Tried that once—failed miserably."

They both laughed.

"This is my road," he pointed to the left. "Park right here."

She parked in the designated spot and then shifted the truck into neutral and turned the key. She faced him and smiled. He was staring at her with a lazy grin, eyes half closed.

"There's something else I can do better than you," he said.

"What's that?" she whispered.

"Come inside with me and I'll show you," he lowered his voice.

Ariel looked away. She liked Derek. She didn't wanna blow this. And she promised herself she wouldn't go there. But it had been so long since a man looked at her the way he was looking at her right now. And she was dying to run her fingers over his broad shoulders and taste his lips.

"I just met you," she said.

Suddenly, he felt his hand on hers. Her eyes snapped back to his.

"You're not like any other girl I've met, Ariel. You're blowing me away. If you leave right now, I'm probably going to call you in the middle of the night—just to hear your voice," he said. "Please stay with me. I don't wanna let you go just yet."

She was spellbound by his words. This was no adolescent boy in front of her. This was a man, who was seeing her for who she truly was. She had to hear more. His words were like bread to a starving person. She craved every ounce of him.

"I'm not like that. I'm not one of those girls that just takes her clothes off with anyone and everyone."

"I know you're not. I'm not asking you to do anything you don't want to do. I just don't want you to leave." He ran the pads of his fingertips over her hand and across her palm.

Butterflies began to flutter around in her belly. Then he straightened up in his seat, cupped the sides of her face and pulled her in for a kiss. It was light at first, but she could feel the heat from his face. Then it turned savage and she found that she couldn't breathe for a moment. When he finally let her go, they locked eyes on each other and didn't say a word for several seconds.

"Okay," she finally whispered. "I'll stay with you."

From that day on, Ariel was absolutely and hopelessly in love with Derek. True to his word, the boy was a rock star in bed. She couldn't get enough of him. During the week, they both worked at their jobs, texting and calling frequently throughout the day. At night, Ariel began spending nights at his house. They would go out to dinner, or just hang out on his couch watching television half naked. On the weekends, Derek took her everywhere. They went to the beach, bowling alleys, roller skating rinks, fishing at the lake, demolition derby speedways, and long walks on the boardwalk. They talked about their lives before they met and shared all their future dreams with each other. Ariel was deliriously happy. She loved every minute spent with him.

About four months later, Ariel noticed that she was late. At first, she thought it was just an irregular period. But when 3 weeks passed, she started to get nervous, so she stopped at the grocery store and picked up a pregnancy test. She drove over to Derek's house and waited for him to come home from work. She went into the bathroom, pulled down her pants, and peed on the stick. Then she remained sitting on the toilet for five agonizing minutes, waiting for the results to come in. When the five minutes were up, she could clearly see two lines on the stick.

"Shit," she said. "Okay, Ariel. Let's get a grip here. This man loves you. Maybe it'll be great. You'll tell him you're having his baby, he'll sweep you up in his arms, put a rock on your finger, and you'll live happily ever after."

Just then, she heard the front door open, and heavy footsteps entering the apartment. Ariel quickly pulled up her pants and exited the bathroom. She found him rummaging around in the fridge.

"Babe, do we have any beer left?" he said when he heard her approaching.

"No, we're all out."

"Dammit!" he said slamming the fridge door and moving over to the liquor cabinet. He pulled out a bottle of Jim Beam and poured some into an empty glass sitting on the counter. Ariel wondered if it was even clean. She watched him carefully, wondering if he was in the mood to hear her news.

"What?" he said, finally meeting her eyes.

"Bad day?"

"You could say that," he replied, moving over to the couch and sitting down heavily. "I had a job in Westgate Commons. You know what that is?"

"No."

"The 'holier than thou' section of town. People there think their shit don't stink. Anyway, I got a call about an osmosis system not working. I got it working. Then the homeowner tells me that I damaged his pipes. The fucking things were rotted to hell and leaking even before I got there. I tried to explain that but do you think he fucking listened? We argued for about 30 minutes. Then I grabbed all my tools and split. I ate about $500 but I don't care. Remind me never to take a job at Westgate!"

Ariel sat down next to him and smiled. Then she put her arms around his neck and kissed him lightly on the cheek.

"What was that for?" he asked.

"I just want you to know how much I love you," she said.

"Okay," he chuckled. "Does this mean you're going to drop your pants for me?"

Ariel pulled away and looked hard at him. "No. It means I haven't seen you all day so I was thinking of making you a nice dinner and having a pleasant conversation with you."

"Wait, what?" he said, raising his eyebrows. "Have you magically turned into June Cleaver?"

"Who?"

"Holy shit, I'm dating myself," he mumbled. "Haven't you ever heard of the show *Leave It to Beaver*?"

"No," she said.

"It's about this pathetically perfect family. The mom is always dressed in heels and making five-course meals."

"That doesn't sound so bad," Ariel whispered.

"What?" Derek looked at her. "What the hell has gotten into you?"

Ariel threw her arms around him again and hugged him tight. He softened for a moment, then he grabbed her arms and held her away.

"Spill. Something is going on," he said.

"Derek," she smiled. "I'm pregnant."

Silence filled the air. He stared at her for a long time, not saying a word. Then he let her go, got up and walked into the kitchen again. She followed him. He went right for the Jim Beam bottle, and this time, he didn't even bother putting it in a glass. He took a giant swig of it and gripped the counter with his back to her.

"I take it you're not happy," she said.

He whirled around and faced her. His eyes were filled with fury.

"Did you plan this?" he asked.

"What? No, I didn't plan this."

"Weren't you on the pill?"

"Yah, but remember that time we got drunk about a month ago and I forgot to take it for a couple days? I think that's when it happened."

"Jesus, Ariel! How could you be so irresponsible!"

"ME?" she countered. "As if I got here by myself, you ass!" She turned and walked back into the living room. She could feel her blood pressure rising. This was not going the way she envisioned. What was she going to do? Have the baby by herself? She rubbed her face and paced. Tears began to well up in her eyes. Derek walked towards her.

"I told you to leave me alone that night, but you didn't listen," she wailed. "Now you wanna blame me for this?"

"I may have been out of line," he replied.

"You think?" she spat out. "I'm 19 years old and I'm about to be a mom. I'm scared shitless!"

Derek put his arms around her. At first, she tried to push him away, but he overpowered her. She was too tired to fight him, so she just relented and sank into him.

"I'm sorry," he whispered. "I've just had a bad day."

"I know," she mumbled into his chest.

"Maybe it won't be so bad," he said. "I know nothing about kids, so you're going to have to take the lead here."

She looked up at him.

"I can do that," she said.

He pulled away from her and sat on the couch again. He grabbed the remote and turned on the television.

"So, about that dinner you were going to make…," he said.

"I'll get right on it," she smiled. But on the inside, all kinds of red flags were shooting up. And she tried really hard to drown out the voice that kept screaming at her to pack up her bags and leave.

■ ■ ■

The first couple of months were fine. Derek went to work every day and Ariel stayed in the apartment and played the part of the happy homemaker. She had fully moved in with him. Jamie had found a daycare she could afford so she didn't need Ariel anymore for the kids. But this left Ariel in a bit of a predicament, since she had to rely on Derek's paycheck for money. He grumbled every time he had to open his wallet.

Then the doctor visits began at her 7th week, but Derek had no interest in going. At first, Ariel tried to shame Derek in not participating. But they got into such a bad screaming match that Ariel quickly decided never to bring up the subject again. Derek's mood swings began to escalate. He began to take Xanax pills for anxiety, but they did nothing to deter his anger.

One time, after Ariel had spent the majority of the day cleaning the apartment, Derek came home to find her laying on the couch, watching TV. When he found out there was no more beer in the fridge, he went into the living room and flipped over the couch with Ariel on it. If she hadn't have scrambled away as quick as she did, it would have crushed her. Another time, Ariel went grocery shopping and forgot to buy Oreo cookies. When he went looking for them, she told him she had forgotten and he slapped her across the face. The red mark stayed on her face for a week.

At the beginning of her second trimester, Derek overheard Ariel talking to her mother on the phone. Her mother was asking her when she would be able to come home for a visit. Ariel told her that she would see her in a couple of weeks, after she had spoken to her doctor. When she got off the phone, she turned to find herself staring down the barrel of a .22-millimeter gun.

"You're going where?" Derek asked.

Ariel only stared at him, frozen.

"First of all, you got no wheels. Second of all, you're spending all my money on this baby so you ain't got any left for no trip up North. Third of all, you try and leave me?" his cold eyes bore into her skull. "I'll fucking kill you. You understand?"

Ariel nodded her head as tears began to stream down her face. She couldn't stop shaking well after he had turned and walked away. She never made the trip to visit her mom that year.

Lila was born on September 10th. She was 7 pounds and 20 inches long. She came out naturally, with no complications, and Ariel was eternally grateful. On the second day of her stay at the hospital, a woman from the records division came to confirm information for the birth certificate. She handed the document to Ariel.

"Can you check this over and make sure that all the information is correct?" she asked.

"Of course," Ariel responded. She scanned her information and nodded. Then she scanned Derek's information and stopped.

"I think there is a mistake on Derek's birthdate," Ariel said. "According to this, Derek was born in 1981."

The woman shuffled through her papers. She pulled out a document and scanned it.

"That's correct."

Ariel looked up. "But that would make him 39 years old."

"Yes," the woman replied, puzzled.

"But Derek is 28," she questioned. "Isn't he?"

"Lila's father is 39 years old."

Ariel's face turned white. She had a baby with a man that was almost 20 years older than her? What else had he lied about? She dismissed the woman and rolled onto her side and released all the tears she had. Her precious baby. What kind of a life would she have with a liar for a father and a mother who had nowhere else to go? Ariel felt like she was in a cage, with no hope of being released. She thought about her mother and how she warned her not to get on a road that would lead to unhappiness. Well, she was on that road, all right! And she wasn't sure she was going to make it safely to the other side. She cried for an hour, and fell asleep completely enveloped in her despair.

= = =

When she woke, the nurse was wheeling in her daughter. Ariel smiled and held out her arms so the nurse could place little Lila on her. Ariel held her daughter, just staring at her. She was so beautiful. She had little pink hands, and feet, and she smelled like warm vanilla. Her dark blue eyes were fixed on her mother's face.

"Hey there, little girl," Ariel whispered. "Soon, we're going to go home and then it'll be just you and me. I should tell you that I'm scared to death. This is my first time being someone's mom. I should also tell you that I'm not sure if you'll have a great dad or not. But I swear to you, on my life, that

I will always take care of you and I won't let anyone hurt you. You are my everything and I will love you forever." Then she kissed her baby and remained like that until the nurse came back a couple of hours later.

On the third day, Derek came to pick them up. He was there for Lila's birth, but not much else. Ariel tucked in her baby in the car seat and walked out of the hospital. Over the next couple of days, she focused on Lila's needs and paid very little attention to Derek. She didn't want to anger him, so she avoided him when he was home from work. She decided not to bring up the fact that he lied about his age, nor anything else that might upset him. She still clung to the idea that Derek might look at sweet, angelic Lila and not only vow to be a good father, but also return to the man she had once known him to be. But after a month of avoiding the two of them, Ariel began to lose hope.

One day, while Derek was at work, Ariel put Lila down for a nap and sat on the couch. She felt alone. She contemplated calling up Jamie and asking for advice, but she knew that her cousin was constantly busy with her own kids and her busy life. Ariel stared at her phone and thought. Finally, she scrolled through her contacts, and stopped on the one labeled "Mom." She hesitated. What would she say to her? *Your daughter is a disappointment and she really messed up big time.* She shook her head to dispel the negative thoughts swirling around in her head. She hit send.

"Hello?"

"Hi, Mama."

"Ariel! How are you?"

"I'm okay."

"Is everything all right with Lila?"

"Yah, she's great. Getting real big."

"Oh, that's great. When can I see her?"

A lump began to form in Ariel's throat and she couldn't seem to talk anymore. Her lower lip trembled and she began to tear up.

"Ariel? What's wrong?"

Suddenly, a wave of anguish swallowed Ariel up and she cried into the phone.

"Mama!" she sobbed. "I messed up!"

"Tell me what happened?"

For the next few moments, Ariel dispelled every horrible memory about Derek to her mother. She described how he punched her, kicked her, slapped her, called her every name in the book. She told her about the gun incident, and how he flipped over the couch. She told her how he wanted nothing to do with Lila and how he isolated her from everyone that meant anything to her. Her mother listened without saying a word. When Ariel finished, she spoke.

"Remember what I told you when you graduated?"

"Every word, Mama," Ariel sniffled. "I got on the wrong road."

"You did. But it's not the only road, girl. When you open your eyes, you're going to notice that there's another road branching off of the one you're on. It's not as wide, not as straight, and not as safe. It's got a lot of bumps and potholes. But it's a good road."

"Tell me what to do, Mama."

"I'll send some money to Jamie. I don't have much but it'll be enough to put a deposit on your own place. Find a job. Jamie can help you get Lila settled at the same daycare she has her kids in. You get the hell out of there, Ariel! And then you get down to that courthouse and file for full custody of that baby, you hear me?"

"I'll try, Mama."

"Baby, you came into this world like a fighting machine. But somebody took away your spirit, your grit, and put out your fire. Light 'em up, girl! I wanna see my daughter back—the one who gave me all these gray hairs on my head. Take back what you are and don't ever let them see you scared."

Something flickered inside of Ariel at that moment. Her mother's words took root and sprouted out a big dose of courage within her. She thought of her innocent little daughter, sleeping in the next room. What example was she giving her? That she too will someday find some jerk to control her and take away her fire? Ariel wanted better for her.

"I will, Mama," Ariel stated, and she hung up the phone.

A week later, Jamie called Ariel to tell her that her mother's money came through. Ariel asked her to hold on to it for a little while so she could search for an apartment. She finally found a reasonably priced, two-bedroom apartment on the east side of town and bummed a ride off of Jamie to go and take a look at it. It had a cute little kitchen, living room, a bathroom, and two small bedrooms. There was even a backyard with an old swing set. Ariel thought it was perfect. She gave the landlord a deposit and told him she'd be back at the end of the month to move in.

Next, she spent an entire day calling various places that had advertised for help in the newspaper. Ariel didn't care what job it was, just as long as it could pay the rent and a few other bills. She was willing to work at McDonald's at this point. She got a call back from the owner of a daycare facility who was looking for a receptionist/daycare provider.

Ariel emailed her resume and set up a time for an interview. The next day, she took the bus with little Lila in tow and arrived at the Little Hands Daycare. She walked in and asked for Mrs. Tripp. A petite woman with short brown hair came up to her and warmly shook her hand. Then she directed Ariel to follow her to her office.

Ariel got the job on the spot, and she swore that it was Lila that made it happen. Anyone could see that Lila was well cared for, and Mrs. Tripp was looking for a person that was skilled with children as well as with computers. Ariel fit the bill. In addition, as luck would have it, Mrs. Tripp was selling her oldest son's Toyota Corolla, since he had enlisted in the Army and didn't need it anymore. Ariel used the rest of the money her mother sent her to purchase the car. She asked Mrs. Tripp to hold on to it until she started her job the following week. She didn't want to alert Derek that she was moving on with her life. He was unpredictable as it was—there was no telling what he would do if he found out.

Ariel began working at the daycare a few days later. Derek left the house an hour before her and came home an hour later than her, so he never suspected that she was working. At the end of the month, she waited until he left for work one Saturday, and packed up her few belongings and moved into her new apartment with Lila. Jamie helped furnish her new pad with some old furniture she didn't want, plus a new bed. The moment Ariel stepped into her new home, she almost fell to the floor and kissed the ground. She was finally free of the monster! He had no idea where she lived or where she worked, so she felt completely protected by the law. If he ever came after her, she wouldn't hesitate to call the police.

That evening, she called him. After all, he was her daughter's father. She didn't think it was right to keep them from each other.

"What?" he answered.

"Are you home?" she asked.

"No."

"Good. You'll notice some things missing when you get there."

"What things?"

"Me and Lila. I moved out today. The place is all yours."

"What?"

"Really, Derek? You didn't see this one coming? I don't think two people could have been more miserable."

"How did you do it? And with what money?" he shouted.

"Don't worry, I didn't take any of yours, if that's what you're asking."

"Yah, right, you liar!"

"I didn't call you to get into a screaming match. I just called to tell you it's over. If you wanna see your daughter, let me know and I can arrange it."

"You fucking bitch! Tell me where you're living now! Are you shacked up with some guy?"

"None of your business."

"Damn right it's my business! My daughter is there!"

"Your daughter? Since when did you begin to care about your daughter? Ever since she was born, you never fed her, changed her diaper, held her, or even talked to her! Just because you donated your sperm doesn't mean you automatically qualify for father of the year!" Ariel could not believe the words coming out of her mouth. Over the past year, she never had the courage to stand up to Derek like this because she feared him. But now that she was away from him, it was like her courage began to sprout from the ground and grow.

"I'll find you, Ariel. Make no mistake about it," he said.

"And do what? Everyone knows what you'll do to me. You'll be in jail for a long time if you touch me," she countered.

"You owe me! I gave you a place to stay and I gave you money!"

"And I paid for it dearly," she said through her teeth. "Goodbye, Derek. Have a nice life." Ariel hung up the phone before he could get in another word.

On Monday, she went into work a few minutes early so she could talk to Mrs. Tripp. She sat in her office and explained the entire situation to her. She wanted to protect her daughter legally, so she asked Mrs. Tripp to advise her on how to reach the court. As luck would have it, Mrs. Tripp had a contact in the courthouse for legal matters. She called her up and quickly summed up Ariel's request. By the time she hung up the phone, Ariel had a court date to present her case to the judge. Ariel couldn't stop thanking Mrs. Tripp. She finally felt that she was on the right road this time.

A week before the court case, Derek called Ariel to see his daughter. They were outside playing so Ariel suggested that he face time her so Lila could see who he was. They spent under five minutes on the phone because Lila grew tired of talking and Derek had to go. Ariel thought it was weird that he got off the phone so quickly but she shrugged it off. When she came home from the grocery store that evening, her gut clenched when she saw the word SLUT spray painted on her front door. She knew Derek had done it, but more importantly, she knew that he had found out where she lived. No wonder he wanted to Facetime—he was able to see the apartment complex she lived in from the background. She didn't park the car in the driveway. Instead, she parked down the street a ways, and called the police.

They came within 10 minutes and took a report. She entered the house only after the officer checked the entire premises. Ariel didn't sleep well that night. She was convinced that Derek would find a way to get to her.

The landlord painted over the spray paint the next day, but the acts of terror continued. A couple days later, Ariel came home from work to find out that her mailbox was destroyed. Again, she filed a report with the police. Again, she couldn't sleep, wondering what Derek would target next. Finally, the date of the court case arrived and she was convinced that justice would prevail. Thankfully, Derek didn't even show up, so Ariel felt at ease to explain the situation to the judge. She presented photographs of the spray painted door and the broken mailbox. She talked about the struggles of being a single parent and fearing for her daughter's safety. The judge listened intently and awarded Ariel temporary sole custody of Lila, until an investigation could be conducted of Derek's mental health. Another court date was set for three months out. Ariel thanked the judge and walked out of the courthouse on feathered feet. Now Derek could never take Lila away legally! It was just one more nail in the coffin to get him out of her life for good!

Ariel continued on a good path for a few more months. Derek got himself a lawyer to prove that Ariel wasn't a fit parent. However, it backfired in his face when the judge ordered Derek to begin paying child support and seek counseling. After that, Ariel didn't hear from Derek all that much. The vandalism and the threats stopped too, and she breathed a sigh of relief. Maybe Derek was finally coming to terms with the fact that acting crazy gets you nowhere.

A year later, when Lila was two, Ariel got into a bind at work. Lila was sick and couldn't come to the daycare. Ariel didn't know what to do because she had used up a lot of sick days going to court and Jamie was not available to take her. She decided to ask Derek for help. After all, he was Lila's father. She called him up and asked him if he could take Lila for at least half the day. To her surprise, he agreed. He didn't have any jobs scheduled that day, so he was planning on staying home and doing nothing. Ariel dropped Lila off with a niggling feeling inside of her that maybe this wasn't the best idea. But she had no other options, so she left her there and went to work. Around lunchtime, she got in her car and went over Derek's house to check in on them. As she neared his apartment, she caught sight of a small, dark-haired child walking up the street. She slammed on the brakes and ran out of the car.

"Lila!" she screamed.

Lila turned towards her and smiled. "Hi, Mommy!" she said.

Ariel picked her up and held her tightly. She then looked at her and checked her for any signs of cuts or bruises.

"Baby, where are you going? Why are you outside near the road?"

"Daddy is sleeping."

"What?"

"Shhh, Mommy. Don't wake Daddy."

Ariel carried Lila to the car and strapped her in. Then she drove to Derek's apartment and parked in the driveway. She told Lila to stay in the car while she ran in and got her things. The door was wide open when she entered the house and the television was on. Derek was passed out on the couch. Ariel could see the bottle of pills on the table so she now knew that he was addicted. She snapped a picture of the bottle, as well as Derek passed out. She then grabbed Lila's toys, threw them in a bag and left. She didn't return to work that day because she was so shaken by what had transpired, but she called Mrs. Tripp to fill her in. Thankfully, it was a Friday, so Ariel had the weekend to take care of Lila before they both could return to the daycare.

Ariel made sure to forward the photographs to the courthouse clerk to add to the file. There was no way in hell that Derek would ever get custody of his daughter—especially if he was addicted to medication. Things settled down shortly after that and she didn't hear from him again. Then one Saturday in early August, Lila was down for her nap when Ariel heard a knock at the door. It was Derek.

"What do you want?" Ariel asked through the closed door.

"Open the fucking door!" he yelled.

Ariel stiffened. Clearly, Derek was not in his right mind.

"Leave or I will call the police!" she shouted.

"Open the fucking door, you fucking cunt!"

Ariel ran to grab her phone but the sounds of wood splintering made her turn around. Derek had kicked the door open and was making his way towards her. He punched her in the face and Ariel went flying backwards.

"When I tell you to open the fucking door, you better do it!" he screamed.

"What do you want?" Ariel cried, holding her face.

"Where's Lila?" he said.

"She's sleeping," Ariel answered.

Derek looked down the hall. "Well, I'm her father and I'm taking her!"

Something inside of Ariel snapped. She feared for her life, and Derek making a mess out of her face, but at the mention of her sweet daughter, she went into Mama Bear mode. She quickly got up and grabbed her phone.

"Touch her and you'll never see the light of day, asshole!" she ground out. Then she quickly dialed 911.

Derek lunged towards her, but he wasn't quick enough. She bounded out the door and ran towards her car with the phone in her hand. Derek reached her before she could open the door and slammed her into the car door, knocking the phone away from her. He then began to beat her. She screamed for him to get off of her, and kicked him away. She then opened the car door, but he grabbed her and slammed her again into the car, breaking the entire control panel with her body. Again, she tried to beat him off of her, but he was double her size. Finally, he grabbed her and slammed her onto the ground.

That's when the world went black.

Ariel woke up to a faint beeping noise, and lights. Her head felt like someone was taking a hammer to it. She squeezed her eyes shut and tried to control her breathing. Where was she? And where was Lila? LILA! Her eyes flew open, and she began to scream for help. Immediately, a nurse rushed into the room.

"Ariel, it's okay. You're going to be okay," she said.

"Where's my daughter! Get me my daughter!" Ariel screamed.

"She's fine. Your cousin Jamie has her!"

Ariel instantly relaxed and sat back against the pillows.

"Where am I?" she asked.

"Portsmouth General. You were beat up pretty badly. Do you remember anything that happened?"

"Yah. My daughter's father came over and he tried to take her from me. When I wouldn't do it, he beat the crap out of me."

The nurse's lips tightened. Ariel could have sworn she saw anger flash in her eyes.

"There's an officer waiting outside. Apparently you called 911 before you had a chance to speak to an agent. They were able to send someone based on your phone's location. When the officers arrived, you were unconscious on the ground."

"And Derek?"

"I'm assuming that's your daughter's father?" she asked.

"Yes."

"He had fled the scene by the time they arrived. You were alone."

Ariel looked away. "What happened to my daughter?"

"The officer found your phone and got in touch with your mother."

Ariel's head snapped back. "My mother?"

"She gave the officer your cousin Jamie's number and Jamie came over to take your daughter. The officer said your daughter was fine."

"Sweet Jesus, what a mess," Ariel mumbled. "Am I allowed to call them?"

"In a minute. The officer needs to take your statement first." She turned to go and call the officer but then she turned back and grabbed Ariel's hand.

"Don't hold back, Ariel," she looked hard into her eyes. "You could have died. You're lucky to walk away with just a concussion. But for the sake of your daughter, don't hold back." Then the nurse left the room.

Ariel sat there and thought about her words. She had had enough. This was not the life she envisioned for her daughter. She had gotten her own place and a job she enjoyed, but it still wasn't enough. With Derek's unpredictable behavior, it was only a matter of time before he would do serious damage to her. And then where would sweet little Lila go? She would be doomed to live with her father and God knows what he would do to her. Rage welled up inside of her. No more! It was time to take the road that led to home!

Ariel's mother arrived two days later. She cried when she saw her daughter laying in the hospital bed. They both held each other for a long time and Ariel spilled her entire sad story to her. Her mother winced at the parts where Derek beat her, but she smiled proudly when she heard about Ariel taking him to court and getting sole custody of Lila. That night, Ariel was released from the hospital and her mother drove her to Jamie's house. It was so good to see Lila again! Ariel scooped her up and couldn't stop kissing her. How she had missed her little girl. Ariel's mother stayed with her a few more days to help her pack up and ship out. Ariel bade a tearful goodbye to Mrs. Tripp, thanking her profusely for all the help she had given her. Mrs. Tripp understood why she was leaving and promised that if she needed a letter of reference, all she had to do was call her.

Within two days, Ariel's and her mother's cars were all packed and ready to go. Ariel made Jamie take back all her furniture, along with the new bed, and advised her to sell everything on Facebook Marketplace. The trip took two days. Lila didn't fuss very much at all, as she switched between driving with her mother and her grandmother. Ariel's mother was delighted to have such a talkative passenger for part of the trip. When Ariel was alone in the car, she thought back over the nightmare she had lived in over the past two years. The further she got away from Florida, the more relaxed she became. She never wanted to see or hear from Derek ever again. But unfortunately, she knew their paths were destined to cross again. Although he was a volatile and unbalanced lunatic, he was still Lila's father.

Ariel moved in with her mother to Lila's delight. Lila quickly became attached to her grandmother and the two were inseparable. It gave her time to settle back into Connecticut and get back in touch with all her old friends and family. When Carly found out Ariel was back in town, she rushed over right away. She had a one-year-old daughter of her own named Riley.

"Girl, you look like shit," she said when she saw Ariel.

"Yah, and you got fat," Ariel shot back at her.

Then Carly threw her arms around her friend and hugged her tight. When she released her, she looked into her eyes.

"Was it awful?"

"Beyond words, Carly," she snorted. "I will never go back there again."

"Good, because you don't belong there. You belong here with us. Who cares that there's sunshine and beaches down South. It's not your home. Never was."

"Yah," Ariel frowned. "I know that now. But three years ago you couldn't have told me that. I had to see it for myself." Then she brightened up and smiled at her friend. "But I'm here now and Lila is going to have the best life—I swear. No one will ever hurt her or me again."

Carly stayed for a while, hearing Ariel's awful tale. Carly then told Ariel about her shotgun wedding and the birth of her daughter. Then she caught her up on the town gossip. Ariel hadn't felt that at ease in a long time. She was truly happy once again.

Ariel walked Carly to her car when she was ready to go home.

"Do you have a job yet?"

"No. That's tomorrow's plan. I'm going to scour the ads."

"Here," Carly whipped out her phone and scrolled through some texts. "I just saw this ad for a garage receptionist and I thought of you. I'll send it to you."

"A garage receptionist?"

"Yah. You love all that grease and tools shit. It would be perfect for you!" Carly laughed.

"K thanks," Ariel smiled.

"Call me later," Carly said, and got into her car. "I gotta feed this kid before she blows her top."

"I know how that goes."

Ariel watched her friend drive away. She walked towards the house and pulled her phone out of her back pocket. She saw the text Carly forwarded to her and opened it up. It was an ad from Marvin Auto in town. Ariel was very familiar with that garage, and with the owner, Eric Steel. He was older than her but he was obsessed with racing. Back in high school, she would sometimes go to the speedway to watch the cars race, and he was always driving one of the fastest cars. She punched in the phone number provided and waited as it rang.

"Marvin Auto," a man's voice answered.

"Hello, I'm calling about the ad in the paper for a garage receptionist."

"Yes?"

"Is the job still available?"

"Yes, it is."

"I'd like to apply for it. How do I do that?"

"What are you doing right now?"

"Right now?"

"Yah. Right now. We close in about 30 minutes so you can come down and pick up an application."

"Great! I will be there in 30 minutes!"

"See ya soon," he said and disconnected the call.

Thirty minutes later, Ariel entered the garage. The mechanics were all milling around a black second-gen Dodge Ram that just had its transmission switched to manual. She smiled. Mechanic boys were always hypnotized by a sweet-looking truck. It would be a tossup which one would hold their attention more—a pretty girl in short shorts, or a souped-up Dodge with a straight pipe.

"Excuse me?" she said to the group of men. "I'm here about the job."

A bald man with killer blue eyes and a muscular physique came towards her.

"Hi. I'm Eric Steel."

Ariel gulped. So this was the professional racer. She knew that he had skill with a wrench, but she didn't realize he was so easy on the eyes as well.

"Hi. I was the one that called you 30 minutes ago."

"Wow, you're quick!" he smiled. "If you don't mind me asking, how did you hear about the job?"

"Oh, my friend saw your ad online and she told me about it."

"I see," he said. "You look really young. Are you in high school?"

Ariel laughed. "No. I'm 22. I just look really young."

"Okay, good. This is a fast-paced garage and we need someone here full time."

"Yes, I know all about this garage. I think my mom brought her car here a few times."

"What experience do you have?"

"Well., I worked as a receptionist of sorts for the past two years."

"Around here?"

"No. In Portsmouth, Florida. But I can get a letter of recommendation if you need it."

"Florida? What were you doing there?"

"Trying to live the dream," she smiled.

"How did that work out?"

"Not good. I'm a big fan of Connecticut now."

Eric chuckled. Ariel noticed that he had great teeth, and she wondered how many women brought their cars to his garage just to get one of his killer smiles.

"Any experience with cars?"

"I know how to change my own oil."

"That's not a requirement. I was just curious," he laughed.

"Oh," Ariel smiled.

"When can you start?"

"Tomorrow."

Eric raised his eyebrows and smiled. "Okay, one final question. If you get this one right, you got the job."

"Okay," Ariel smiled. "I really need this job."

"Then answer correctly. You ready?"

"I'm nervous but ready."

"Okay. If you had the choice to drive a 1997 Dodge, 12 valve, 5.9 Cummins versus a 2005 Chevy Dually, Duramax, which one would you choose?"

Ariel smiled. She knew that this question was not related to the job itself, but merely thrown out there to toy with her.

"Dodge Cummins, all the way," she responded.

"You're hired," he smiled.

"Seriously?"

"Yah. Actually it had nothing to do with the way you answered that last question."

"You're kidding," she rolled her eyes.

"I'm sure you knew that. You're hired because you came down here quickly when I asked. This job involves a lot of dedication and work ethic, which you seem to have."

"Yes, I do. I'm not afraid to get dirty either so if you need me in the garage, I can do that as well."

Eric chuckled. "We'll start with answering the phone and typing up some invoices, okay?"

"Okay."

"See you tomorrow at 8 A.M. sharp."

Ariel thanked him and left in a hurry. She couldn't wait to tell her mother the news. Next on her list would be to enroll Lila in preschool at the local elementary school, which happened to be right down the street from the garage. And then maybe she could save up enough money to get a little place of her own, just for herself and Lila. But as she drove home, she thought about her selfless mother. What did she want for Ariel and for herself? She had to know.

She pulled into the driveway and found her mother pushing Lila on the swings. She got out and walked over to them.

"I got a job, Mama."

"That's wonderful! Where?"

"Marvin Auto."

"Oh, really? Working for Eric Steel? I'm jealous."

"Mama!"

"What? I can still look," she chuckled.

"Mama, can I ask you something?"

"Of course."

"Are you happy?"

She looked at Lila and smiled. "I am now."

"Remember that talk you gave me after high school? About being on the right road and all?"

"Yes?"

"When you told me to never forget which road leads to home, were you talking about me coming back home to get back on my feet or were you talking about something different?"

Her mother stared at her for a moment, as if she were reading her mind. Then she stopped pushing Lila and carefully placed her on the ground so she could run to the sandbox. She turned to Ariel.

"When your father left, he took with him a piece of my heart. I gave him my all, but it turns out, it wasn't good enough. I never wanted the same fate for you." She sighed and went on. "But the one good thing he gave me was you. Even though you were a handful back then, I still loved your spirit—your bad-ass spirit. I never wanted to see it go away. But this man you were with—he took it from you, and I was afraid I would never have my daughter back again."

"He told me I wasn't good enough, Mama," Ariel whispered. "I began to believe him. He told me I was a selfish bitch."

Her mother grabbed her by the shoulders and faced her. "But you aren't! You took his abuse for so long and then you left. You protected your daughter from him. You got your own place and you got the hell away from him. And when he came to you and put you in the hospital, you still didn't back down. You packed your car and left him in the dust. You have the courts on your side, you have full custody of your daughter. You have a job now, and you have people here that care about you. Coming back home doesn't mean you're running away—it means you're getting back to the place that made you who you are. Selfish bitch? Not even close! Bad-ass bitch? Now we're talking! And don't you ever let any man take that away from you again."

Ariel threw her arms around her mother and hugged her tightly. She let the tears flow freely down her face as her mother rubbed her back and soothed her. After several minutes, she faced her again.

"How long can we stay here, Mama?"

Her mother cupped Ariel's face with both hands and smiled. "Forever." She then let go and looked at the house. "This is your home, Ariel. Long after I'm gone, you will have this place for yourself." She looked at her daughter again. "If you want it."

Ariel smiled and reached for her mother's hand. She glanced at Lila digging a hole with a shovel, singing a song about unicorns.

"We're home, Mama." ▪

■ CHAPTER NINE ■
Julia

"I wish Papa was here," Julia sighed as she smoothed back the white lace gown she admired in the mirror.

"He is here with you," her mother smiled and kissed her daughter lightly on her forehead.

"Now, there is no time for sadness, my daughter. Today is your wedding day! Only happiness."

She pulled Julia away from the mirror and held her hands. They both smiled at each other. Then her mother took a red rose from the dresser and gently placed it in her hair.

"There! Now you are ready!"

Julia laughed and turned one more time to the mirror. "Okay. Let's go!" she said and made her way to the door.

Suddenly, the door burst open and her friend Pepe appeared, sweating and out of breath.

"Julia! It's Tony! There's been an accident!" he yelled.

"What?" Julia gasped.

"He was on his way to the church! She stabbed him, Julia!" Pepe cried.

"What are you saying?" her mother declared, frown lines etching her face.

"Come, Julia! Quickly!"

Pepe grabbed Julia's hand and led her out of the room and out of the house, with her mother right behind them. He led her down the street, towards the church. Her heart was pounding and it seemed like she was running in a blur, trying to go as fast as she could in her white heels.

When they turned the corner, she could see a mass of people staring at something in the road. As she approached, they looked at her and backed up, bowing their heads. She could see a body lying in the middle of the cobblestone way. It was Tony and he wasn't moving.

"Tony!" she knelt down and noticed the crimson stain taking over his white button down shirt. She put her hand to her mouth as tears began to pool in her eyes.

"Tony!" she screamed and took his hand. It was cold. His eyes were open, but there was no life left in them. They stared off into the distance.

"Oh my GOD, TONY!" she screamed again, and held his body close to hers, rocking him gently.

"Please get up! We were supposed to be married today!" she cried and held him tightly for what seemed like an eternity, her mother and the other townspeople weeping on the side.

Finally, the paramedics arrived and they gently tried to coax Julia away from Tony's body.

"No! First my father was taken from me, and now Tony! I won't let you have any more of them!" she blurted out, breathing erratically, flames dancing in her eyes.

Slowly, her mother and Pepe pulled her gingerly away from Tony's body.

"He's gone, my daughter. Let him go," her mother said.

Julia looked at her mother, tears smearing her makeup, her dress disheveled.

"Why, Mama? Who did this?" Julia wailed.

"It was Mimi. She couldn't bear to watch him marry another, so she stabbed him. The police have her now."

"What am I to do now, Mama? I have no father, and now, no husband."

"We go home, Julia. We'll put away the dress, and you can lay down for a while. I'll make you a cup of tea, and then we'll talk. It will be okay, you'll see. Someday, you will forget," her mother smoothed back a tendril that had come loose in Julia's hair.

"No, Mama," Julia said adamantly, ripping the rose out of her hair. "I will never forget." She threw the rose onto the ground and began walking woodenly towards her home.

"Never."

■ ■ ■

A year later, Julia was on her way to the market to do her daily shopping for her mother. The sun was beating down and she raised her face towards it so she could feel its warmth. She closed her eyes and breathed in the summer air. A smile formed slowly on her lips. She kept her eyes closed while she was walking, so she didn't notice when she ran into someone.

"Oh, I'm so sorry!" she gasped, her eyes flew open.

"I should have made more noise," the man chuckled.

"Joel? Is that you?" Julia asked.

"It is," he smiled. "How are you, Julia?"

"I'm fine. When did you get here?"

"Oh, I just arrived yesterday."

"Ah. Are you staying for the summer?"

"For a few weeks, at least. I'm staying with Uncle Lorenzo."

"I see. Well, I am on my way to the market. I really must go," and Julia walked around him and waved goodbye. She continued to walk.

"I heard about your Tony," he called after her.

She stopped cold in her tracks. There wasn't a day that went by that she didn't think of her beloved, but to hear his name being said out loud, sent arrows shooting back into her heart. Joel walked up to her.

"I'm so sorry, Julia."

She glanced at him. She didn't know if he was being sincere or if he was taunting her. She met Joel right before she became engaged to Tony. He came to visit his uncle that summer, and became smitten the moment he saw her. She had long golden hair, sultry brown eyes, and a very well-endowed chest. He had asked her repeatedly to leave her boyfriend for him, but she refused. She was in love with Tony. Finally, he went back to the United States where he came from, and she stayed in her warm little, Italian village, dreaming of the day she would become Tony's wife. Life couldn't have been better.

But that was an eternity ago, and now she felt alone. She went through the motions every day of cleaning the house, making dinner and working at the local bakery a few hours a week. But there was no joy in her eyes anymore. After losing her father at age 10 to pneumonia, and her fiancé at age 18 to a jealous girlfriend, Julia had convinced herself that she was cursed, and stayed away from any man that asked for her attention.

"Thank you," she replied. And continued to walk towards the market.

"May I see you later?" he asked.

"I'm very busy," she said over her shoulder, and picked up her pace.

Later that day, she was exiting the bakery when she noticed Joel, leaning against a streetlamp waiting for her. She sighed and tried to ignore him as she headed towards home.

"Ignoring me?" he asked.

"No. I'm just very busy. I don't have time for this," she mumbled.

"Julia, please," he said, grabbing her arm.

She whirled to face him, with fire in her eyes.

"What do you want?" she demanded.

"Just five minutes of your time," he pleaded. "I swear I will leave you alone if you just hear me out."

Julia tamped down the anger and breathed in.

"Fine. You can walk with me as I go home. That will take five minutes."

"Okay."

They began walking towards her house in the late, summer evening. A warm breeze swirled around them both as he spoke.

"When I first met you, you took my breath away. I have never met a more beautiful girl. I tried to steal you away from Tony, but I was a fool. I was a boy, and it was a game to me." He looked at her to see her reaction, but saw nothing but annoyance.

"I went back to the United States and things changed for me. I went into the military and fought in the war. It changed me. I saw so many atrocities. We may have gone in as young boys, but we came out like old men. I did a lot of thinking about my life and what I wanted. The war ended and I got out of the military. I got a job at a gun factory in the city. It pays good and has good benefits. I'm saving money for a house now." He glanced at her again. This time, the annoyance was replaced with interest. Maybe he could get through to her after all.

"I'm here because I want to settle down with someone. You have always been on my mind. I heard that you were single, so I decided to take a chance. I can buy us a house, provide for us, and we can live a good life in the States. We can have a family. It would be a dream for me, Julia." At this, he stopped and faced her. "Please consider my offer, Julia. I could take you away from the ghosts that surround you every day. I see the sadness in your eyes and I know I can fix that. Please just think about it."

Julia looked away from him, towards the buildings that she had known all her life. She noticed a giant crack in one of the apartments that she had not noticed before. Time and weather patterns had doled out a beating to its concrete mass. She thought about the beauty of the town, and wondered how much longer would it be able to stand the test of time before it began to wither away. She looked at Joel.

"I will consider your offer," she said.

He grinned from ear to ear.

"Thank you, Julia!" he said. "You will not be disappointed!"

"I am going home now. You can wait for me again tomorrow at this time and we can talk some more."

"Okay, yes!" he said. "I will be here!"

"Goodnight, Joel."

"Goodnight, Julia." She left him standing outside of her house and hurried inside. When she closed the door behind her and looked out the window, he was gone.

■ ■ ■

Over the next couple of weeks, Joel waited for Julia outside the bakery as promised. They chatted as he escorted her home. Julia enjoyed his conversations and found herself looking forward to his company. She didn't love him the way she loved Tony, but she appreciated his ambition. He had so many dreams he wanted to fulfill, it was refreshing to talk to someone who lived in a place that offered so many opportunities. The more he talked, the more she longed to be in a place like the United States. It sounded fantastic!

On the third week of his stay, Joel announced that he would be leaving in a couple of days. He asked her again if she thought of his proposal.

"What do you say, Julia? Be my wife and come with me to the States?"

"I will," she replied.

He wrapped his arms around her and swung her around. She smiled weakly, wondering if this was the right thing to do. But then she shook away her apprehension and told herself that she needed to move on, rather than rotting away in the little Italian village.

Two days later, they were married in the church she was supposed to marry Tony in. She repeated her vows to Joel as if she were speaking to Tony. She couldn't seem to shake the niggling feeling inside her brain that something wasn't right. In the end, she just chalked it up to superstitions and dead ex-fiancé's whispering in her ear.

On the third day, Julia kissed her mother goodbye and headed off to the airport with her new husband. This was the first day of a new chapter in her life and she couldn't help but feel a bit excited. She enjoyed new adventures and she couldn't wait to see what this one had in store for her. She took her first trip in an airplane, squeezing his hand the entire way. She closed her eyes when the plane took off and when it landed. She thanked God when it finally touched the ground safely.

Joel's father came to pick them up in an oversized Buick. She couldn't believe that cars were made this big! She was used to the small Fiats and the horse and carriages of Italy. This was amazing! In fact, everything about the United States was enormous. There were giant cites, giant stretches of land, and big houses everywhere! It was like something out of a movie.

They arrived at Joel's parents' house around six o'clock P.M. that evening. Joel took Julia inside and introduced her to his mother. She had dinner waiting for them and Julia was famished. After a dinner of steak and potatoes, Julia whispered to Joel that she was exhausted and wanted to go to sleep. He immediately got up and grabbed her suitcases. She told her new in-laws goodnight, and followed Joel down a flight of stairs. Were they going into the basement? But she kept silent and continued to follow him. Sure enough, they were in the basement, but it was remodeled to assimilate a small apartment. There was a mini kitchen, a sofa and a television, and off to the side was a small bathroom and a bedroom in its own walls. She grabbed one of the suitcases and headed into the bedroom. She placed it on the bed.

"Well, what do you think?" Joel beamed.

Julia looked around.

"It's nice. Did you make this?" she asked.

"Yep. When I came home from the war. I figured this would be good for my own place and to save money for a house."

"Oh," she said, not looking at him, digging into her suitcase for her nightgown.

"You don't seem to like it," he said, coming closer to her.

"No, it's fine," she said. "I'm just really tired. I'll check it out tomorrow morning." And she began to walk past him to get to the bathroom.

He grabbed her arm.

"I hope you're not that tired," he gave her a slimy grin.

She stared at him.

"Really? I can barely move," she whined. "How about tomorrow?"

"I've waited years for you!" he said, anger flashing in his face.

"And one more day is not going to kill you," she shot back at him.

He raised his hand and slapped her across the face. She fell backwards with the blow of it.

"You're my wife now! You do as I say!" he yelled. Then he turned on his heels and walked out.

She could hear his footsteps go up the stairs, as she struggled to get up. She made her way into the bathroom and locked the door. She looked at herself in the mirror and saw the giant red welt forming on her face. Tears sprang up.

"What have I done?" she whispered.

BAD-ASS BITCHES

■ ■ ■

Over the next few months, things went from concerning to holy hell. Julia made dinners, cleaned the little apartment, and helped Joel's parents with their chores as well. At first, Joel went to work every day, and things were okay. But then he began taking days off for no apparent reason. He stayed in the little apartment and watched television or slept. By the end of the first year, he got fired. His parents begged him to get another job so that he could move out and have a decent life. But Joel refused. He grew fatter by the day and took out his frustrations on his new punching bag—Julia.

He called her names whenever he was dissatisfied with the taste of a certain dinner item or the way she folded his clothes. He told her that the apartment was filthy and she should learn how to clean better, when he, in fact, was the one causing the mess. She got punched in the mouth or slapped in the face for talking back to him so she learned how to ignore him and speak to him as little as possible. She saw no evidence of the man she knew in Italy, that wooed her relentlessly. The man that she married was a monster and she regretted ever leaving her safe home. She wished she could go back in time to make a different decision.

One day, she asked Joel if he wouldn't mind if she took a job down the street at the laundromat. She tried to tell him that she wanted to use her own money to buy groceries, and not depend on his parents. He punched her in the head so hard that she fell unconscious. Joel's father heard the commotion and went downstairs. When he saw Julia lying unconscious on the floor and his son sitting on the couch watching television, he called the police. They came in less than five minutes, handcuffed Joel and hauled him away to jail. Julia was taken to the hospital where she suffered from a bad concussion. When she finally awoke, she cried that she could not see. For seventeen days, Julia lived in a hospital room in total blindness. Finally, her sight came back when the swelling in her head went down and she was released. It was the most blissful six months of her life, living by herself in the basement, while Joel stayed in jail. She began working at the laundromat.

Joel returned home from jail in a somber mood, and at first, it seemed that he was returning to his original charming self. Julia became pregnant, with a set of twins, but she continued to work at the laundromat.

Joel was not interested in becoming a father. He spent his days watching television or out with his friends. He never helped Julia with anything around the house. But she was happy when he was gone so she could have peace in her life.

One night, Joel came home from hanging out with his buddies and didn't like the fact that his dinner was cold. He began to verbally abuse Julia so badly that she began to experience shooting pains in her belly. While he continued his verbal assault, she doubled over from the pain and collapsed on the floor. She crawled her way to the bathroom while wetness oozed onto her underwear. She managed to hoist herself onto the toilet and pulled down her pants. Blood and chunks gushed out of her, and she knew without a doubt, that her precious twins were gone. She stayed in the bathroom for a long time, weeping pitifully, until every last drop was out of her.

"Julia?" her mother-in-law knocked on the door. "Are you all right?"

There was silence from the inside.

"Julia, please open the door," she pleaded.

Three minutes later, Julia slowly opened the door, tears staining her face.

"Can you give me a ride to the hospital? I think my babies are dead."

■ ■ ■

The following year, Julia became pregnant again. Another set of twins. She was worn out from verbal, and physical abuse, and she swore that once her babies were born, she would leave the bastard and go back home to Italy. As the months wore on, Joel remained inside the apartment with nothing to do all day, and he again began to take his frustrations out on Julia. One day, she returned home from work exhausted, her ankles swollen.

"I'm starving. When's dinner?" He greeted her from the front yard.

"I haven't even gotten in the door yet, Joel. Give me a minute!" she spat out, annoyed.

He rushed towards her.

"You shouldn't be working anyway! I never approved this!" he countered.

"Where the hell else do you think we'll get money from? You?" she laughed.

Then he pushed her with such force that she fell on her ass. Thankfully, she landed on soft grass, but the embarrassment of his actions teared her up.

"Now get inside and make me something to eat!" he yelled.

She scrambled to her feet as quickly as a seven -month pregnant woman can, and went inside the house. She silently prayed to God that she would deliver these babies before he ended up killing them all.

That night, Julia began to experience labor pains. She knew that it was too early but she was as big as a house. She got a ride to the hospital from her father in law, because Joel was too tired to go anywhere. She delivered her first babies with no family around her. Perry and Jesse were born in the wee hours of the morning but they were awfully small. They had to stay in the hospital for at least a month. Julia made sure to spend as much time as she possibly could at the hospital, without pissing off Joel. They were so precious—growing bigger by the day. And they had each other, which Julia was thankful for.

One month and fifteen days later, Julia took her twins home. She was ecstatic that her babies would be home, but what kind of home was it? She lived in a dank, dark basement with a lazy ass husband, a couple of in-laws who pretended everything was fine, and now she had no job. Julia once again gritted her teeth and took care of her family. All the while, she spent a lot of time thinking about how to change her situation. Finally, she wrote a letter to her mother.

> *Dear Mama,*
> *You have two grandbabies now. Their names are Perry and Jesse. They are amazing! I want so badly to show them to you. I hope you are doing well.*
>
> *Life here has become unbearable. I fear for my children if something happens to me. Could you please send me some money for a plane ticket? The babies are free, I already checked. I want to come home to Italy. I cannot bear being married to this ogre for another day.*
>
> *Your loving daughter,*
> *Julia*

The following month, Julia received the money, wired from her mother. She bundled up her babies and hurried down to the travel office to purchase a plane ticket. They were scheduled to leave on Friday, four days away. Those four days took forever to pass, but she spent her time packing some clothes and hiding them under the bed. Joel never suspected what she was doing. On the fourth day, she waited until Joel left for the afternoon and quickly called a cab. She had her babies ready to go with her luggage in hand when her mother-in-law came downstairs and saw what was going on.

"Please, don't try and stop me," Julia said.

Her mother-in-law bowed her head and took a deep breath. She finally looked up and faced her.

"I'm amazed you actually made it this long," she said. "Where will you go?"

"None of your business," Julia snapped.

"Not too many places will take in a woman with two babies who can barely speak English," she countered.

"You underestimate me," Julia said. "I'm a little smarter than you think."

Her mother-in-law raised an eyebrow and just stared. A car honked outside.

"That's for me. Now get out of my way or I'll plow you over," Julia stated, between clenched teeth.

Her mother-in-law turned and went back up the stairs. Julia followed with her babies and luggage in tow, holding her breath the entire way. When luggage and babies were safely in the car, Julia got in the front seat and closed the door. Her mother in law stood in the doorway watching. While the cab drove away from Oakland Street, Julia, breathed a sigh of relief and smiled. She vowed to never again return to that vile house.

■ ■ ■

For two years, she lived happily in her hometown in Italy. Her mother absolutely loved spending time with the boys and it gave Julia the freedom to get back her old job at the bakery. It was perfect! She took care of her babies in the morning, then put them down for a nap and went to work for 4 hours. By the time she came back, they were awake, fed and ready to spend time with her before bedtime. Joel finally figured out where she went and began to write her letters asking her to come home. At first, the letters were pleasant, as he apologized profusely for his actions and promised to change. After two years of no response, he got the authorities involved.

"Hello?"

"Good afternoon. May I please speak to Julia Dimitri?"

"Speaking."

"This is David Shapiro from the US-Italian consulate. I've gotten notification from your husband, Joel Dimitri, that you reside here with your children Perry and Jesse."

Julia's heart dropped.

"That is correct."

"Ma'am, the children are citizens of the United States and they are requested by their father. Now according to policy 12-35, they are to be returned to their birth country immediately."

"What if I refuse?" Julia seethed.

"We will have to send the local authorities to take your children into custody and fly them out to the States."

"I'm their mother! They belong with me!"

"Unfortunately, ma'am, they belong in the United States. However, you do not have to go, if you choose to stay in Italy."

"What? Who would do that?"

"You'd be surprised."

Julia sighed and closed her eyes. "How much time do I have?"

"They need to be back in the States by the end of the week."

Julia spent the rest of the evening crying on her mother's shoulder. Just when she believed all her problems were finally over, Satan reared up his ugly head and dragged her back into the pits of hell. There was no way she would ever leave her children with their pitiful father. She had no choice but to go back. She packed up her boys, said a tearful goodbye to her mother, and made her way back to the States before the week was over.

Joel met them at the airport. They barely exchanged any words on the car ride back to Oakland Street. She sat in the backseat and chatted with her sons in Italian, the only language they knew how to speak.

Time went by slowly for Julia. She returned back to the damp basement where no one bothered to buy a crib for the boys to sleep in. Julia put the boys in bed with her, and if Joel decided to join them, she slept on the floor. To avoid Joel's rage, she swallowed her pride and pretended to be the happy little homemaker. By the year's end, she found herself pregnant once again. Joel beat her up when she told him and it landed her in the hospital. Thankfully, her baby was fine and she escaped with only a broken finger.

A few months later, when her baby was born, she found joy once again. She named him Tony, after the love of her life, and her husband never guessed the connection. She snuggled up with him at night and talked to him when no one was around. She promised her little son that someday she would buy him a big house with gardens and they would live in it, just the four of them.

Shortly after Tony came home, Joel was in another one of his rages and decided to take it out on Julia. He punched her in the face and when she fell over, he kicked her in the ribs. In the morning, she had trouble breathing, so she packed up her kids and walked down to the doctor's office. Dr. Musuco took one look at her black eye and narrowed his eyes at her. She followed him into the examining room.

"What was it this time, Julia? Was his dinner too cold or did you not sweep up the floor right?" he grumbled.

"I wanted money for groceries," she sighed.

The doctor looked at her, flabbergasted and shook his head.

"There's not too much more of this that I can take," he stated. "You have a black eye and a couple of bruised ribs. I fear the next time you come in, it will be in a body bag!"

"C'mon, Doc, just patch me up," she said. "I gotta go feed my kids."

"Fine. But I'm getting you a ride home. You shouldn't be moving too much in your condition."

"All right," Julia winced as he moved his hands over her abdomen. A few minutes later, Julia left with some strong painkillers.

"Julia? This is Mrs. Fields," the doctor said, extending his hand to a petite woman sitting in the waiting room. She rose and smiled warmly at Julia.

"Hello, Julia," she said.

"Hello."

"I'm going to take you and the children home. Would that be all right?"

"Yes, thank you."

Mrs. Fields carried little Tony and Julia held onto the hands of both her boys as they walked to her car in the parking lot. She placed all the children in the backseat and motioned for Julia to sit in the front. Once they were on the road, Mrs. Fields began to ask questions.

"How long have you lived in this country?"

"Too long," Julia replied.

"Your English is not that bad."

"I spent a lot of time learning the language," Julia replied.

"Do you have anybody to help you over the next couple of days?"

"No."

"How about your husband?"

Julia looked incredulously at Mrs. Fields without saying a word. "He's the one that did this to me," she finally said.

Mrs. Fields pursed her lips tightly. She didn't ask any more questions until they reached the house.

"This is Joe and Tina's house," she said.

"Yep," Julia said, opening the door to get out.

"I know them well."

Julia ignored Mrs. Fields' comments and hurriedly took her twins out of the backseat. Mrs. Fields grabbed the baby and followed Julia into the house. Julia led her inside and down the flight of stairs to the basement. Halfway down, she noticed that Mrs. Fields was waiting at the top.

"Are you leaving now?" Julia asked.

"Oh, no, I'll wait till you come back upstairs so I can help you get something to eat."

"But I live down here," Julia responded.

Mrs. Fields cocked her head and stared at her.

"In the basement?" she asked.

"Yes."

Mrs. Fields slowly descended the stairs and took in the room. She noticed how damp and cold the room was and how meager the furniture was. While Julia fixed the children with something to eat, Mrs. Fields continued to look around.

"Why do you live here and not upstairs?" she asked.

"That's where my in-laws live," Julia replied.

"But you have three children!"

Julia stared at the woman who brought her home. She didn't quite understand why she was so upset, but she was too tired to question her.

"If you don't mind, I'm tired and I'd like to lie down," Julia said.

"Of course, dear. If you need anything, please call me," and she handed Julia a small piece of paper with her name and number on it. "I'll see myself out," she smiled. She waved at the children and ascended the stairs, and then she was gone.

The next day, Julia was outside watching her babies play in the yard when she noticed an official-looking car stop in front of the house. Two men wearing uniforms got out, along with Mrs. Fields, and walked towards the front door. Tina came out to greet them.

"Why, Jane!" she said. "To what do I owe this surprise?"

"Hello, Tina. Is your husband home?" she answered.

"Yes. Is there a problem?"

"Oh, I would say there is," Mrs. Fields stated coldly. "A big one."

Tina turned to call her husband. In a flash, her husband came to the door.

"May I help you?" Joe asked.

"Good morning, Mr. Dimitri. My name is Brad Johnson from the town of Manchester Civil Services Department. This is my partner Larry Tomes, and I'm sure you know Jane Fields very well."

"Yes. What is this all about?" Mr. Dimitri answered.

"We know you are very busy so we'll get right to the point. Are you housing your daughter-in-law and three grandchildren in your basement?"

Joe stood stunned and looked oddly at the men.

"Why, yes," he answered. "They live downstairs with our son, Joel."

"She was recently treated by Dr. Musuco for bruises on her face and ribs. Any idea how she got that way?"

"Uh, no, I don't," Joe lied.

"Did your son do that to her?" Mrs. Fields asked.

"I'm not quite sure."

"We understand you own three apartment buildings in town, is that correct?"

"Yes, that is correct."

"Mr. Dimitri, you have until the end of the month to vacate one of your tenants from one of your properties. By September 1, Mrs. Julia Dimitri will be moving in with her three children. We believe that her living conditions in your basement are not suited for young children. She needs a proper living environment, preferably away from her abusive husband. If you have any objections, we can get the department of children and families involved."

"Now wait a minute! You may have gotten your information wrong. Julia doesn't even speak English!"

"Then I'm sure you won't object to us taking a look at her living quarters for ourselves. I'm sure we were misunderstood when she told us that there were no beds for her babies."

Joe's face turned white, and he swallowed loudly.

"Uh, no. There is no need to see the basement. The truth is, we were planning on moving Julia out of there soon. We've been looking for a place for her and the kids."

"Like I said, Mr. Dimitri, you have until the end of the month. We will be back on September 1 to pay her a visit in her new apartment. If you do not comply, we will be pressing charges." Brad got right in Joe's face. "Am I making myself clear?"

"Yes, sir," Joe replied.

The men turned to leave but Mrs. Fields remained.

"Oh, by the way," she spoke. "Please make sure your son is under control. If before September 1 Julia has any evidence of physical abuse, your son will be put in jail. And this time, it will be longer than six months. If you would like us to tell him directly, we can return this evening."

"That won't be necessary. I will tell him," Joe said.

"Then we have an understanding. Good day, Mr. Dimitri," and she walked down the pathway, got in the car with the men, and drove away.

Julia watched the scene from the side yard. She couldn't make out what they were saying but she knew it had something to do with her. She hoped the men and Mrs. Fields had not come to cause trouble for herself and her children. Later that day, she could hear Mr. Dimitri screaming at his son from the basement. They argued for a long time. Finally, Julia heard the front door slam and Joel never came back that night.

Joel stayed away from Julia for the rest of the month. She packed up her few belongings along with the kids, and was ready to leave by the end of the month. Mrs. Fields provided a secondhand crib for little Tony and a couple of mattresses for the twins. Julia was ecstatic about her new home. She couldn't wait to move in and provide a better life for her kids. The first night she spent in her new apartment was like a dream. She slept soundly for the first time in over four years. Joel had no intention of living with her, nor was he invited. He was more interested in spending his money on travel anyway, rather than being a father and a husband. Four years of being verbally and physically abused, and being utterly alone came to a halt that day. The only thing that she had to worry about now was providing for her children. First she had to find a job. Then she had to find someone to watch her kids when she went to work. She had heard at the grocery store that the Spin Mills in town were hiring a night crew. But who would watch her children during the night? She prayed to God that someone would be able to help her.

And just like that, God heard her and responded.

Early one morning, Julia awoke to a knock at the door. Groggily, she padded over to the door and opened it. A petite woman stood outside the door. She had a very thin coat, short brown hair, and she kept her eyes fixed to the floor.

"Can I help you?" Julia asked.

"I'm Susie," the woman looked up and said.

"I'm Julia. What can I do for you?"

"Mrs. Fields sent me. She said you needed help."

"Oh," Julia responded. "Please come in." She held the door open as Susie came into the apartment. Julia led her into the kitchen and they sat down.

"I have three children," Julia began. "The twins are three years old and the baby is six months old. I need to get a job or we are all going to starve. I have no money to pay you right now, but I'm sure we can work something out." She paused to take in Susie's reaction.

Susie just stared. It seemed like her thoughts were in a foreign land and Julia couldn't make out what she was thinking. Finally, after a few seconds, Susie took a deep breath and looked at Julia.

"My husband died last year. He took care of everything, including me. When he died, I didn't know what to do. I didn't have a job or anyone to take care of me. I lost my home—the home we made together. I've been staying with friends, and sometimes I've had to stay at the shelter. I don't know how to get a job—I'm very shy. But I love kids. I met Mrs. Fields at the shelter. She told me you needed someone to watch your kids and that maybe I can help you out."

Julia watched Susie carefully as she told her story. She could see the sadness in her eyes and wondered if her heart would ever mend. She extended her hand and placed it gently on Susie's hand.

"We'll help each other, then," Julia smiled. "You come and live here with me. I'll go to work at night and you can sleep in my room. During the day, you can watch my babies while I get some rest. I can make all your meals—I'm a very good cook. I might be able to give you some money once I see how much I can make. How does this sound so far?"

Susie looked up at her and smiled sheepishly. She grabbed both of her hands and shook them.

"I would like that very much," she said.

That morning, Julia headed down to the Spin Mills to apply for a job. She was hired on the spot as a nighttime yarn maker. Susie began living with her and the boys that night and Julia began working the next day. The work was good but the money she earned seemed to pay for the apartment and groceries only. Julia wished that she could earn more for Susie and other things the kids might need. A month later, she got wind of another job opening at a restaurant called Garden Grow. They needed a waitress to work on the weekends. She applied and got the job almost immediately. Now she was working nights and weekends, but with the money she earned at Garden Grow, she was able to buy a stove and proper beds for the twins. If there were any leftover dollars, she gave them to Susie so that she could buy herself toiletries or clothes from the thrift store.

Over the course of the year, Julia began to make a home for herself, the boys, and Susie. On her way home from work one morning, she noticed that someone had thrown out a perfectly good couch. It had a small hole in it, but otherwise it was in good condition. Julia and Susie and the boys dragged it to the apartment and put a cover over it to hide the hole. It served its purpose well for the small family. Julia also bought fabric with leftover money and made clothes for the boys. She couldn't afford shoes for them, so she covered their feet in cloth. It was almost as if they were wearing moccasins, like the Indians—very comfortable and protected them from the harshness of the ground.

The twins entered school the following year. They were used to speaking Italian with their mother so they entered knowing very little English. For this reason, they were teased and bullied by the other kids. Julia listened to their accounts of their days at school with a broken heart. She wanted her boys to have friends and get a good education. She decided to begin speaking English at home so that all her children would not have to face any more obstacles than they already had. By the end of the year, all three of her boys were speaking perfect English.

It had been nine years since she left her terrible life on Oakland Street. The boys saw their father very little. He was too busy traveling to different places in the world on his parents' dime to care about his sons. Julia was perfectly fine with this—the less she saw of him, the better. She got her driver's license and made friends with all the local policemen and town officials. She continued working her two jobs and saving as much money as possible. She was determined to keep her promise to little Tony—to live in a big house with beautiful gardens. Then one day, on her way home from work from the Spin Mills, she decided to take an alternate route through Eldridge Street. It was a bit out of the way, but something pulled her in that direction. As she walked up the street, she noticed a huge white house with a For Sale sign in front of it. Julia could tell that the house was sadly neglected. The paint was peeling, the grass was overgrown, and the clothes line was broken and flapping in the breeze. There was a phone number on the sign, so she hurried home to make the call. She learned that the house was listed for $15,500, and it needed a lot of repairs. She made an appointment with the real estate agent to see the house the following day. Sure enough, the inside was in need of updates—from the kitchen to the bedrooms. But structurally, the house was sound and had a good heating system. There was also a new roof. She instantly fell in love with the house. It was big enough for all her boys to have their own rooms, including herself and Susie as well!

She had $9,000 saved in the bank, all from tips she earned at Garden Grow. She credited it to a combination of being attractive and being extremely kind and diligent to the customers. She quickly discovered that they gave her more money in tips when she smiled a lot. The only items she bought for herself were uniforms and shoes, and that was not very often. She directed the real estate agent to make an offer on the house, for full price, with $9,000 as a down payment. The next day, the real estate agent returned back to her with the disappointing news that she was denied. The reason—because she was a single woman.

Julia saw red! How dare they deny her a decent place to live all because of her social position? She was a hardworking woman, who was willing to give over 50% as a down payment? Were they crazy? She dared them to find a man that could outwork her, while raising three children at the same time! She did not accept their reasoning calmly, so she called the bank and made an appointment to speak to the entire board. She made up her mind that she would not leave the bank until they heard her out. She put on her best dress, her wedding high heels and marched into the meeting on fire!

"Mrs. Dimitri. We understand you would like to speak with us concerning the purchase of the property on 39 Eldridge Street," a man in a very stiff brown suit said.

"That is correct," Julia answered.

"Mrs. Dimitri, we are impressed at your desire to speak with us directly, but the fact remains..."

"Stop right there!" she blurted. "I already know your reasons for denying me. Now you're going to hear mine."

Immediately, the all-male board members, sat up and looked at her with open mouths.

"This is a man's world—you guys get to be in charge of your homes, you get the better jobs, drive the better cars, and you think it's perfectly fine to beat your women," Julia began. She heard some of the members gasp faintly.

"But I have three sons and I need a house. I have more than enough cash to cover the down payment and I work two jobs. I have no doubt in my mind that the mortgage will be paid every month. Now I know that you are all educated men, or else you would not hold the positions that you hold right now. I am not a homeless person off the street, and I am very smart and resourceful. And I am not leaving here, until you sign the document that will approve me for a mortgage with your bank!" Julia fiercely stated.

The board members looked at each other.

"We'll have to vote on this matter," the stiff brown suit man said.

"I'll wait," Julia replied.

The six board members shifted in their seats and cleared their throats. Then the chairman began the voting.

"In the matter of Savings Bank versus Mrs. Dimitri, what is the pleasure of the board on allowing a single woman to hold a mortgage?"

"Calloway?"

"Approved."

"Jenkins?"

"Approved."

"Peters?"

"Approved."

"Moriarty?"

"Approved."

"Flannigan?"

"Approved."

"That is unanimous, Mrs. Dimitri," the chairperson smiled. "You may have your mortgage."

"Thank you," Julia smiled. As she turned to walk out the door, she stopped and turned to face them again. "Out of curiosity," she asked. "How many other single women have you given a mortgage to?"

The chairperson pursed his lips and stared at her. "You are the first, Mrs. Dimitri."

Julia beamed and walked out the door with her head held high that day. She had won, not only for herself and her predicament, but maybe for all women to come. She had opened a door. If they were willing to work hard, they too could purchase a house without the assistance of a man. At that moment, Julia felt that there was nothing she couldn't do. She had stared down the devil for the last time and crushed him like a bug. No more would he ever tell her how to live, or beat her to a pulp when she didn't agree. The chains were broken that day, and Julia spread her wings and flew high up over the world. She saw her mother smiling up at her, she saw her children and Susie waving to her, and she saw her father and her beloved Tony blowing kisses to her from the heavens. Julia was unstoppable. She had power, determination, and honesty all wrapped up in self-worth and respect. And she achieved all of this with a little help from her friends and the man upstairs.

■ ■ ■

Four years later, Julia entered the bank office once more to purchase another house that went for sale on Eldridge Street. It was listed at $13,000. She used the equity from her first house to put as the down payment. Once again, the bank approved. She fixed up the little house and rented it for $160 a month. Now she was a landlord! She continued her waitress job at Garden Grow but added hours when they asked her to wash pots and pans for additional pay. After a while, the owner discovered Julia's amazing cooking talents and asked her if she wanted to be one of the chefs. She accepted.

Five years later, another house went for sale on her street. This one was a two-family house and not in need of as many repairs as the other two. It was listed at $50,000. She was approved for the mortgage and rented it for $200 a month, per side. She stopped working at the Spin Mills when the Kimberly Hall convalescent home asked her if she would like to be the head chef in the kitchen, preparing meals for 350 people a day. She worked from 3 A.M. to nighttime. Julia's children all graduated from the private high school in town. All her extra money went to giving them a good education.

By the time Julia reached her 35th birthday, she owned 6 houses on the same street. Garden Grow had gone out of business, leaving her with just the one job at the convalescent home. She decided to begin selling baked goods at the farmer's market in town, where she averaged about $10,000 a year. One day at the market, a familiar face greeted her.

"Julia?"

"Dr. Mausuco?"

"You remember me," he laughed. "How have you been?"

"I've been just fine, Doctor," she laughed as she took his hand.

"Please, you must call me David," he said. "I'm not your doctor anymore, Julia."

"All right," she smiled. "David it is." Then she told him all that she had accomplished—the boys growing up, the various jobs she held, and the houses that she was able to purchase through her hard work.

"My God, Julia," he exhaled. "There were times I was honestly worried that something bad was going to happen to you. It kept me up some nights."

"Oh, David, there were times when I thought the same," she sighed. "But I never thought I would surrender. I'm from Italy, and where I come from, the women there are like blocks of steel. We carry our families on our backs while we work all day long. I think that is what angered Joel the most—he could never break me."

"I admired you so much, Julia."

"I was doing what any mother would do."

"No, Julia, not what any mother would do. I've been practicing for a long time and sadly, I have met a lot of mothers that gave up on their children."

"I cannot imagine that."

"I know," David stated. "You were the woman that I respected the most. You were so very different from all of them. I admit, I had a giant crush on you."

Julia's eyes widened and she blushed.

"I don't know what to say," she smiled.

"My good friend, Tom Moriarty, told me about the day you came in the bank and demanded they give you a mortgage."

Julia laughed out loud.

"Ah, yes. I was a bad-ass bitch back then!"

"You may have been bad-ass, but never a bitch, Julia."

"I did whatever it took to make a good life for my children. And if that made me a bitch every once in a while, so be it. But no one was ever going to tell me what I could and couldn't do anymore. Not after Joel, anyway."

"Do you still see him?"

"No. The boys do sometimes, but I want nothing to do with him. I never had the money to divorce him so technically, we're still married," Julia chuckled.

"Oh! Well, I'm sure you have the money now."

"I am old, David. I have no intention of ever getting married again. So what is the point of getting a divorce now?"

"What if someone came along that wanted to marry you?" he whispered.

Julia stared at him for a few seconds, trying to understand what he was trying to say. This man was nothing but kind to her throughout the years. In fact, if it wasn't for his intervention, she may have had to endure more than the four years of abuse she faced with Joel. But she was a powerful woman with many responsibilities now. She preferred to remain married to her aspirations and her goals rather than a man.

"Would you accept sharing a dinner with me instead? I'm afraid I can only offer you my everlasting friendship," she said.

David smiled and took her hand once again. "I would be honored, Julia." She smiled back at him.

"Would this evening be too early?"

"Not at all. I finish here around three. You could pick me up at five."

"Perfect!" he said. "I'd love to hear about Italy. You must have been something when you were growing up."

"Ha! You have no idea. I didn't get where I am today because I was shy."

"I can imagine!" he laughed. "Oh, by the way," David handed her a small bouquet of flowers that he had picked up from one of the other vendors. "These are for you. I picked them up because red roses are my favorite."

Julia stared at him, open mouthed. She was instantly taken back to the day she was to marry Tony, and she was speechless for a moment.

"Is something wrong?" David asked, frown lines creasing his forehead.

Julia smiled at him, tears welling in her eyes.

"Red roses are my favorite as well." ▪

▪ CHAPTER TEN ▪
Noel

Narcissism—self-worth—It's like taking a pile of shit and wrapping it up in a shiny metallic blue superhero costume. At first glance you think, *Wow! He's amazing! I'm so lucky to have him in my life!* But as you get closer to him, you begin to smell things coming from him that are not too pleasant. He derails you by spraying some more freshly smelling lies upon you. Until you wake up one day and realize that you have lost your identity and cannot even recognize yourself when you look in the mirror. He has successfully stripped away all of your friends, your family, your ambition, and your drive to live out your dreams. You have become nothing more than his puppet and his slave, and if you don't do what he tells you to do or be what he wants you to be, he will inject you with a foul smelling dose of "you suck" until you are apologizing profusely and begging him for forgiveness. The six characteristics of a narcissist are:

- Frequent lies and exaggerations
- Rarely Admit Flaws and Are Highly Aggressive When Criticized
- False Image Projection
- Rule Breaking and Boundary Violation
- Emotional Invalidation and Coercion
- Manipulation

You cannot fix a narcissist. They will never change no matter how much love and devotion you give them. They cannot love people—they only aim to control. They will never admit that they are wrong. They are fueled by any attention you give them—whether it be praising them or arguing with them. The only thing you can do with a narcissist is to leave them and never talk to them again.

And you pray to God that your children don't grow up to be like him.

Steve was a predator, and Noel had no idea that she was the prey. When they first met, Noel had just built a house in a farming town. She was 32 years old and she was a teacher for a public school system. Her front yard was devoid of plant life and it was a hot day in July. So she put on her bikini and boots and began raking rocks. Steve happened to be haying the lot across the street from her. His tractor conveniently broke down so he could spend a minute taking a closer look at the pretty newcomer in town.

In the following weeks, Noel spent time with her only friend in town, Reggie Dalton. He was a 70-year-old man that liked to shoot guns and drink. They often sat in his front yard and he filled her in on all the pertinent information regarding the town and its inhabitants. That's where she heard about Steve. Reggie informed her that Steve would be haying his lands in a few days. Noel loved farms and farmers! She grew up watching *Little House on the Prairie* and secretly wished she lived on a farm. She moved to the agricultural town because she couldn't get enough of the endless corn fields and the old red barns. Farmers were the epitome of honor, diligence, and respect. Their devotion to the land and bringing forth life was enough to make any farm loving woman want to hang up laundry on a clothesline and have babies.

"I wanna meet this guy," Noel said.

"No, you don't," Reggie frowned.

"Why not?"

"He has ... baggage."

"What kind of baggage?"

"Well, he's got a kid."

"That's not baggage!"

"He was never married."

"Well, is he still with her?"

"No. She left him."

"Oh," Noel said. She sighed and looked away. Then she shifted her eyes back to Reggie. "Well, maybe he needs a nice girl in his life." She smiled and began to think of ways to go about meeting Steve—what she would wear and what she would say to him. She was so absorbed in her thoughts that she didn't catch the worried look fleeting on Reggie's face.

Against Reggie's better judgment, he called Noel when Steve arrived. She jumped right up on his tractor and boldly introduced herself. Steve was taken aback by such a brash woman, but he was curious to get to know her better. He had to take a quick trip back to his farm to gather some supplies, so she invited herself to go with him. He stopped his pickup truck in front of his farm and she got out. She quickly ran inside and began to pet the little baby calves in the pens.

"Oh, they're so cute!" she squealed.

"Yep," he answered. Then he turned his head towards a gray truck that was just pulling up. "Hold on a second, I'll be right back."

Noel noticed that Steve went to lean on the truck's door and spoke to the driver in hushed tones. They carried on for quite a while, but Noel didn't mind because she had fallen in love with the babies, stroking their faces and allowing them to suckle on her fingers. After a while, Steve moved away from the door and a blonde woman got out of the truck. She shot daggers at Noel and jumped up into the bed of the truck. She began to slide down sawdust bags so Steve could pile them up inside the barn. After a few minutes, the blonde woman got in her truck and left.

"Who was that?" Noel asked.

"Just a friend. She went and got sawdust for me," he answered.

"Is she your girlfriend?"

"Uh… no, not really."

"She looks young enough to be your daughter," Noel smiled as she walked to his truck.

"She's not that much younger than me," he replied.

"Oh, yah? How old is she?"

"Twenty-four."

"And you are?"

"Thirty-six."

"Twelve-year difference? In most third-world countries, you could be her father. But that's your business. That and the serious cottage cheese she's got forming on her thighs," Noel shot back.

Steve gawked at her but said nothing. She was told by others that she had no filter, and she certainly wasn't going to hold back with this guy, no matter how blue his eyes were.

Noel did not see Steve for the rest of the summer. Reggie had given her reports about seeing the gray truck at the farm on a daily basis. Noel sighed and gave up thinking about Steve. Clearly, he was taken. There was nothing she was going to do about that. The beginning of another school year started and she focused her attention on that.

One evening in early September, after returning home from the Hebron Fair and being scolded by her cousin for wearing a tube top with no bra, Noel decided to engage in a task that brought her the most joy—baking cookies. She spent hours mixing dough and placing trays in the oven, while blasting songs from *The Fray* on her CD player. The phone rang around 8:00 P.M.

"Hello?"

"Hello. Is this Noel?"

"Yah. Who's this?"

"Steve."

Her heart stopped beating. What the hell was he doing calling her?

"How did you get my number?"

"Reggie gave it to me. I hope you don't mind."

"Not at all. Why are you calling me?"

"I was wondering if you wanted to get something to eat."

"At 8:00 at night?"

He chuckled. "Yah, I know it's late but I just finished working."

"Oh, well, what about your girlfriend?"

"She's not my girlfriend."

"You seemed pretty chummy the last time I saw you."

"She's just a friend. I've known her for a while."

Noel sighed. "Well, I can't leave right now. I'm baking cookies."

"Oh? What kind?"

"All different kinds. Why? You wanna come over and sample some?"

"Yah!"

"Well, come on over." She disconnected the call and smiled. *Hmmm. Up against a 24-year-old and he's calling me instead of her? Damn, girl, you still got it!*

Half an hour later, Steve came over. He entered her house and sat at the island which was covered in cookies of all different flavors.

"Holy shit, you weren't kidding!" he exclaimed.

"Yah, it's my hobby. Someday I'd love to have a bakery of some sort."

"But aren't you a teacher?"

"Yah. But I love to bake. Always have."

He stayed for a couple of hours, chatting about various aspects of his life. She learned that he was the sole owner of a dairy farm that used to be owned by his grandfather. But his grandfather died before it could get passed down to him, so he spent the last 18 years buying up all the pieces from different family members. Noel was impressed by his dedication and ambition. She also learned that he had a five-year-old son named Kenny. Steve had told her that he had full custody of him because his mother had a mental illness. A dedicated, hardworking old-fashioned farmer who was raising a child by himself? Instant attraction!

In the days that followed, Noel and Steve spent an ample amount of time on the phone. It usually happened after she returned from work or when he was getting ready for bed. One beautiful fall evening, she had the overwhelming urge to sit with him under the stars. He invited her over to sit on the porch with him.

"Where's Kenny?"

"He's watching TV on the couch."

"He doesn't wanna come out here?"

"No."

Suddenly, she noticed a gray truck pulling into the farm driveway.

"Who's that?"

"You know who that is," he glanced at her.

"Why is she here?"

"She's just picking up the last of her stuff. I left it by the barn."

Noel thought it was odd that they hadn't done this a month ago. Why would a girl leave her "stuff" at a friend's house and pick it up a month later? Unless they weren't finished until recently? But she shrugged it off and didn't think much else about it. She never saw the gray truck again.

A month later, Steve and Noel were lounging in his living room, watching TV and chatting about various things.

"So obviously I know about Miss Gray Truck and Kenny's mom. How many others have there been?" Noel asked.

"Just a couple. One in high school and maybe one more after Kenny's mom left."

"So you could basically count on one hand how many women you've had?"

"Yah," he said. "Why? Is that strange?"

"Kinda."

"Why? How many have you had?"

"Shit! I could probably count on both hands and both feet!" Noel chuckled. "But most of them were losers so it's not really worth repeating."

Steve sat up and pulled away from her.

"What's wrong?" she asked.

"You've been with over 20 guys?"

"Yah, why?"

"That's a lot!"

"Who cares? That's part of my past. There's nothing I could do about it now."

"Jesus. Maybe you're not who I think you are. Twenty guys?" he looked at her in disgust.

Noel didn't understand what she said that was so wrong.

"It's not like I'm a teenager. I'm 33 years old!"

"Yah, well, I'm older than you and I still didn't have that many!"

"For someone who acts like they like me, it sure doesn't seem like you wanna know anything about me—about my past. I would think that when two people like each other, they wanna know everything about each other."

"Not that!" he shot out.

She got up from the couch and walked into the kitchen and grabbed her jeep keys. She wanted him to stop looking at her like that—like she was the biggest whore in the world. She knew she wasn't, but maybe she was. Was she? She said goodbye and left. She didn't call him for a couple of days. She was convinced it was over.

A few days later, she was on her way home from work when her phone rang. It was Steve.

"Hi."

"Hi," she answered.

"I bought you a present."

Her heart instantly softened. She didn't wanna fight with him. She really liked him. And it seemed that this was his way of saying "I'm sorry."

"You did? What is it?"

"Well, it's kind of a surprise."

"Just tell me."

"Okay, I bought you a book. I know how much you like to read."

Noel was delirious. He bought her a book! How sweet is that? "What kind of book?"

"It's a book that Mrs. Nelson wrote. It's her life story. I'm even in it!"

Noel knew about Mrs. Nelson. She was like a second mother to Steve. She was a spunky city girl who ended up marrying a wonderful farmer. She learned how to work hard and she became one of the most respected citizens in town. Noel was fascinated with local history, but she couldn't help but wonder if he was trying to tell her something else by buying that particular book for her. Again, she shrugged off the weird feeling and thanked him for the gift. They were back on track again. That's all that mattered.

The next few months were good. Noel spent a great deal of time doing farm-related activities. She rode the truck with him during corn chopping season, they visited old people that had small farms of their own, she even made a farmhand teach her how to milk cows when Steve came down with the flu. On weekends, when he had to get up at 1:30 in the morning to go milk cows, she would either go with him or pack him his coffee and a couple of cookies to get through the early morning hours. She got very attached to a certain cow named 1228, or so it was written on her ear tags, and she spent time in the barn stroking her while Steve scraped the barn or pushed up cows. Their relationship was good, but she spent all her free time with Steve, and no time with her friends or family. She chalked it up to "the honeymoon period" of a relationship—and made a conscious effort to meld the two more often—Steve and the people she cared about.

One evening, they were driving home from dinner at her parents' house.

"That was nice, right?" she asked.

"Yah. Not bad."

"Not bad? What was not good?"

"The food was good. Your dad is very talented with wood."

"But?"

"Your mom is very opinionated."

Noel chuckled. "She's always been that way."

"Yah, but don't you see how dangerous that is?" he glared at her. "Her entire opinions about the government and politics are wrong! We are working our asses off so the government can tax us more and take away our livelihoods! I get no aid from the government because they don't care about farmers! And what about religion? People who go to church are hypocrites! They sit there and pretend they're good people but then they come home and judge other people. Church is filled with liars and cheaters!"

Noel was taken aback by this statement. She didn't look at church that way. Surely she knew that no one was perfect, but she didn't think of humankind as being a collective disappointment. There had to be good people in this world, and she always thought that her mother was one of them. Now she wasn't so sure anymore.

"My mom doesn't lie and cheat," she said softly.

"Oh, but she defends people that do! This is what happens when you don't watch the news! All those priests that have abused little kids? Your mom defends those people. They are disgusting! They have hurt little children, but yet, she still goes to church and listens to every word those priests have to say. And God forbid you don't go to church! You'll never hear the end of it from her!"

"Why are you being so mean to her?"

"Because your mind has been poisoned all these years by a woman you trusted. I'm not saying she's a bad person, but just question what she says sometimes. She's not always right."

Another evening, Noel was entertaining a friend and her husband for dinner at her house. She hadn't seen the friend since college so she was overjoyed to see her. The four of them sat down to a wonderful meal Noel had prepared. When dinner was over and they left, Noel and Steve sat on the couch and chatted.

"That was awesome," Noel beamed. "I'm so glad I got to see Meg. She looks great!" When Steve did not respond right away, she turned to him. "What did you think?"

"There's something wrong with her husband."

"What? How do you know?"

"I have a sixth sense about people—I can read them pretty good. That guy is on something."

"What?" Noel looked at him, appalled.

"Yep. Not sure what it is—prescription drugs or maybe he smokes weed, but he is definitely on something."

"Oh," Noel frowned and looked away. She never invited Meg and her husband to dinner again.

A couple months later, Noel and Steve were getting ready to go to sleep in his house. She hugged him and brought her face close to his. He turned away just as she was getting ready to kiss him, so her lips landed on his cheek instead. She instantly jerked up.

"Why do you keep doing that?" she asked.

"Do what?" he replied.

"You keep on turning your head to avoid kissing me."

"Just forget about it."

"No, I really want to know!" she sat up.

"I don't want to hurt your feelings."

"Just spit it out!"

"Well, the first time we kissed, you had bad breath."

"Bad breath? And you never told me?"

"Well, I didn't want to hurt your feelings."

"So not kissing me was the way to solve that problem?"

"Kissing is very personal. I only kiss when I'm in love."

Wham! And there it was. The real reason why he wasn't keen on kissing her.

"So you don't love me," she whispered.

"Look, it takes a long time with me," he sat up and faced her. "I've been through some terrible relationships, and it's just really hard to trust someone. I want to. I honestly want to trust you, and all I can tell you is that you're on the right road. But I just need more time."

She immediately softened. There was no arguing this point. People had a hard time trusting, and according to Steve, there were more bad people than good people in this world. She just had to prove she was one of the good ones, that's all.

"I will use mouthwash from now on. That ought to help."

Steve smiled at her and kissed her on the cheek.

"Okay," he said.

≡ ≡ ≡

That summer, Noel offered to work on his farm feeding calves for no pay. She wanted to show him what a good and dedicated worker she was. So every afternoon, from 2:30 to 5:00ish, she fed about 60-70 calves. New ones were born almost daily, so the number kept on fluctuating. She began by scraping the old bedding and putting new sawdust down. Then she filled water and grain buckets, and bottle fed the newly born babies. There were groups inside the barn, as well as out back. At first, she enjoyed the work. But as the temperatures increased and her boss turned from her boyfriend into a slave driver, she found that she didn't like it so much. One day she was passing the time by giggling with another farm hand while they were working together. He was very childlike in nature, although he was in his twenties. But Noel was an imaginative person, so she thought he was hilarious. Steve happened to walk by while they were pretending they were speaking another language.

"What the hell do you think you're doing?" he bellowed.

"I'm doing my job," she replied.

"No, you're not! You're fooling around with Ricardo! This is how mistakes are made, and I cannot afford any mistakes on my farm. Do you understand?"

"We were just talking while we're working," she said.

"If you can't listen to me when I tell you something, then I'll find someone else to do the job."

She stared at him. Ricardo had slunk away to the opposite end of the barn. She almost didn't recognize the man before her. Not only was he embarrassing her in front of someone else, but he was threatening to replace her. As if she were expendable! As if she didn't matter to him at all. She lowered her head and carried on with her work. Anger filled her head and she tried very hard to make sense of it all. She was a hard worker, and she was doing the job for free! What was his problem? Surely he must be having a bad day. That's it! He was just having a bad day and taking it out on her. But she was careful not to speak to Ricardo again. At the end of the summer, Noel happily announced that she was returning back to school and that she would no longer be available to feed calves.

"Why?" he asked.

"What do you mean, why? I'm going back to work."

"You come home at four, you could continue doing the job if you wanted to."

"Well, I don't want to."

"Well, this puts me in a very difficult position. Who is going to replace you?"

"You knew this day was coming. You knew this was only for a summer!"

Steve shook his head and frowned. "See, I knew it. I knew I shouldn't have done that. I never should have agreed for you to work here."

"What are you talking about? I gave you three months of free labor!"

"That doesn't help me now, does it? You'll have to find a replacement."

"Me? I don't know anything about running a farm business!"

"I had plenty of high school kids before. Call the high school. See if they have anyone available."

"Who would I call? I don't know anything about these schools?"

"You're a smart person. You can figure it out."

Noel was convinced that poor Steve was put in a difficult predicament because of her. She should have helped him solve this problem sooner. She was not proving to him that she could be trusted. She was determined to get back into his good graces. She dialed up the high school and was put in touch with the Ag teacher, who recommended a young freshman. Steve grumbled at his lack of experience, but agreed to take him on. Noel breathed a sigh of relief.

One day in late fall, Noel had spent a whole Saturday cleaning Steve's house. Kenny was at his mom's so she had the house to herself. While she was cleaning Steve's bedroom, she found a bunch of photographs of random women in a photo album as well as old love letters from Kenny's mom. She read them. Her heart tugged for the poor woman. In the letters, she basically pledged her undying love to Steve and begged for him to continue their relationship. Noel felt sorry for Kenny's mom. She had met her on a couple of occasions and she liked her. But Steve warned her not to believe a word that came out of her mouth because she had a mental illness and she was a terrible mother. The proof was in the fact that Steve had full custody of Kenny. Noel had no reason to doubt him, so she believed him when he said that Kenny's mom was a bad person. Still, the letters made Noel feel sorry for her. She was just uncovering Steve's yearbook when he came into the room to check up on her.

"What are you doing?"

"I found your yearbook!" she announced happily.

"I'll take that," he said, as he advanced towards her and grabbed the book.

"Why won't you let me look at it?" she asked, puzzled.

"Because it's embarrassing."

"That's silly! I wanna see your senior picture. C'mon, show it to me."

Steve hesitated. Then flipped open to the class pictures. "See?" he said pointing to his picture.

Noel giggled. "Wow. You look pretty mad."

"I was," he said. There was no humor in his tone. "I hated school and everything about it. I couldn't wait to get out."

"Oh," she replied. "Well, can I at least read the comments your friends wrote inside?"

"No," he stated. Closing the book and sliding it under his arm. "That's private."

Noel was stunned. Since when are things about your past private from your girlfriend? Unless he was trying to hide something. Was he? Again, she decided to shrug it off. If he didn't want her to know, then she should obey him. She spent the rest of the afternoon cleaning. By the time 5:00 rolled around, she was exhausted. She just wanted to go to her house, take a warm bath and relax on the couch. She got in her car and turned on the ignition. She could see Steve walking towards her from the barn. She waited until he got close.

"Where are you going?"

"I'm going home for a while. I'm tired."

"Did you finish cleaning?"

"Yes."

"Well, I was hoping you would help me finish up my chores so I could be done too."

"What would you have me do?"

"Maybe finish feeding the calves, and pushing up cows with me."

"I think I'll pass. I'm seriously wiped," she sighed.

"I worked circles around you today but you don't hear me complaining."

Stunned, she stared at him. He was trying to make her feel bad. Normally, she would have given in. But this time, she was genuinely tired. It was cold and damp outside and she had no desire to be outdoors.

"I really don't want to," she answered.

"Kally always stayed and helped me. No matter how tired she was."

Anger welled up inside of her. How dare he throw Kenny's mom at her? He didn't even like her!

"I am not Kally, nor will I ever be Kally!"

"No, you're not! Go on home and relax!" he shouted, walking away.

"I will!" she shouted back.

"YOU'RE A FUCKING BITCH!" he turned and shot back at her. Then he stormed away.

Noel stood dumbfounded. She had been called names before, but never one this strong. She stepped on the gas and put as much distance as she could from herself and Steve's farm. She was never going to shed tears over this, and she wasn't angry either. She was scared. Steve had shown her his mean side, and she wasn't sure how to handle this. Did this constitute abuse? Should she run now? All she did was to refuse to work an extra hour when she had put in a full day already—cleaning his house. For free! She didn't deserve this. Of this she was sure.

Noel didn't speak to Steve for the rest of the day. The following day, he came to visit her at her house. He smoothed things over the best that he could, promising never to call her that again. He also gave the excuse that he was cold and hungry and tired, and he had dealt with a lot of problems that day. She listened to his reasoning, but did not forgive him easily.

"I think we need some help. I don't think you and I are on the same page," she finally said, when he was done talking.

"What kind of help?"

"I'd like us to go and talk to someone. A professional. Someone who can be neutral enough to tell us what to do."

"You mean a shrink?'

She winced at that word. "Yes. A therapist."

"I've been to plenty of them when my sister was in trouble. I know all about it."

"You've talked to a therapist before?"

"Plenty of times. They don't work."

"Well, I don't know what else to do. All I know is that I am unhappy with some things. I'm willing to meet you halfway, if you can meet me halfway. I know that relationships need work and I'm willing to try."

He looked at her hard, then sighed. "Fine. Find a person and I'll go."

The following week, Steve and Noel were sitting in Penny Royce's waiting room at 4:00 P.M. sharp. A short-haired woman dressed in a suit greeted them and escorted them in the room. A soft light glowed in the corner. They were instructed to sit in chairs forming a triangle.

"What can I do for you?" Penny asked.

"Well, my boyfriend Steve and I are having some problems. We're hoping that you can help." She glanced over at Steve who was reading something on his cellphone.

"Tell me more," Penny asked.

"I don't feel … respected. I also don't feel loved—he's not very affectionate towards me, and I feel that he doesn't pay any attention to me."

Penny glanced at Steve, who was putting his cellphone in his pocket. "And how do you feel, Steve?" she asked.

"Well, as you can see, I run a dairy farm. I don't have a lot of free time on my hands. I work seven days a week, and I'm pretty much on call 24 hours a day. So I'm sorry that she feels I don't give her attention, I just don't have a lot of time to give."

Penny shifted her eyes to Noel. "What would you like from Steve?"

"I am not asking him to give up his farm. I love the farm too. But all we talk about is the farm. We never talk about my dreams and my ambitions. It's like he doesn't care about anything else."

"I have a responsibility to the farm, Noel. It comes first."

"And Kenny comes second. Which leaves me … last. I always thought your boyfriend or girlfriend was supposed to come first," she snapped back.

"Before we get into that," Penny interrupted. "What about the other two things you mentioned? Why don't you feel respected?"

"Well, if you put in a full day cleaning your boyfriend's house and then he turned around and called you a fucking bitch, would you feel respected?"

"I already explained why I said that and I already apologized. It was one time!" Steve retaliated.

"What about the affection part?" Penny asked.

"He never kisses me. He never hugs me. He never holds my hand. But I'll tell you what he does plenty of with me and that's sex. To me, that's not affection. There is no emotion in it."

Penny's eyebrows lifted, then she glanced at Steve.

"If you want the answer to that, then you'd have to go back to my childhood. Let me tell you all about that."

And for 30 minutes, Noel had to listen while Steve monopolized the hour-long session, describing in great detail all about growing up in a house devoid of any affection. His father was an alcoholic and his mother was an enabler. He was expected to work as a young boy at various tasks and that was why the outside world couldn't hold a candle to him as far as work ethic is concerned. He had conflict with his father, which prompted him to get kicked out of the house by the time he was 17 years old. He spent his senior year of high school living in an apartment by himself. His older sister was a drug user and his little sister was spoiled rotten. When he was finished, he had painted a picture of a sorrowful young boy who grew up hardened and untrusting of anyone around him.

"Well, that's all the time we have for today," Penny announced. "Same time next week?"

"Yes," Noel mumbled, as she fished out a twenty from her wallet. She handed it to Penny and walked out the door. Steve trailed behind her, smiling.

The following week, Penny began the conversation by turning to Noel and asking her to describe her childhood. Noel told her about her immigrant parents and how they worked very hard and instilled a robust work ethic in their children. She went on to explain that she and her two brothers lived a pretty happy life. Steve interjected.

"Now see, she says she was happy, but I really think a lot of her problems came from her mother."

Noel snapped her head at Steve.

"What do you mean by that, Steve?" Penny asked.

"I mean that her father is very quiet, and her older brother is okay, but her mother is overbearing. When I first met Noel, she wasn't even speaking to her mother. There is definitely a lot of friction there, and I think Noel is desperately trying to break away from her mother. But her mother meddles in her business and screws her all up in the head."

Noel furrowed her brows. What the hell was he talking about? Why were they discussing her mother anyway? This wasn't even about her!

"Hmmm, is this true, Noel?"

"Well, my mother is very protective of her children. But I think we're getting off topic here."

"See? This is what Noel does. When she doesn't want to talk about something, she'll change the conversation. How can we ever get to the bottom of things if she is not willing to discuss this?" Steve added.

"This is not about my mother! This is about you and me! Why don't we talk about that!"

"Okay, hold on, hold on," Penny interrupted. "Noel, breathe, please. Count to 10 and just breathe."

Noel complied and began to cool off.

"You can obviously see why this is a touchy subject," Steve stated. "This is why we're in a mess. I firmly believe that if she could rise above her mother and not let her control Noel so much that we would be in a better relationship. I'm willing to trust her, but she has to show me that she's on my side."

Noel suddenly felt like she was Luke Skywalker being called to the dark side by Darth Vader. Just like Luke wanted to believe in the good of his father, Noel wanted to do the same of Steve. But did that really make her mother Emperor Palpatine?

■ ■ ■

For the next couple of months, Noel and Steve continued to attend their therapy sessions. And each time they ended, Noel left frustrated. She continued to appeal for help, while Steve continued to deflect all of her requests and place the blame squarely on the shoulders of her mother. It was maddening! One time, Penny asked Steve if he could give Noel more respect, affection and attention. "I will try," he said, and then continued to dive into Noel's head to point out all of her shortcomings.

At the final therapy session, Noel walked out saying, "I'm all done going there."

Steve simply chuckled behind her and said, "I knew it."

Noel spun around and stared at him. "What do you mean by that?"

"I saw the same thing happen with Kally. The minute the therapist tells you something you don't want to hear, that's the end of therapy."

Noel saw red. "It has nothing to do with that! For the entire two months, all you two have talked about is my mother and my issues. Never once did we discuss your issues and the real reason why we even went!"

"That's because I'm not the one with the issues," Steve said. "I've been trying to tell you this but you are so stubborn you don't wanna listen. Your mother really screwed you up. She did such a good job at it that you have no idea how screwed up you really are. We were trying to help you in there, but you just didn't want to hear it."

"I'm not Kally! I have three college degrees, a good job, and I own my own home!"

"But who helped you get all of those things?" he purred. "You didn't get them all by yourself, did you?"

"No, of course not!"

"Did you ever think that getting all those college degrees was just so your mom could go bragging to all her friends about her educated daughter? And that house? It was just so your parents could keep you confined in your little glass box. They never wanted you to find someone. They were perfectly happy with you being all alone."

Noel didn't know what to think. Why was he saying all of this? None of it made any sense. Parents not wanting their daughter to ever find someone? That's absurd. But they did help her with all of it. Her mother had convinced her to move forward with her education when she wanted to drop out. Was he right? Was this all part of her plan? Noel didn't know anymore. All she knew was that she was exhausted and wanted to stop talking about all of it. It was close to Christmas anyway. She wanted to enjoy the holidays, not avoid them. But somehow, all the Christmas joy seemed to have disappeared that year.

Gaslighting—at its finest.

■ ■ ■

Over the next three years, things did not improve much. Noel began to have problems with Kenny as well. She couldn't blame him, really. He was a little boy who had a controlling father and a mother who was barely in the picture. Noel tried to help raise Kenny using her views and beliefs of a strong respect for authority while still having a fun childhood. She created the "Fun Friday nights," where the three of them participated in kid-like events such as roller skating, bowling, and watching movies. When Kenny would act out in school, Noel threatened to take away the Friday nights as punishment. But Steve wouldn't hear of it. Thus, Kenny got away with being disrespectful in school with no consequences at all.

In addition, there was no talk about a future between them. They still resided in their separate homes and the lack of attention and affection continued. Noel felt like she was at a standstill. She needed something more. She was slowly ebbing away into depression. She didn't want to involve her friends and family so she decided to find a new therapist. Her name was Barbara Zane, and Noel liked her the moment she saw her. She was tall, thin, and had a pretty smile, and when she spoke to Noel, she oozed strength and self-worth. After the first session, Noel realized that her relationship with Steve was pretty much over. She went to his house with a heavy heart, that Friday night, and sat at the kitchen table and told him.

"I'm leaving you," she said quietly.

"Why?" he asked.

"I can't do this anymore. You're mean to me, you don't want to listen to anything I say, and all you do is complain about the things I do wrong. I'm a good person, in case you don't know. I've managed to keep my job for the past 13 years and I own my own home. I'm pretty well liked by everyone and yet, you don't see any of that," she stated, while tears formed in her eyes.

"I know I'm hard on you. It's because I'm hard on everyone."

"I'm not one of your farmhands!" she blurted out. "And I don't want to be treated like one anymore."

There was a moment of silence, then Steve spoke.

"Please don't do this," he choked out. "We can talk about it."

Her heart shattered into a million pieces. Not only was she broken, but now she felt the guilt of breaking another human being as well. But despite all that, she found the courage to stand up and push in her chair.

"Goodbye, Steve." Then she walked out the door.

The weekend was absolutely miserable. She couldn't stop the tears from flowing. She tried to distract herself by visiting various family members, but it didn't help. Her five-year-old nephew even sat next to her on the couch and offered to marry her in Steve's place. She smiled sadly at him, but it still couldn't quell the pain. Her mother was relieved. She couldn't stand Steve. She didn't like the way he treated her daughter—like she was his chattel. She wanted so much better for Noel.

Noel spent the weekend thinking about the ultimate reason for the breakup—it was the fact that the relationship was going nowhere. She was 36 years old and her friends around her were already married with multiple children. What did she have? A boyfriend who was fine with the way things were. Her age was worrisome. Who would want such an old lady? And where would she find someone closer to her age who wasn't already married? Surely a man for her did not exist. She should have settled for Steve, and those were exactly the thoughts that prompted her to pick up the phone when he called.

"Noel, just hear me out, okay?" he began.

"Yes?" she replied.

"What if we renovate this house to your liking? We'll get an engineer to draw up some plans and we'll do this together? I can't live at your house because I need to be on the farm, but we can sell your house and live here once this house is completed."

"What else?" she asked.

"I'll agree to marry you."

"What else?"

"And we can have a kid. But just one, okay?"

Noel searched her heart. Was this what she really wanted? Marriage, a kid, and a house with a white picket fence? It was pretty much all she ever wanted. But was he the right man for this dream? What the hell. How bad could it be? "Fine," she answered.

They agreed to marry in three months, on February 12. If they were going to spend money on renovating a house, there was no need to spend money on a glorified party. When Noel told her parents the news, her mother was furious. She wanted so much better for her daughter and she tried like hell to convince her otherwise. But Noel stuck to her guns and proceeded with the wedding plans anyway. She paid for pretty much everything—the suits that both Steve and Kenny would wear, the marriage license, the white gold wedding bands (she refused to wear a diamond ring), and the flaming red wedding dress (who was she kidding at 36 years old) in which she paid ninety dollars for. The entire gig cost about $2,000.

Then tragedy struck. A month before the wedding, Steve collapsed at a pizza restaurant. After rushing him to the hospital, Noel was told that Steve needed to have a pacemaker. His nerve endings were not functioning properly. She stayed with him at the hospital, and returned to the farm at night to make sure it was running properly. She also made sure that Kenny was okay.

They performed the surgery a couple of days later and released him within the week. But Steve was not okay. He complained of chest pain and insisted that something was wrong. Noel brought him back to the hospital again where the doctors performed multiple tests. They were told that the pain was normal and that he should just rest. One night, Steve was in severe pain, but he refused to go to the hospital. Noel was exhausted and couldn't keep her eyes open. She just needed to lay down for two hours, and then she'd be fine. When she woke up, Steve was barely functioning. She drove him to the emergency room and insisted that something be done. The doctors discovered that the pacemaker was installed wrong and Steve had to be operated on again. They transported him to Hartford General and performed the operation. Noel waited for hours in the waiting room. She was relieved when he woke up with no pain in his chest.

For the next few days, Noel sat by Steve's side in the hospital room. The stress of the events were beginning to take a toll on her. Her boss was furious at her for taking off so many days from work. She was constantly running back and forth between his house, her house and the hospital. She wasn't sure what to do about the wedding, which was only weeks away. And Steve, loud and thunderous Steve with the strength of a bull, seemed so small lying in the hospital bed, mostly sleeping throughout the day. On one such visit, she broke down and sobbed long and hard by his bedside. Steve was oblivious to her despair, but the Spanish lady visiting in the next room heard her. She came over and smoothed back Noel's hair while she let it all out. When she was done, Steve had opened his eyes and the Spanish lady walked out.

"Why are you crying?" he whispered.

"I'm so terribly sorry," she sniffled.

"For what?" he asked.

"For all that you're going through. You should have been home by now, most likely back on your feet. This is awful."

He stared at her and looked away. "Well, I'm glad you're crying."

"What?" she frowned.

He turned back to her. "This was awful and it happened to me! If you had paid more attention to me, it might not have happened."

"Wait, what?" she recoiled. "I've been doing nothing BUT paying attention to you."

"Really? I've woken up plenty of times without you here. I'm the one that's scared, and I'm the one with a hole in my chest! Try seeing if you'd be in good spirits if that happened to you."

"I've been here as much as I could. But I've had to run back and forth to the farm to make sure everything was running smoothly!"

"The farm doesn't need you! I do. And I expect more from the woman I'm about to marry."

That shut her up. Noel had no words to retaliate with. All of a sudden, she felt selfish. He was absolutely right. She should have been by his side the entire time. Other people did it. They camped out all day long in their loved one's room and didn't move at all. And God knows what emotional toll it took on Steve, almost being at death's door. Surely she should be more sympathetic to him. She wasn't the one lying in that hospital bed. He was.

"You're right. I'm sorry," she whispered. "I'll try harder."

A few days later, Steve was released from the hospital and feeling much better. Noel carried on with the wedding plans and life went back to normal, somewhat. Steve was not back at work yet, but at least he was taking care of business from his phone.

One Friday evening, Noel was watching a movie in his living room. It was a horror movie and the scene involved a girl getting raped. For some reason, Noel couldn't handle it. She had never been raped before, but she couldn't watch a scene with a man overpowering a woman. It disturbed her badly. She jumped up and shut off the TV. Steve stared at her.

"What's wrong?"

"I can't watch that," she replied.

"Why not?"

Her face jerked to his. "What? The girl was getting raped!"

"She probably deserved it," he replied.

Noel was beyond appalled. "No woman ever deserves to be raped!" she seethed.

"All right, calm down," Steve laughed. "Let's talk about more important things, shall we?"

"Yes, let's," she responded.

Steve walked into the kitchen and returned with a very thick document. "So I went to my lawyer today and he suggested that I have this written up," he said as he handed her the papers.

Noel took one look at the title and her heart fell. *Prenuptial Agreement.* She looked up at him.

"Why do you want me to sign this?" she whispered.

"So nothing will ever happen to the farm. I'm basically taking it out of the equation so it will go on forever."

"I would never do anything to your farm. It's not mine."

"I know that. But I've been around a long time to see people do some crazy things. You may say that now, but you might change your mind if you were seriously pissed at me."

"But what you're saying is that you don't trust me. And if you don't trust me, how could you marry me?"

"I do trust you. But you have to remember that this farm has been in my family for generations. I never want it to be anyone else's but mine."

"But I'm not that kind of person. Surely you should know that about me."

"Again, I understand what you're saying, but I know how people can change if they get angry enough. I've seen so many people lose everything in a divorce. It happens."

"So you're assuming we will divorce?"

"No," Steve sighed, getting irritated. "I just think it's a smart thing to do. That way you and I can just focus on getting married and renovating this house."

"What if I don't sign this?"

"Then we don't get married."

"You would do that?" she replied, aghast.

"Yes," he stared at her coldly.

"I guess I'll have to think about it," she said, flipping through the pages.

"YOU'RE A SELFISH BITCH!" he shot up from the couch and stormed into the kitchen.

These were words that she had heard from his lips many times before. But the intense amount of anger attached to them was undaunting. She couldn't believe he was asking this of her. She would never be that kind of person. But did she know that for sure? This was his farm, she should understand that. Maybe she was being unreasonable again. She had a habit of doing that, according to Steve. Woodenly, she got up from the couch and walked into the kitchen. He was sitting at the kitchen table, drinking a beer. He never drank beer. Her words and actions most likely drove him to do that. She placed the document in front of him.

"I'll sign it," she said.

■ ■ ■

On the day of their wedding, Steve spent the day working on the farm. Noel took the day off of work and went and got her hair done. The stylist was running late so she spent almost 30 minutes in the waiting room. A good looking man in his 40s struck up a conversation with her. Noel announced that it was her wedding day and the man congratulated her. Then he went on to describe his views of marriage and how the last 25 years of his life had been the greatest ever. He talked about his children and how his wife looks just as beautiful today as the day he married her. No doubt, from the way he spoke with the twinkle in his eye, the man was clearly still in love, after all those years. Noel looked away. Steve never spoke about her that way and she didn't think he ever would. She wondered if they would even make it to twenty-five years of marriage.

When she left the salon, she went back to her house where her sister-in-law was waiting for her. It was just the two of them. They both changed into their dresses and got ready. Noel looked around. Was this how it was supposed to go? Where was all the cackling from her girlfriends, and her mom giving her advice on marriage? Where was the champagne bottle being passed around, and swooning every time her future husband's name was mentioned. More importantly, where was Noel's smile?

An hour later, she sat in the back of her parents' car staring at the church. Her father had already gone inside to take his place at the doorway. Her mother turned around to look at her from the front seat.

"Say the word, and I'll put this car in drive and keep going," she said softly.

Noel glanced at her, then looked at the church again.

"No, Mom. I promised to marry him. I'm going to go through with it," she sighed.

"Why? Why are you doing this?"

"Because I gave my word."

And with that, she opened the door and walked to the front door of the church. She observed the small group sitting down in the pews. She saw Steve pacing in front of the altar. She saw her brother and her sister-in-law standing near each other in the front, laughing at some funny comment they were sharing. She closed her eyes, to try and regain control of her insides screaming at her. *THIS IS WRONG! DON'T DO THIS! WALK AWAY NOW!* But she didn't have the courage. How could she disappoint all those people in front of her? She wasn't that kind of person. She made a promise—and she would keep it. No matter what. She reached for her father's arm and began her long trek down the aisle.

The reception took place at the local restaurant in town. They had reserved the room set aside for small parties. Putting on her party face, Noel chatted with her family members, cut the cake, and drank one alcoholic beverage after another. By the time her family left, she was seeing double. But she wasn't done yet. She wanted to end the evening at the bar, so she and Steve, and their close friends John and Felicia walked over to find a couple of stools. The place was packed and there were only two stools available, so Felicia and Noel sat down while the boys hung out near the wall.

"Ah, isn't this great?" Felicia asked, after receiving a couple of Long Island iced teas from the bartender.

"Yah, it's great," Noel said, as she proceeded to slurp down half of the drink.

"Woah, girl. You better slow down! Or you'll end up spending your wedding night in the bathroom."

Noel looked at her friend hard. "And that would be a bad thing?"

"But then you can't… you know," Felicia giggled.

"I've already seen it," she slurped again. "Not a big deal."

Both women erupted in laughter, then drank some more.

"You know what, Felicia?" Noel turned to her and said. "You're a really good friend."

Felicia smiled. "Aww, girl. I love you too."

Something primal moved inside of Noel at that moment. She had just married a man she wasn't sure she loved anymore and she was three sheets soaked. Suddenly, she caught a glimpse of herself when she was in her twenties—carefree, head held high, full of dreams, and crazy as all hell. She longed to see that girl again. She longed to be that girl again. Not the one she was now—a beaten animal with a brand-new, thicker chain around her neck. She couldn't bear the look of sadness in her own eyes. Like a volcano erupting, she leaned over to Felicia.

"I'm going to kiss you right now, okay?" she said, staring her down.

Felicia's head whipped over to her and she returned her stare. "Bring it."

In the next instant, Noel brought her lips onto Felicia's. At first, it was a simple kiss you'd give your sister. But then Noel moved her tongue into her mouth and really tasted her. She had never kissed a girl before, nor did she ever have the desire to. But this wasn't about being attracted to the same sex. This was about finding something to get rid of the pain she had in her heart. The pain of binding herself to a man she didn't fully trust. It was also about tapping into her badass. Did that girl still live inside of her? Apparently she did.

Noel broke off the kiss and smiled at her. Felicia smiled back.

"What the hell are you guys doing?" Steve demanded.

Noel gulped down the last of her drink and eyed him.

"I kissed a girl."

Steve stared at her, dumbfounded.

"Yah, Steve," Felicia giggled. "You wanna go in the bathroom with me and take a crack at it too?"

"Oh, Jesus," John sighed. "She's drunk." He moved over to his wife, and took her hand. "I better take her home. I'm sure we won't make it past the parking lot before she pukes all over the side of the car."

"We'll follow you out," Noel giggled. She began to follow them out when Steve grabbed her arm.

"What was that all about?" he asked.

"Aww, c'mon, babe," she purred. "Two girls kissing? Isn't that what every man dreams about? I just gave you a wedding present."

Steve stared after her, open mouthed. Nothing else was said as they left the bar. Noel had proved her point—she still had fire. But she also knew that Steve didn't like her fire, and he would do everything in his power to extinguish her flames.

■ ■ ■

Two weeks later, Noel discovered she was pregnant. She was overjoyed! She had always wanted a baby. She quickly called up Steve to tell him the news.

"I'm pregnant!" she announced.

"Oh, shit," he replied.

"Uh... that wasn't the response I was going for."

"We're beginning a major house renovation, Noel! This is going to cause me some serious stress!"

"Well, I didn't plan this!"

"You shouldn't have thrown away your birth control pills in December. That was too early."

"How the hell was I supposed to know I was so fertile? Usually it takes months after the pills are gone."

"Well, this is what you wanted. You're going to have to take care of it."

"You mean you're not going to help me at all?"

"Who's going to renovate the house? I'm taking care of a farm at the same time. Where's my help?" he shouted through the phone.

Noel didn't say a word. Was she being unrealistic again? She knew he didn't want any more kids—this was all her. But would he even love this baby? It didn't matter, because she wanted this baby. If it was only the two of them in this world, that would be okay with her. She vowed in that moment to be the best mother possible. "Don't worry. I'll take care of this baby all by myself," she told him.

Noel's pregnancy was easy. She had no nausea and she was moving around like usual in her first trimester. She attended all the doctor's visits by herself, since Steve wasn't interested in joining her. In the second trimester, the house was completely gutted and being worked on full time. Steve convinced Noel to buy a 32-foot camper using her money, and they moved into it while the house was being worked on. Noel's brother offered to buy her house to Noel's delight. No price tag could be put on having family nearby, so Noel gave him a very reasonable price for the house. When Steve found out, he was furious. He did not agree with the price and wanted her to ask for more money. Noel refused. No matter what temper tantrums Steve threw, she would not budge. This was her beloved house and he couldn't tell her what to do with it.

"You're a fucking loser!" he spat out at her.

"It's my house! And it's my brother! Just because you don't care about your family, doesn't mean I don't!"

"You're putting us in a very tough spot. Now we don't have enough money to pay for this one! If I had known this, I would have never begun the renovations!"

"I didn't ask you for all the upgrades! Lifetime shingles and central air? That wasn't part of the original deal! You're the one who added all these costs!"

"You lied to me! This is why I knew all along you can't be trusted. You never even included me in the discussions about selling your house to your brother!"

"That's right! Because I knew you would give me the bullshit you're giving me now. I will never inflate a price on a house that isn't justified, just so it can make your life easier. I got quotes from two real estate agents on the value of that house. And I trust THEM over you!"

Steve shook his head and looked away. "I can't believe we're starting our marriage this way. You deceived me. You're just like your mother—

manipulative. This marriage doesn't stand a chance. You're not like my sister and her husband. They're a real team. They do everything together and there are no secrets between them." He shifted his gaze to her and bore his eyes into her skull. "We're not a team at all. I'm not sure if this marriage will survive."

Noel was jolted. What was he saying? That the cause for the problems in their marriage were completely her fault? She should have at least talked to him about her thought process with selling her house—he could have disagreed with her. But Noel knew how he operated. He wouldn't be satisfied with simply disagreeing with her. He would have manipulated her in such a way that she would end up losing the sale to her brother. She had already put a strain on her relationship with her parents, she couldn't do that to her brother as well. She put her head down.

"I'm sorry," she said. "I'll try harder."

"You better believe you'll try harder. We're going to have to save some costs so you're going to have to pitch in. Good thing your summer vacation is coming soon because you'll be working here!"

"What am I going to do?"

"We'll have to rip up the old wooden floors, and then you'll have to paint all the exterior doors. There are seven of them. Then you'll have to scrape the compound off the floor in the office. They're coming to lay those floors soon so you'll need to move fast."

"But I'm pregnant. Is all that safe for me to do?"

"I don't give a rat's ass! You owe me big time! You wanna be a team player? This is your chance to prove it!" and he stormed away.

True to her word, Noel performed all the tasks he requested and then some. She was on her feet all day long during that long, hot summer. If she wasn't physically working on the house, she was driving around the state of Connecticut gathering quotes or picking up materials. She was exhausted at the end of each day. Steve ignored the fact that she was pregnant. He never offered to talk to the baby or help her when she was in discomfort. He also didn't show her any affection whatsoever, telling her that pregnant women were disgusting. They were fat and swollen and super lazy.

One day she felt shooting pains in her belly because she had carried a 50-pound grain bag. She had asked Steve to help her, but he refused, because he had to finish his conversation with the contractor. When she complained to him, he told her to go soak in a bath. Noel complained that the house was gutted, and there was no bathtub. He instructed her to drive herself to her old house and take advantage of it before it was sold to her brother. As Noel hobbled away, she could hear the two men laughing about something stupid. They were not worried in the least about her condition. As she sat in the tub waiting for the pain to subside, she stared at the phone and wondered when Steve would check in with her to see if she was alright. But he never did. It was evident that he didn't care about her or the baby. She let the tears flow freely down her face. She had never been more miserable in her life. Noel fell further and further into depression.

At the beginning of her third trimester, Noel had conflict at work. Her boss, a ginormous loose cannon, attacked her verbally, and promised to terminate her if she didn't comply with his demands. Noel was very stressed and turned to Steve for comfort.

"You probably did something wrong," he said.

"No, I did not!" she seethed. "He's making false accusations against me! He's lying!"

"Listen, I'm a boss myself so I know how ridiculous employees can get. You obviously did something wrong."

"You're taking his side over your own wife's? Without even knowing the situation?" she shot back.

"I'm just putting myself in his shoes."

"What if the stress of the situation causes me to lose my baby? Will you still be on his side?"

"Now you're getting dramatic. You're upset. It doesn't help that you're pregnant—your emotions are everywhere. Just relax."

Noel never felt so alone in her entire life. The fire raged inside of her. She knew she wouldn't get any help from this buffoon in front of her so she had to think clearly. Every boss had a boss, so she would call the Superintendent in the morning and set up an appointment. Noel would take care of this all by herself.

"Hey, I'm going over Randy's house for a while," Steve said. "Don't wait up—I'll be there for a while. He got a new pair of oxen."

"Of course. Oxen are way more important than your wife," she shot back.

Steve's nostrils flared. "Like I said," he said through clenched teeth. "Don't wait up."

■ ■ ■

On the first day of school, Noel was on her feet all day and it was blazing hot outside. She had a huge belly and her ankles began to swell. Her horrible boss was keeping his distance, thankfully. The chat the Superintendent had with him must have done the trick. To be on the safe side, Noel put in for a transfer, but at the moment, nothing was available. She had to stick it out for the year. When she went home that evening, she did her usual round of chores which included making dinner, feeding the animals and cleaning up after everyone. She then walked over to the house, almost completely renovated, and washed the brand-new wooden floors. Steve was going to begin moving furniture the next day so she wanted the floors to be spotless. Steve was already asleep when she entered the camper that evening. She could barely stand up. She crawled onto the small couch in the kitchen area and fell asleep. An hour later, she awoke to the feeling of wetness rushing down her legs. She looked down and noticed a giant wet spot seeping into the couch. *Holy shit, my bladder stopped working. I can't stop peeing!* She waited a few seconds for the rush of fluid to stop, but it didn't. She reached down, touched the liquid, and brought it close to her nose. *Oh my God, this isn't urine! My water broke!*

"STEVE! STEVE!" she shouted.

For the next couple of hours, Noel panicked. She had called her sister-in-law to give her a ride to the hospital since Steve could not leave Kenny by himself. She wore a towel like a diaper to catch all the escaped fluids while her sister in law put the pedal to the metal. Once inside, the doctor examined her. He told her that she was seven weeks early and the baby would be premature. He told her she would have to be bedridden in the hospital for the next two weeks. They immediately transferred her to a larger hospital in Farmington, where there was a NICU for babies. Noel was terrified of losing her baby, and the stress of it caused her heart to beat out of control. Once they gave her medication for the erratic heart beats, her contractions began, and with that, there was no stopping her little baby from making his entrance.

For four hours, she pushed. But the baby was too large so he got stuck in the pelvic region. They called for an emergency C-section but it took a while for the anesthesiologist to arrive. As they waited, the baby's heartbeat began to drop. Steve crumbled up on the floor next to her. Witnessing the horror of the event before him rendered him immobile. Noel cried. Her precious little child was dying. She closed her eyes, and the world went black.

When she awoke, her mother's face was the first thing she saw.

"Gil is alive!" she beamed.

"What?" Noel whispered.

"He's a fighter, Noel! He looks all beat up from being stuck so long, but he's doing fine."

"Where is he?"

"He's in the NICU. They're waiting for you to wake up so you can see him."

Noel sat back and closed her eyes. At first, small tears formed in her eyes and she allowed them to cascade down her face. But then she thought about all she had endured in the past year and she sobbed uncontrollably. She allowed all the pain and turmoil to exit her body with each pitiful wail. Her boss, the house, her uncaring husband, being pregnant and utterly alone, the sale of her house, her job, and nearly losing her baby—all of it was too much to bear, so she cried out in despair while her mother stroked her hair and tried to comfort her with words.

Three long weeks, Noel went back and forth to the hospital where Gil lay. She had named him that because his name meant "happiness." Steve hated that name. Gil was doing well—getting bigger and holding his own heat. She spent entire days at the hospital and held him all day long. At night, she sadly went home, where she distracted herself by unpacking more boxes. They were living in the new house now, and she was determined to make it spotless before her baby came home. But the pain of being without Gil was too much to bear. Mothers should never be separated from their babies—it's unnatural.

One evening, she was organizing the living room when a wave of anguish washed over her and she began to sob. Steve came into the room.

"What happened?"

Noel collapsed down to her knees. "I miss my baby."

"Jesus, Noel, I thought someone was dying!" He made no moves to get closer to her or comfort her. He just stood there watching her, for several moments.

Suddenly, Steve's mother entered the room. She stopped for a visit and heard Noel crying from the driveway.

"What is happening here?" she said, and immediately placed her hands on Noel's shoulders.

"She's overemotional again," Steve grumbled.

His mother straightened up and glared at him.

"No, she is not! She misses her child. Your child, I might add! Show her more respect!" she shot at him.

Steve snorted and walked out of the room. Her mother-in-law continued to comfort her until Noel stopped crying. Then she thanked her, and continued organizing the room.

After 23 days, Gil was released from the hospital. It was the happiest day of Noel's life. She spent the entire day showing him all the rooms in the house, in between his naps, of course. She pumped her milk when he was sleeping and froze it for later use. Steve continued to ignore them both. He did not offer to get up for nighttime feedings, nor did he help change diapers. He ignored them both, and spent late hours in the barn. He only came inside to eat dinner, sleep, and grab money from the cupboard. He gave his full attention to Kenny during dinner, and never once looked at Gil. This infuriated Noel, and her hatred of him grew deeper by the day.

When Gil was 9 months old, Noel planned to take him to Michigan to visit her younger brother. Steve refused to go because the farm came first. Noel was relieved. She didn't want him to ruin her good time. It was one of the happiest memories with Gil. He slept with her every night, and in the morning, they would take long walks with the stroller into town. They ate ice cream, watched her brother race cars, and hung out at the beach. It was amazing! One night when she was singing him to sleep, she looked at his beautiful, peaceful face and immediately thought about Kenny. Kenny did not have a tight relationship with his mother, and he looked miserable every time she came to pick him up. The boy had no joy in his life. Noel wondered if he felt alone or abandoned. She didn't want the same fate for Gil. The age difference between Kenny and Gil was ten years. Kenny would not be around to protect Gil. He needed someone closer to his age. Noel was sure that her marriage to Steve would not survive. She didn't know exactly when it would fall apart, but she was sure it would.

When they returned from Michigan, she knew she was ovulating. Steve had barely touched her for months, so she knew this was her only chance. She seduced him easily, and all it took was his 30-second performance to do the job. She announced she was pregnant in early August. Steve was beyond furious when she told him. He refused to speak to her for two full weeks. Thankfully, it was the end of summer vacation when she told him. She tried to focus her attention on starting a new school year and Gil turning one year old. But the black hole of sadness that enveloped her was unreal. She wished for a different life.

Around her tenth week, Noel felt wetness on her underwear. When she looked down, she was horrified to see a giant blood stain on her panties. Panicked, she convinced Steve to drive her to the hospital. The emergency room doctor examined her and explained to her that she was having a partial miscarriage—meaning that the baby was still alive, but barely holding on. Noel leaned back against the hospital bed and closed her eyes. Tears cascaded down her face, as she gently rubbed her belly.

"I told you," Steve spoke.

Noel snapped her eyes open and stared at him. "What?"

"Women your age should not be having babies. You're too old."

Anger flared up inside of her. If ever she wanted to punch someone until their face was unrecognizable, this was the moment!

"Get out of this room right now," she seethed.

He didn't move.

"GET OUT!!" she bellowed.

The doctor rushed in to see what was the matter.

"She's out of control," Steve explained. "Do you have any sedatives you can give her?"

"I'm not taking any medication!" Noel screamed. "When can I get out of here?"

"Uh, I can put the paperwork through right now," the doctor replied.

"Good. Make it as quick as possible, and hand me my cellphone while you're at it, please."

The doctor did as instructed and Noel dialed up her mother.

"Mom? Do you mind if Gil and I come and stay with you over the weekend? I think my baby is dying and I need some help."

Noel spent the weekend at her parents' house. She knew full well that Steve would not assist her at all in her delicate condition. She spent a great deal of time laying down in her old bedroom. If there was any hope of saving her baby, she was going to try like hell. Her parents entertained Gil so that she could rest. Finally, Monday came and Steve came to pick them up. They barely spoke in the car on the ride back to the farm. Once she got home, she fed Gil, then packed him up to go to the OBGYN. Steve didn't offer to watch Gil and she didn't care to ask him. She was used to taking him everywhere with her anyway.

"Is he gone?" Noel asked, choking down the lump in her throat.

"Is who gone?" asked the doctor.

"My baby."

"No," she replied, confused. "Why would you think that?"

Noel blinked. "But the emergency room doctor told me I was having a partial miscarriage."

"No, you weren't!" the doctor chuckled. "From what I can tell, your placenta was starting to detach. It's pretty common in women your age. But your baby is just fine."

"Oh my God," she smiled and closed her eyes. "I thought he was dying."

"Not at all!" the doctor replied. "But to be on the safe side, I'd like you to start progesterone shots on a weekly basis. They will fortify your amniotic sac. Let's try and avoid having another premature birth, shall we?"

"Yes! Let's!"

■ ■ ■

In the months that followed, Noel moved through life more at ease. She focused on her job and Gil, and felt confident that her baby would survive. After all, there were no houses to renovate or horrible bosses to fight with. The only thing she had to avoid was her wretched husband, but since he spent so much time in the barn, it was easy to do. One night, around her 31st week of pregnancy, Steve woke her up in the middle of the night.

"The crop reports were due today," he said.

"So?"

"So they weren't done!"

"And you woke me up to tell me that?"

"Yes! This is no joke! If those reports aren't done, I could lose valuable funding for my farm!"

"It's your farm. You're the one that needs to handle that!"

"You've always helped me with them!"

"Listen, I've got a little bit more on my mind these days, if you haven't noticed. I don't know what dates your reports are due unless you tell me."

"Well, you should know them. That's what would make you a team player. You never engage with the farm. Have you ever wondered why I never come inside the house anymore?"

"Yes."

"It's because I'm sick of your bullshit. All you do is complain and whine about things. I'm busting my ass to make sure that this family is provided for, but that's not good enough for you."

"That is not true! You do NOTHING to be a part of this family. The only person you talk to is Kenny. You ignore Gil and I. Is this how you think a father is supposed to act with his children? By playing favorites?"

"I am not playing favorites. I just don't like you. And since Gil is always with you, I avoid you both. If you would just help me out more often, I would probably change my attitude."

Noel was too angry to argue with him at this time. The man was never satisfied with anything she did. She cleaned the house, left him a warm dinner every night, and took care of his child, while working a full-time job! Even if she milked cows in the morning, he still wouldn't be satisfied. Her heart began to beat uncontrollably again. She spent the rest of the night breathing evenly, just to try and make her blood pressure simmer down. She was worried about her baby. Steve was obviously not concerned. Within minutes of issuing his verbal beating, he was snoring loudly next to her.

Later that morning, at work, Noel did not feel any better. Her chest hurt badly and she honestly thought she was getting ready to have a heart attack. In addition, there was light moisture on her underwear. She panicked, as it was exactly the same week that her water broke with Gil. She alerted her principal, who begged her to call for an ambulance. Noel stubbornly refused, insisting on driving herself to the doctors that knew her well. If she was going to deliver, it was going to be in a familiar place. She quickly called Steve to let him know and made sure to tell him that if anything happened to this baby, it would be entirely his fault and that he would be subjected to her wrath.

Once she arrived, the doctors examined her and told her that it was a false alarm. Obviously, she had gotten so worked up from her conversation the previous night that her body had given her nothing more than a fair warning. When they released her, she stormed over to the barn and tracked down her husband. With fire blazing in her eyes, and her body shaking, she got right in his face.

"You EVER wake me up in the middle of the night for your own carelessness and stupidity, I will punch you in the face until you bleed. Do you UNDERSTAND ME?" Then she walked away and heard him chuckling softly behind her.

▰ ▰ ▰

Maverick made his debut entrance into the world on time. He was only ten days early. Noel was as big as a house when her water broke. The doctors moved fast before the contractions set in because Noel wanted a C-section. Shortly after midnight, Maverick came out screaming and blazing mad, his black hair glistening in the LED lights.

"That's my boy," Noel whispered. No doubt, the nine-pound, 4-ounce baby was an Italian beast, who seemed to stare down anyone in his path. She knew he would be a force to be reckoned with.

Noel took care of her baby over the next couple of months. When summer vacation hit, it was just the three of them spending time together—Noel and her two babies. Steve had bought Kenny a pair of oxen that summer, so all of his free time was spent teaching Kenny how to pull. Noel became frustrated with this. Surely there was a way to divide attention evenly amongst all the children. Lots of men did it! Even ones that were just as busy as Steve. But he would not entertain any of her pleadings, convincing her that she was being unfair to Kenny. Obviously, the two babies had someone seeing to their needs, but poor Kenny had no one but his father. She was being ridiculous and unreasonable.

By the fall, Noel began to worry about her children's wellbeing. Any type of communication with Steve ended up in screaming matches, with the kids caught in the crossfire. What kind of an example was she showing them? That this was how a normal family functioned? Full of anger and hate? And what if they carried on like this? Would her boys grow up to be abusive to their wives as well? Would they learn how to lie and manipulate people just like their father? Would they end up in failed marriages as well? *Failed marriage.* The words echoed in her brain.

Noel had finally had enough.

She filed for divorce that fall. At first, Steve didn't understand what prompted her to do that. She explained that they had lost connection, and if he was interested in trying to repair the damage, she was open to the idea of seeking out a counselor. But it would have to be for a minimum of one year. Steve refused. He argued that he wasn't the one with problems. The only reason why they had reached this point was clearly because of her mother. Noel was aghast. She had kept her distance from her parents for the past year, not wanting them to see her in such a low state of mind. But Steve continued to argue that Noel's mother still had influence over her daughter, and that the only way to save the marriage would be for Noel to cut all ties with her. Raging against his absurd request, Noel continued with the proceedings.

Shortly after Christmas, Noel began to doubt her decision. She continued to see her therapist, Barbara Zane. Barbara advised her to slow down—that divorces took months to complete and that oftentimes, women had to live in apartments because the settlements were either too small or delayed. Apartment? Her children didn't deserve an apartment! They deserved a warm home with a big backyard and good children to play with. She began to worry about the effects of her decision. Was she making the right choice? Uncertainty filled her brain, and Steve, being the mastermind at reading people, saw this. He swooped down from his surmountable perch and pinned her with his pitiful stare.

"What do you want?" she asked.

"I'm really worried about you," he replied.

"Why should you care?"

"Believe it or not, I do. I know you're angry with me, but I think you're heading down a bad road right now. I'm afraid of what will happen to the kids."

"The boys will be just fine—as long as they're with their mother," she defended.

"Oh, of course they will. But are you in the right state of mind to take care of them? I feel like you're on the edge of a nervous breakdown. The stress you've had the last couple of months has done this to you. You're barely holding it together."

"It hasn't been easy, that's for sure."

"I just want you to think about it. I just don't want to see anything bad happen to you," he said softly. "If you wanna talk, I'm here."

What the hell is he saying? Is he actually being nice to me? WHY? Does he really care? And why now and not before? Is he changing his ways? Am I making the wrong decision? Is he right? Will I end up hurting the kids? Am I on the brink of a breakdown? Noel couldn't breathe. The weight of the divorce came crashing down on top of her, and she needed to get away. She grabbed her jacket and quickly put it on.

"The kids are taking naps. I need to go for a walk," she said, as she ran out the door. She didn't even wait for him to respond.

≡ ≡ ≡

Noel called off the divorce a few days later. Steve just looked at her, like a card shark that just won a high-stakes poker game. The worst thing Noel had to face was her mother, who cried when she told her. Her mother begged her to reconsider, stating that she was just scared and that things would turn out alright in the end. But Noel refused, telling herself that the boys needed to be on the farm. She would just have to change her ways and become a more subservient wife. Once she did that, her marriage would get better.

Over the next couple of years, Noel focused on her little boys. Gil started preschool and needed speech therapy. Maverick attended an in-home daycare and was making friends. Noel was pleased that her boys were surrounded by kids their ages and developing social skills. She wondered if that's why Kenny was so sad all the time—the only people he ever talked to were grownups. He never did anything fun, and he really didn't have any friends.

One night, Steve and Noel were having a discussion about Kenny while they were lying in bed. Steve was concerned about his deteriorating behavior in school. At first, Noel just listened to him. She knew very well how these conversations ended up. She had learned over the years to keep her opinions to herself when it came to Kenny. Steve was not open to any of her ideas, and he made that perfectly clear to her.

"I just don't think the school is doing a good job with him. He's failing classes, he hates going there, and it just seems like everyone is out to get him," Steve complained.

Yah, well, if you had made more of an effort to get involved with his education, it probably could have gone much better for him. Instead, you've given him the message that school is useless!

"I think I'm going to call up the director lady tomorrow and give her a piece of my mind!"

Good Lord! That's right—pass the blame onto someone else!

"He's probably going to end up like Rudy. He'll be able to do so many cool things with his hands but he won't be able to add 2 plus 2! It just pisses me off how they get away with shit like that!"

That poor kid doesn't stand a chance with a father like you. It's too bad, really.

"You're awfully quiet. You have nothing to say about this?"

"Not really," Noel replied.

"Why not?"

"I just don't think that comparing your kid to the guy with the mental illness down the street is right. Kenny isn't like him."

"You don't know that! He could have a whole lot of problems like him! But I'm the only one seeing it. And I'm the only one that's going to do something about it."

"Well, you're his father. You gotta look out for your kid."

"Oh, I see, so this is my problem?"

"I've been down this road before. You don't want my opinion about things that involve Kenny, so I'll respect that and keep out of it."

"Again, acting like the non-team player. He's got a terrible mother and now he's got an even worse stepmom."

Something snapped inside of Noel. This insult was more than she could take. "First of all, I would take a long, hard look at myself before I go blaming someone else for your shortcomings as a father," she seethed. "After all, you are the main parent. Not his mother, and not me! So if there is something *wrong* with Kenny, the only person you have to blame is yourself!"

Steve bolted out of bed. "GET UP!" he bellowed at her.

Noel lay frozen in bed.

"I SAID GET UP!" he screamed again.

"Stop shouting. You'll wake the boys," she managed to squeak out.

At that point, Steve walked around the bed and came over to her side.

"GET UP!" he yelled again.

When she wouldn't move, he grabbed her arm viciously and yanked her onto the floor. Noel scrambled to her feet and walked quickly out of the room. She knew a confrontation would end badly, so she got as far away from him as possible. She fled down the stairs and reached the phone hanging on the wall. Quickly, she picked it up and managed to dial 911 before Steve came and yanked it out of her hands. With his actions, the entire phone ripped out of the wall.

"Calling the police? I don't think so," he spat at her. "Don't even think of getting back in that bed either!"

Noel was shaking. She had seen Steve mad before, but never to the point where he would lay his hands on her. His eyes were blazing and his nostrils were flaring. Tears sprang up in her eyes, but she refused to let him see the fear in her. She walked into the living room and sat on the couch.

"Good. You can sleep here tonight. I'm not laying in that bed with such a piece of shit!" he said. Then he stomped up the stairs.

Noel remained on the couch for a long time. She couldn't stop shaking, and no matter how many blankets she wrapped around herself, she couldn't get warm. Steve had turned into a demon, of that she was sure. She knew she didn't love him anymore, but she had to stay in this marriage for the kids. She had had many divorced kids in her classes over the years, and she knew that they struggled with insecurity and anger management issues. She couldn't let that happen to her boys.

Suddenly, blue and red lights pulled into her driveway. Steve leaped downstairs and stalked over to her.

"Get rid of them, Noel," he warned. "You better not say a word."

Noel walked over to the door and opened it. Two uniformed men stood on the porch.

"Ma'am?"

"Yes?" she croaked.

"Someone made a call to 911 from this address. Is there a problem?"

Noel stared at the officer. If she said yes, all hell would break loose. But if she said no, then the officers would go away and leave her all alone with her nut job husband. There was no telling what he would do to torture her for the rest of the night. She had no idea what to do. But she did know that if she didn't say anything, he would put his hands on her again. And the next time, things would be worse.

"Yes," she answered.

The next few minutes happened in a blur. The two men pushed their way inside. One steered Noel into a dark corner of the living room and the other grabbed Steve and pushed him farther into the kitchen. Both officers began to interrogate them. Noel spoke in a whisper and told the officer everything that had happened. She could hear Steve in the next room pinning the blame on her. He painted her out to be a crazy psychopath that had gotten under his last nerve. Thankfully, it didn't look like the officer was buying it.

They hauled Steve into the back of the police car with handcuffs on. He wouldn't even look at Noel. The officer warned her that she would have to go to court to iron all of it out, but for tonight she would be safe. She closed the door behind her and took a deep breath. She had no idea what the repercussions of her actions would be, but she was sure of one thing. If he ever put his hands on her again, she wouldn't think twice about calling the police again. No man should ever do that to a woman! Despite the fact that Steve wasn't around that night, she didn't sleep soundly at all. Her mind was too busy racing with all sorts of ideas on how Steve would get back at her.

And he would get his revenge.

≡ ≡ ≡

The incident smoothed over within a week. Steve returned the next day and ignored Noel. He was very subdued when it was necessary to be around her. They both went to court and the case manager advised them both to seek counseling. Since Noel was already seeing Barbara Zane, Steve agreed to go with her a few times, to appease the court. After about three visits, he decided that his time was better suited fixing his farm, rather than fixing his marriage. The crack between Steve and Noel began to widen.

While Steve was paying attention to his farm, Noel decided to focus her attention on her community. She joined the PTA and even ran for the Board of Education. When she got elected, she felt like she was on top of the world. Even though Steve seemed pleased with her success, he cautioned her on spending too much time with the school system and not enough time doing her "duties"' at home. She swore she could balance both. Then came the opportunity Noel had been waiting for all her life—getting her baking license. She joined a commercial kitchen one summer and applied for the license. She was very nervous the day the State came down and observed her. Thankfully, she was awarded the license and made plans to sell her cookies at the town's farmer's market. She couldn't have been more overjoyed! This had been her dream since she moved to town! Again, Steve cautioned her. This time, he had a problem with Noel using the farm for liability insurance. What if someone sued her? They could bankrupt the farm, and this didn't sit well with Steve.

Noel spent the summer selling her cookies and avoiding Steve's worried eyes. She even brought the boys with her to help out. But when the summer was over, Steve had made life miserable for Noel once again. He argued that not only was she ignoring her family and the farm, but she was pocketing all the money from the market for her own needs. After all, wasn't it the farm's insurance that allowed her to become so profitable? And now that the farm was falling into hard times, why wasn't she pulling her weight more? Day after day, and night after night, Steve did what he did best—put an incredible guilt trip on Noel. She couldn't take it anymore, so she took her entire cash box down to the town hall and paid the house taxes with it. Normally, this was something Steve took care of every year. But as a show of good faith, she emptied every last dollar she made, after working so hard all summer long at the farmer's market. Steve didn't even thank her.

When Gil turned 4, Noel had a birthday party for him in the backyard. It was an unusually hot day, and she sat with all the other mothers under the shade tree, watching their children play outside. Suddenly, a red pickup truck pulled into the farm and a young girl got out. She had long brown hair, short shorts, and a tank top.

"Who's that?" asked Tyra, Noel's best friend.

"Oh, that's the girl that comes and gets silage for her cows," Noel replied.

"She comes every day?" Tyra asked.

"Every other. Why?"

Tyra shifted uneasily in her seat. "I don't know. I wouldn't want no young thing tramping around my husband."

Noel giggled. "Please. Steve may be an asshole, but one thing I know he'd never do is cheat on me. He's got a reputation to uphold in this town. Can you imagine if he did? They'd castrate him."

Tyra giggled. "That's for sure. Still, I wouldn't want Cupcake around him too much."

"Who's Cupcake?" Noel laughed.

"That cheap thing hanging onto his every word. Look at them."

Noel turned to look at the girl talking to Steve. She was smiling and tossing back her hair and he was smiling back at her. She shrugged it off. Lots of girls came to the farm. But he was married and that was the end of that. Not even Steve would be that stupid.

As the months progressed, Steve became different. He was more agitated, more argumentative, and more withdrawn from Noel. Noel found herself asking one of the farmhands if they had noticed a change in him as well.

The man chuckled and responded, "No. He's always an asshole."

She went on with her life, hoping that this was nothing but a phase. But the milk prices dropped even further and paying all the expenditures of the farm was becoming even more difficult.

One evening, Steve had the audacity to tell Noel that she should be handing over her teaching paycheck to him every week, so that he could pay for the farm. Flabbergasted, Noel refused, asking him what would she use to pay for groceries and phone bills and everything related to the kids? Steve erupted at her and called her a selfish bitch once again, and stormed out of the house.

Another evening, Steve had a cow slaughtered, and piled all the meat in the freezer, on top of her cookies. Noel was disgusted and moved all the meat into another freezer, so that meat and baked goods would be separated. When Steve found out, he called her a fucking loser in front of all the kids. Noel was so embarrassed that she grabbed her coat and rushed past him, tears blurring her vision. She got in her car and drove as far away as she possibly could. She ended up at her friend Mary's house. Mary was going through a divorce from her husband at the time.

"I just don't understand," Noel sniffled. "What did I ever do to deserve this treatment? Am I that terrible of a human being?"

"Absolutely not!" Mary frowned at her. "This has nothing to do with you. The fault is your husband's. He is a horrible human being and no one in this town likes him. But you knew that all along."

Noel straightened up. "I know. But my poor children don't deserve this. They deserve a better father and a better example of a good marriage."

"Yes, they do," Mary offered. "But are you ready to take that step?"

"I absolutely hate him, Mary."

"As do I of mine. But mine cheated on me. I had no choice but to leave—that is, if I wanted to keep my dignity."

Suddenly, Noel's phone rang. It was Steve.

"Don't answer it," Mary stated sharply. "He's trying to guilt you."

Then a text came through. Maverick had stapled his finger with a stapler. He needed medical attention.

"Doesn't his father birth calves? I'm sure he knows where to find a pair of tweezers," Mary warned. When she saw the nervousness growing in Noel's eyes, she faced her friend. "Listen to me. You will know when the time is right. You're incredibly smart and kind and you will do the right thing in the end. Remember these words—we are led where we need to be at the time we are supposed to be there. Do you understand?"

"Yes," Noel nodded.

"No one can tell you what to do—only you can. And you will know, when the time is right."

Noel left Mary's house shortly after. She returned to her house and found everyone sitting on the couch watching a movie. The boys rushed up to hug her when she entered the house. She smiled at them and examined the Band-Aid on Maverick's finger. She didn't even look at Steve. Even later that night, when he halfway apologized to her, she ignored him. She was too busy thinking about Mary's words. Was this where she was led to be?

The next day, she informed Steve that she needed a separation from him. She was going to begin making arrangements to find somewhere else to live with the boys. Maybe they just needed a break. Steve did not argue with her. Noel found a house for rent down the street. It was old, and not as pretty as her current house, but she could make anything beautiful. Noel had that gift. Later that month, she received a call from Melvin. He was friends with Steve, and oftentimes accompanied him on trips out of state or to the auction to sell animals. He was a jovial man and fun to talk to, so Noel smiled and answered the phone.

"I have to tell you something," Melvin began.

"Oh? What about?"

"Your husband."

Noel swallowed and took a deep breath. "What has he done?"

"As you probably know, I went to the auction with him on Monday."

"Yes, I know."

"We weren't alone," he said.

There was a pause on the phone, as Noel desperately tried to understand the meaning of his statement. If there was another man that tagged along for the ride, Melvin wouldn't have called her. So the mystery passenger must have been a female.

"Who was it?"

"Cupcake."

Alarm shot through Noel, as she heard Melvin recount the story of how he arrived at the farm and found her waiting in the truck, next to Steve. Throughout the entire ride to the auction, Melvin had to be subjected to the giggles and flirtatious behavior between Cupcake and Steve. It was enough to make his insides want to hurl. The reason why Melvin called Noel was so that she would do something to stop the inappropriate relationship from continuing. He did not think he could continue his friendship with a man who cheated on his wife. Noel told him she would get back to him, and then hung up the phone. She then called Steve and told him she had to speak to him immediately. He made her wait over 30 minutes before he appeared in the garage, where she was waiting, sitting on the stairs. She had a coat on, but all the blood had drained from her face and she was frozen solid.

"What?" he asked.

"Are you cheating on me?"

"You're gone! I don't even know why you care."

Noel stood and faced him. "Is. There. Another. Woman?"

"I have a friend."

"Last I checked, you are still married," Noel said.

"You're leaving me."

"Separating! Not divorcing! Separating to try and save our marriage. All we do is fight!"

"Well, I'm not even sure I want to save it."

Wham! The blow of his words went straight through her heart. Even though she hated him, she was certain that he wouldn't do anything as hurtful as replacing her while she was still living in the same house!

"How old is Cupcake anyway?"

Steve stared at her. "She's young."

"In her twenties, I believe. And you're 50," Noel threw out.

"It's not about that."

"Well, then please tell me, what's it about?"

"She gets me. We have really good conversations, and she is interested in farming so it's very easy to talk to her."

"I'll bet," Noel mumbled.

"Look, it doesn't matter anymore. The flame I had for you is almost out. You did so much damage to this relationship—you and your mother. I'm just tired of it all."

"So cheating on me is the way to go?"

"I'm not cheating."

Noel looked away. She wasn't about to hand over her children over to a kid that was a child herself, and a father that acted like a 14-year-old boy. He barely spent any time with them as it was. What would their lives become? Although she hated the man in front of her with a passion so deep, she loved her precious children even more. She would walk through fire for them, and lay down her life for their happiness. She would even sell her soul to the devil himself.

"I'm not leaving anymore," she said softly.

"What?"

"You heard me. I'm going to stay and change my ways. I'll do whatever you tell me to do and be what you want me to be. I'll even stop talking to my mother."

Steve was taken aback at her words. He eyed her carefully. "I'm not sure this is going to work."

"There is nothing I wouldn't do for my children." Then she turned and walked woodenly back into the house.

■ ■ ■

Christmas that year was the worst ever. While she saw the joy in her children's faces, opening up presents, and friends and family experiencing the joy of the season, she secretly wished that God would take her life and end it. She had sunk to the pits of depression, and began to isolate herself from everyone. Ripping her heart out of her chest, she quit the Board of Education, the PTA, and the beloved farmer's market. She spent her days going to work, and cleaning the house until it shone. She tried desperately to win back Steve by performing any sexual desire he had. But after a month of that, she couldn't help but wonder if he was thinking of Cupcake when he had sex with her. That and the numerous vaginal infections she was getting every time they did. One day, she tapped into the Verizon account to see if he was communicating with her. To her horror, Cupcake's number appeared several times a day, and for as long as 70 minutes sometimes. She felt sick to her stomach and waited until the kids went to sleep to confront him.

"What the hell do you guys have to talk about?" she demanded, thrusting a copy of the phone records towards him.

He looked at the records and then took a deep breath. "I know this looks bad, but she's just a friend."

"Just a friend? I don't talk to my best friend this much! What the hell do you guys talk about if it's just as friends?"

"Farming and other stuff."

"What other stuff?"

"Well, like owls and other random trivia facts. She's a bird lover."

"Owls?"

"Yah. Did you know that 200 pennies is equal to two pounds?"

"I DON'T GIVE A RAT'S ASS ABOUT OWLS AND PENNIES! All I know is that you're spending a lot of time talking to a woman who isn't your wife!"

"Calm down, you'll wake the kids."

"You will end this immediately," she glared at him.

"No, I won't," he calmly stated.

"Excuse me?"

"Not until things between you and I get better. When that happens, then I'll stop talking to her. This all hinges upon you, Noel. You brought me to this, and now it's your responsibility to fix it."

Noel couldn't believe her ears. Did other men respond like this when they were confronted by angry wives? Did she thrust him into Cupcake's arms? Was this all her fault, like he said? She didn't quite know. She marched up the stairs and got into bed. She tried desperately to go to sleep, but she couldn't. She spent the entire night staring at the ceiling. Was it just a friendship like he said? Lots of men had girls for friends. Maybe she was making a big deal about nothing. But as much as she tried to shrug the whole thing off, she kept on picturing her husband and Cupcake frolicking in the barn when no one was looking. Men got a kick out of forbidden relationships.

Steve's disagreeable moods increased. He was annoyed with anything and everything that Noel said and did. She was losing ground to a ditzy 20-year-old that had a reputation for bending over for any farmer in the state of Connecticut. She decided to restore Steve's beloved high school truck. Certainly Cupcake couldn't rival her on issues of money. Since it wasn't running, she arranged for a garage to pick it up and give it a paint job. The job would cost about $10,000. But the $10,000 turned into $23,000, because the truck was so old that the entire interior had to be replaced as well. A simple paint job turned into a full-blown restoration. Any wife would be applauded at bringing back to life a man's high school truck. But not Steve. He grumbled the entire time, that she spent way too much money and the job was mediocre at best. When she refused to spend any more money or time into the project for fear of losing her employment, Steve called her a phony fuck, and told her she was the most selfish person in the world.

■ ■ ■

Around Easter, Noel decided to go out to dinner with her parents instead of going to their house for a party. She just didn't feel like celebrating the holiday. Since she had spent so much money on the truck, she decided to cash in on some old gift cards she found at the bottom of a drawer. They had been collecting dust for over two years. She gathered them up and used them to pay for dinner. When Steve found out, he was furious.

"Who said you could use those cards?"

"I didn't know I needed permission. They were given to both of us."

"What if I wanted to use them?"

Noel thought about this for a moment. *To bring your girlfriend out on a date? I don't think so.* "When were you planning on using them?"

"It doesn't matter! See? This is the kind of shit you pull all the time! You're sneaky and you lie! You told me you weren't speaking to your mother anymore!"

"I have a dad too."

"You're just like her! You're just as devious as your mother! You can thank her for ruining our marriage! She did her job well!"

The following month, Noel spent an entire Saturday completely consumed in tasks. She woke up at 5:15 A.M., made Steve coffee, vacuumed the pool, fed the chickens, did 3 loads of laundry, spent about 5 hours outside raking and mulching the yard, fed the boys, got them ready for baseball, attended their game (alone), came home and gave her niece a pep talk about her own failing marriage, transplanted strawberry plants around the pool, cooked dinner, went to the barn to fix the time clock, burned a bunch of rotting lumber in the fire pit, and then spent until 11:00 at night cleaning the kitchen from a mess she didn't make.

When she crawled into bed that night, Steve said, "It's about time you start pulling your weight around here."

By the summer, Noel was losing weight and falling deeper into depression. She left her boys with Steve while she took an hour-long reprieve to go to therapy.

"Are you throwing in the towel yet?" Barbara asked.

"Do you think I should?"

"I can't tell you that. Only you can. But you're living in an abusive marriage and you're emotionally starving. Either you'll leave him, or you'll end up cheating on him."

"I'm not like that," Noel said softly. "Besides, I can't handle any more of them."

"What are you working on now?"

"Well, I'm just about finished with his truck, I have to pay the car insurance, and the house taxes when I'm done here. Then I have to call the septic company to come and pump out the septics for both the farm and the house."

Barbara raised her eyebrow. "Hmmm. And what is on Steve's agenda?"

Noel looked away. "I don't know. All I know is that he calls Cupcake three times a day now."

"Noel."

She snapped her eyes back to Barbara at the sound of her name. "Yes?"

"Have you ever heard the term 'narcissist'?"

"No."

"That's your homework. Google it, research it, talk to people about it. It's important."

"Why?"

Barbara looked sadly at Noel. "Because you're married to one."

That evening, Noel Googled "narcissism" on her phone. She scanned the various articles and medical diagnoses surrounding the term. The more she read, the more her heart dropped into her belly. Every single characteristic described Steve to a tee. She wanted to vomit. How could such an educated and level-headed girl fall for this? Why hadn't someone told her earlier? Would she have believed them? Suddenly, Mary's words came flashing back to her—*we are led where we need to be at the time we are supposed to be there.* She didn't know what the next step was, but she did know that she didn't have a marriage anymore. She looked down at her left hand. Slowly she eased her wedding band off her finger and placed it in the drawer of her desk.

≡ ≡ ≡

The summer bled into the fall which bled into the winter. The holidays were not merry and bright, as the saying goes. Steve became more and more dis-attached from his family, spending unusually long hours in the barn talking on the phone with his girlfriend. Noel still was undecided about what to do, since she had no proof that the relationship was sexual in nature.

One morning in early February, Noel had come down with the flu. Even though she had a raging fever and could barely move, she forced herself to go outside and feed her animals, which took an act of God in itself. Steve refused to help her with anything. But he did manage to tell her on his way out the door that he had given Cupcake a job at the farm on Wednesdays and there was nothing that Noel could do about it.

Oh, hell naw! Noel blazed. *The bitch is gonna go!*

She waited until Steve went on an errand in his truck. Then she printed out 5 sheets from the phone account, highlighted all the times Cupcake and Steve communicated, and marched right over to the barn where she was working. Jose, one of the farmhands that was friends with Noel, saw her stalking over to the barn, and tried to derail her.

"Noel!"

"Get away from me, Jose!" she barked.

"Don't do it, Noel!"

"Mind your own fucking business!"

Noel turned the corner and found Cupcake wheelbarrowing sawdust in the barn.

"Hey! I gotta talk to you," she said.

Cupcake immediately dropped her wheelbarrow and stood facing Noel, her eyes filled with terror.

"Do you see this?" she said, thrusting the highlighted document in front of her. "This is a typical week in Steve's cellphone account." She began to flip through the pages, showing her. "See this one? 40 minutes. Another one—50 minutes. Oh, look at this one—70 minutes! Do you see what time it is? It's the same time that Maverick usually calls his father to come inside so he can see him before he goes to bed. But on this particular day, he didn't come in because he was too busy! Now what do you think he was too busy doing?"

Cupcake's face paled. She looked like she was going to vomit.

"Is this what you would want your husband to do to you?"

Immediately, Cupcake shook her head and looked down.

"I wanna know what the fuck you two talk about for 70 minutes?"

Cupcake looked up. "I mean no disrespect."

"Disrespect? Bitch, you've gone beyond disrespect! You've become the biggest barn whore in the state of CT!"

Cupcake began to retreat, shaking her head.

"I want you to get in your piece-of-shit truck, and get the fuck out of here and never come back. Do you hear me?"

Cupcake nodded vigorously.

"I'm going back to the house now. By the time I get there, you better be gone! Do you understand?"

Noel didn't even wait for a response. She knew she had made her meaning very clear. She turned on her heel, and stalked back to the house. By the time she opened the front door, she could see Cupcake's truck driving by. Noel went to the couch and collapsed.

But she should have known better. Narcissists don't play by the rules.

■ ■ ■

A couple weeks later, Noel was at Maverick's basketball game when she got a call from her friend, Sheryl.

"Where are you?"

"I'm at the elementary school. Why?"

"Do you know where your husband is?"

"Yah, he's in New York at a farm show. Why?"

"I'm looking right at him."

"In New York?"

"Yup. And he ain't alone."

Noel's heart slammed into her chest. Suddenly, the world began to spin and she had to lean against the wall. Deep down inside, she thought that her talk with the whore made their relationship stop. She still believed that people were good. When faced with immoral choices, people generally say they're sorry and move onto a better path. Right? There was no such thing as devious people, who strike against families with small children. Right? How did she end up surrounded by horrible, selfish people who didn't think twice about spending the weekend with a married man—a married man that was 25 years older too! The whole thing made Noel want to vomit.

"Snap a picture of that."

"I can't do that!" Sheryl wailed.

"Snap a picture, Sheryl, or so help me God, we are no longer friends!"

There was silence on the other end.

"Done. I texted it to you." Then she hung up the phone.

For a long while, Noel wouldn't open up the text. When she finally did, she saved the picture to her photos. It was a picture of the two of them laughing together inside the farm show. Noel did the only thing that a decent wife could do—she texted the picture to Steve's number and hit send. Then she ignored his calls all day long.

Hell hath no fury as a woman scorned, and Noel was officially done.

When Steve returned, he tried to feed Noel a story that included him bumping into Cupcake at the farm show and their meeting was nothing but platonic. But Noel was not that stupid. And Steve was. His truck conveniently broke down on the way, so when she found the work slip in Steve's truck, she called the garage and they confirmed that a female was accompanying Steve that day. Noel also found the bill for the $100 flower arrangement that was delivered to Cupcake on Valentine's Day. Noel made sure she texted the bill to Steve as well. On Monday afternoon, right after work, Noel filed for divorce. This time, there was no turning back.

That night, Noel moved Steve's mattress and belongings into his office. He would never again share a bed with her. But Steve didn't make things easy for Noel. He intended to stick his knife further into Noel's heart with no remorse. He threatened to tell the court that she was a bad mom and that he would fight for custody of the boys. The only way he would stop is if she agreed that he didn't have to pay her any money, including child support. But Noel wasn't thwarted because she had an attorney who knew the law pretty well. His stupid requests were denied.

Steve was relentless. He began to diagnose Gil with all sorts of issues to prove that Noel was a neglectful mother. The first was that there was something wrong with Gil's tonsils. Noel brought him to a throat specialist, only to confirm Noel's analysis—Gil had a cold. Strike one!

The second was when Steve diagnosed Gil with sleep apnea. An overnight study was made in which Gil had to spend the night in a hotel with 24 wires hooked up to him. The outcome? Gil didn't have sleep apnea. Strike two!

The third and final blow was when Steve and Noel attended Gil's PPT. Steve ranted and raved that the school system was misdiagnosing his son and he wanted to sue them. Noel calmly stated that based on his reading behaviors and low test scores, it appeared that Gil might have dyslexia, and would the school offer some testing to determine that? The special education teacher agreed with Noel and began to outline a timeline when the test could be given. The teacher went on to explain that the test would be given over a few days since they didn't want Gil to suffer from test fatigue. Before Noel could confirm, Steve spouted out that this measure was not adequate enough and he demanded that Gil be tested in an outplacement facility away from the biases of the school system. He was certain that this went beyond something as simple as dyslexia. To appease him, the school officials agreed and made arrangements for Gil to receive neuropsychological testing in another town. Gil had to endure seven grueling hours of testing, in the middle of the summer when kids were supposed to be on vacation. At the end of the afternoon, Steve and Noel sat in the doctor's office awaiting the results of the tests.

"Your son has dyslexia."

STRIKE THREE! YOU'RE OUT!

As the months wore on, Noel anxiously awaited the court date that would set her free from her jailer. While school was in session, the days moved by fast. She began running as a means to alleviate stress. Steve only increased his torture. He would come in from the barn early on Friday nights and go into the bathroom. Then he would shower and perfume himself up. Then without a word, he would get in his truck and drive off. He wouldn't return until midnight. One of those Friday nights, Noel decided to follow him. He became aware that she was behind him, so he tried to lose her by turning into a dirt road and hiding behind a giant rock pile. But Noel was too smart for that. She parked further down the road at the library, knowing that he would have to go that way eventually. He did and she continued to follow him. She followed him all the way to Cupcake's hometown, when he again discovered she was behind him. He pulled into a gas station and got out of the truck.

"What are you doing?" he demanded.

"I'm going for a drive. Why?"

"I think you're following me."

"Well, where are you going?"

"To Dunkin' Donuts."

"All the way in Chaplin? I think we passed ten of them on the way here."

"I like this one."

"Hmmm. Will you be bringing Cupcake a Coolata? She lives around here, right?"

"It's none of your business where I'm going! We're done!"

"Ah, but sweetheart, you're still married to me. So anything you do before you sign on the dotted line is considered adultery. Try explaining that one to your kids."

"This is all your fault, you know! The whole marriage failing is your fault! I did everything I could to help you and you just got worse and worse. You drove me to this! You and your mother!"

"Tell me something. You never intended me to find out, did you? You were going to keep your slave wife and your dumb girlfriend forever, weren't you? You honestly thought you could get away with this, didn't you?"

"She's not my girlfriend."

"Still trying to shove that one down my throat, eh?"

"Believe whatever you want."

Noel stared at him for a moment, anger bubbling up inside of her. She really hated him. Nine years of marriage ended up at a gas station trying to cover up a lie. Noel didn't think she ever met a more pitiful human being.

"I wouldn't make an enemy of me if I were you, Steve. I could get pretty ugly and you know it," she pierced his eyes with one of her "I dare you to mess with me" looks. Then she put her car in drive and peeled out, leaving him in her dust.

■ ■ ■

The summer was brutally long. Noel tried to begin packing some things to pass the time. But when the court date got delayed until September, she stopped. She had found a house to buy that had the perfect square footage and amenities. The only problem was she didn't have the money for a down payment until Steve settled with her. In addition to that, Steve was winning an Academy Award for his portrayal of an absent father. He would constantly throw his boys over for a date with Cupcake instead. Noel did her best to compensate for their disappointment by taking them to a friend's house or on little excursions. Overall, she worried about their mental wellbeing once they had to move out of their house.

The insults and mental abuse continued. Steve refused to give up the title to the camper, even though Noel had the bill that proved she bought it. He refused to go to parenting class, even though the court ordered it. But the worst of it was when he would cut through Noel's bedroom to get to the office. She would be in bed reading, and he would stop in front of her, pull down his pants and reveal his hard penis after spending time on the phone with Cupcake.

"You want some of this?"

Without looking up, Noel responded, "No, thanks."

"Why not? It would feel so good," he purred.

"I'm all set."

He would then saunter into his room, calling out to her every ten minutes. When she got up to go close his door, he told her to leave it open, in case Gil needed something.

"Gil won't be going anywhere near you in your current state of need," she said, closing the door. But then once she got into bed, he stormed over to the door and flung it back open. These mental games continued throughout the summer.

In September, Noel and her lawyer went to court. They had an appointment with a couple of master lawyers who would hopefully be able to sort the divorce out quickly. Steve and his lawyer showed up late, as usual. Both men seemed to be oblivious to people's precious time. Once the four lawyers went into a room to hash everything out, Noel closed her eyes and prayed. She wanted nothing more than for this nightmare to end. Steve kept pacing in front of her. Noel occupied her time by answering emails. But that didn't take long at all and she was back to going crazy in her head in no time.

Finally the lawyers came out and filled their clients in.

"He's trying to get out of paying child support," her lawyer said.

"Is it going to happen?"

"Not likely."

"What about custody?"

"You still have residency and four nights a week."

"Thank God. Okay."

Suddenly, a young man with glasses came out and escorted everyone in. Noel and her lawyer sat on the left side of a large desk, occupied by two very annoyed-looking men shuffling through papers. Steve and his lawyer sat on the right.

"We've reviewed the case," one of the men said. "I'm curious. Why do you feel that you should not be paying child support?"

"My client feels that he can provide for the boys himself. He is also worried about the financial stability of his farm. This could put his dairy operation under."

The annoyed man looked at Steve. "The minimum I recommend is $200 a week."

"With all due respect, sir, that is too much," Steve's lawyer answered. "My client has fallen under hard times. Surely you can understand that."

"What I understand is a man trying to weasel his way out of doing what's right for his kids. Now, he can try to dispute this in court, but I guarantee he will get laughed right out of there. We could end this right now if your client takes the deal. Or he can try his hand before the judge and take his chances."

Noel held her breath as Steve and his lawyer spoke in whispers. *Please let this be over, please let this be over! Please free me from this ogre!*

"My client will take a court date," Steve's lawyer reported.

Noel deflated. How much more could she possibly take of this? Who knows how much longer they would continue to live in the same house, while they battled this out. She didn't think she would live to see Christmas. But one thing was certain—Steve was not done with her yet.

The next day, Steve approached Noel and said, "It's too bad that we can't sit down and work this out. But you're so hostile that I just can't talk to you. I mean, I don't wanna go to court. But I have to because I can't even sit down and talk to you. It's such a shame. You should at least do it for the sake of your kids."

Noel did not respond.

■ ■ ■

At the end of the month, Noel was putting Gil to bed one night and she noticed that he was a bit melancholy.

"What is it, Gil?"

"I don't think Dad will buy me a cow anymore."

"Why not?"

"He told me he will only buy me a cow if I sleep at his house every night."

Noel suppressed the level-5 hurricane swirling around in her head. It was one thing to propose these ridiculous ideas in front of a judge, but to manipulate your innocent children into pathetic schemes was another thing entirely.

"No worries, Gil. I will get you a cow."

"But how, Mom? You don't even have any land?"

"I have plenty of friends with farms. I have no doubt that they would allow me to rent some space to have an animal."

Gil's face relaxed a bit.

"Your father should not be making deals like that with a nine-year-old. It certainly is not fair to you. If you have any other problems, talk to me about them. I will do my best to fix them."

Gil smiled at Noel. Then she hugged him and kissed him and proceeded to read to him. He fell instantly asleep.

■ ■ ■

The month of October toyed around with Noel's sanity. The bank was giving her a hard time because they needed a separation agreement to issue her a mortgage. She was forced to put off the closing for yet another month. The next court date was scheduled for October 17. Maverick was beginning to suffer from anxiety. He wouldn't allow Noel to go anywhere without him. She couldn't even go to the end of the driveway to get the mail without him glued to her side. Steve continued to ignore the boys. When Noel had to participate in meetings or functions, the boys preferred to stay with Nana or Aunty or some friends, rather than with their own father. How on earth would the boys survive when they visited their father three nights a week? Noel's stress levels rose to an all-time high that month. She woke up every morning, praying, "Please, Lord. Just let me get through this day." She felt incredibly alone. But she knew she had to carry on for the sake of those precious boys. She dug down deep, every day and put one foot in front of the other. She had to keep moving.

October 17 finally arrived. Noel trudged over to the courthouse like a soldier making her last stand in the final battle. Ripped and tattered, Noel sat next to her lawyer and took a deep breath. For four hours, Noel's lawyer shuttled back and forth from the private room Steve was in, then back to Noel's to relay the terms of the separation agreement. By the time 2:00 rolled around, both lawyers were exhausted and fed up. Child support was agreed on at $175 a week. Noel rolled her eyes at the pitiful amount, but bit her tongue and moved on. Two installments would be made as far as the settlement was concerned. The first half would be paid the day before Noel moved out, and the second would be made six months later. If there was any delay in payment, Steve would be taken back to court in which he would have to pay all court expenses. Noel thought this was fair. Residency was given to Noel with four nights a week. Noel was to keep both her jeeps and the camper, as she paid for all three. Both Steve and Noel were instructed to return to court one more time on October 24 to sign the divorce decree.

Seven days of torture ensued. Noel's dog peed on the floor and Steve bellowed at Noel in front of the boys. Apparently, Noel had cleaned up the mess, but not to Steve's satisfaction. He ordered her to do a better job, and if she didn't he would not sign the divorce papers. Seeing that Steve was losing his marbles, Noel quickly shoved the boys out the door and then drove them to school.

Another night, Steve walked through Noel's room on his way to go to bed and pulled down his pants again.

"How about a one-night stand?" he asked.

"No, thank you," Noel answered.

"Are you sure? This may be your last chance."

"Yup, I'm sure."

Then he strutted away.

On October 24, Noel sat in an office close to the courtroom and waited for the judge to call them inside. Apparently, Steve was throwing a temper tantrum because he wanted Noel's Jeep Wrangler. He threatened to withhold his signature if he didn't get it. With one foot out of her jail cell, Noel was not about to delay her release one minute longer. She sold the Jeep to him for $3500. Then Steve had a problem with both children being named beneficiaries on his life insurance policy. If something happened to him, Noel was their guardian, so she would get the money. Rolling her eyes and looking up to the heavens, Noel agreed to allow her lawyer to scratch that article from the separation agreement. Finally they were called before the judge. Noel held her breath, as the judge reviewed all the information. Finally, the divorce decree was issued and Noel was finally free of Steve.

But the elation she should have felt was not there. As she walked to her car, she felt an incredible sadness wash over her. She wasn't rejoicing in her freedom—she was mourning the death of a marriage. Nine years she gave to him, and upheld all the vows she took that day. She did everything she possibly could to be a good wife and a good mother. But it was never good enough. The marriage had almost killed her. Even though she was happy to be rid of Steve, she couldn't help but feel like a failure.

The following weekend, 8 friends with trucks and cars came to move Noel out of the farmhouse. They began at 8 A.M. and by noon, the house was practically empty. Noel left Steve the bed and the contents of the living room. Sheryl stayed by Noel's side the entire time, making sure that Steve didn't try anything stupid at the last minute. When the dog and cat were loaded into the car and the last items packed up, Noel removed her house key from her key chain and laid it on the counter beside the picture frame of the family. *Fiercely loyal. That's why you stayed. Not because you were stupid and easily manipulated. You were loyal to your family when others were not.* She ran her finger over the five faces, and then turned and walked out the door.

When she reached her house, there was a frenzy of activity. The last of the boxes and furniture were being unloaded from a truck. Noel walked into the house—her house—and immediately fell to her knees. All the anguish and misery she had lived in for the past few months finally caught up with her. She let the tears fall freely down her face and placed her hands on the ground to brace herself. Her body spasmed and shook while she exuded every horrible memory of her past life. Her mother immediately tried to console her, but Noel halted her.

"I need a minute, Mom," she cried.

No one made a move to console her. They only watched in silence. It seemed like a lifetime ago that Noel dreamed of this very moment—and she was finally here. Never again would Steve threaten her, or wake her up in the middle of the night to complain about something ludicrous, or tell her that she shouldn't join a committee, or try to convince her to pay one of his bills. Steve had no weight over her anymore. She was finally back to being herself. But who was she? It was too far back to remember when she was her own person, free from the influences of a man. She couldn't wait to meet that girl again. She had missed her so much.

Noel got up from the floor and wiped her face with the back of her hand.

"Well, this place is a mess," she smiled. "Let's get to unpacking!"

■ ■ ■

A couple months later, Noel drove up to the hardware store to refill her propane tank. She walked over to an employee waiting outside. He looked at her strangely and she looked at him.

"Why do you look familiar?" he said.

"Are you Larry Bonner?" she replied.

"Yes."

"I'm Noel Masterson."

Larry sighed and closed his eyes. Then he opened them and looked at her for a long time. "I was hoping I would have the chance to talk to you."

"About what?"

"I wanted to apologize to you."

"Apologize? You weren't the one that did anything wrong. Your roommate was the one that ended my marriage."

"I know that. But I was the one that pushed her towards him."

Noel smiled and looked down.

"I gave her a place to live, but she was really after me. My wife was ready to leave me. I didn't want to end my marriage, so I sent her over to Steve's farm to buy feed. I knew they would … get close."

"Well, then I guess I have you to thank. If it wasn't for Cupcake, I would still be married to that degenerate."

"You do know that it was going on for a while, right?"

"At least a year, right?" Noel answered.

"Try three."

The blood drained out of Noel's face. Now it all made sense. The numerous yeast infections, the sightings of their vehicles parked in fields together—they had been having an affair for much longer than she suspected. "Ugh. They definitely deserve each other."

"It won't last. You also know that there were three other marriages, right?"

"What?"

"Yours, she actually succeeded at terminating. She tried to break up mine and two others before yours."

"Real prize, isn't she?"

"Oh, mark my words. She will cheat on him in the end. It's who she is. She can't help it."

Noel thanked Larry and drove away. She smiled. All this time she had thought she was not pretty enough, not skinny enough and not young enough to hold the attention of her husband. But the truth was, Steve needed someone to control. What better victim than a dumb slut? He could hold that against her forever! She would have no choice but to do his will. She almost felt sorry for Cupcake. She had no idea what fate awaited her.

■ ■ ■

A year later, Noel was reading to Gil in his room. She looked upon the green walls and smiled. She remembered when she painted the boys' rooms—green for Gil's favorite color and blue for Maverick's. The house was quiet and clean. Maverick had fallen asleep an hour ago.

"Mom?" Gil interrupted.

"Yes?"

"I wrote you a letter today in school."

Noel stared at her ten-year-old son and smiled. "You did?"

"Yah."

"Why did you do that?"

"The assignment was to write a letter to one of the most important people in your life. I chose you."

Noel looked down, hoping that she could hold off the tears. "What does it say?"

"It just says thank you for being my mom and buying me new sneakers and painting my room green, and renting a gaming trailer for my birthday."

Noel chuckled. "Aw, that was nice."

Gil then threw his arms around his mother's belly and snuggled her. She stroked his hair.

"We had a tough year, kid. I'm sure getting used to living between two houses couldn't have been that easy for you. But you seem to be doing alright."

Gil nodded and sat up. "I still don't like it," he said. "But I have to be honest—even though I love my cow and the farm, it's not the same there. The house is … different."

"I know it is," Noel replied. "Your family is not complete there. But it isn't here either, I suppose."

"But I like coming here more," Gil said.

"Why?"

"Because you took care of me since I was born. You're always there for me, Mom. You fix everything. And I always relax when I'm here. I never want to go to Dad's. But I guess I have to."

Noel smoothed back his hair. "But someday you won't have to. You'll get to choose where you want to go. Someday you'll be on your own and you won't need me anymore."

"I'll always need you, Mom."

Noel swallowed the lump that was beginning to form in her throat. She finished reading him the chapter, tucked him into bed and kissed him goodnight. Then she tiptoed into her office. She pulled out her red journal and flipped to an empty page in the back. Then she took out her favorite black pen from the pencil can and began to write:

Dear God,

Today my son told me he will always need me. Those words hit me right in the gut. I realized that I never let him down throughout this whole transition. I never forgot about my kids and what they needed. I forgot about myself for a minute, but now I feel like I've come back. I'm not like I once was. I feel stronger, wiser, calmer, and empowered. I'm a teacher, a baker, a Board of Ed member, a PTA mom, a gardener, a chicken farmer, and a mother. I juggle all these things and never drop them. I don't keep any friendships that are toxic, and I have no desire to ever marry again. I guess that one could change over time, but the point is—I will never let any man knock me down again. I fight for a better education for my students and I fight for better schools for my children. I keep my home sacred for my boys—this is their home with me, and no one else. I live among the trees and the wild creatures that live in my woods. I own a quad and a chainsaw, and I'm not afraid to run both. I make rock walls and gardens and I love to shovel my driveway just as much as I love to mow my lawn. I bake cookies till midnight during the summer and I can't bake enough banana breads for the demands of my customers. Look at what I've done, God—without the help of any man! I'm a bad-ass bitch, and I'll take on anyone who tries to take that title away from me again!

But I will continue to thank you each and every night for this amazing life you've given me. Although I would never want to experience that pain again, I can't help but wonder if it led me to where I am right now. Watch over my boys for me, when I cannot. Keep the joy alive in their hearts and help me to find ways to add to it. My kids are the most important people in my life, and they always will be.

Sincerely,

Noel
Queen of the Bad-Ass Bitches ▬

CPSIA information can be obtained
at www.ICGtesting.com
Printed in the USA
BVHW011009060222
628231BV00002B/205

9 781638 671640